He wanted her, but not at the price she was asking...

You want this, don't you, little one? His voice purred seductively, although his lips did not move. *You came here for this, didn't you?* He began to gently suckle on her neck.

"Yes," she whispered, as her arms lifted to clutch his shoulders and pull him closer to her body. Her eyes were tightly closed.

William drew back slowly, wondering about the woman's motives, about her willingness to surrender to a monster.

Then he remembered what she'd said. "You wanted me to kill someone for you." It was a statement. What he had taken as a jest before suddenly seemed very serious. Who was this woman? And why did she seek the Angel of Death?

"Yes," she whispered again, refusing to open her eyes.

Look at me. The command came unbidden. The full force of his will was behind the order. He would know what the woman in his arms wanted, what dangers she presented to him. Then he would deal with her.

"Who do you want me to kill?"

Her lashes lifted slowly, languorously. Her breathing was ragged. Her chest rose and fell jerkily. "Me. I want you to kill me."

WITHDRAW from records of Mid-Continent Public Library

F
Eden, Cynthia.
The vampire's kiss

MID-CONTINENT PUBLIC LIBRARY
Raytown Branch
6131 Raytown Road
Raytown, MO 64133

RT

D0424716

Mom, after all of the books you
bought for me over the years,
this one is finally for you.
Thanks, Mom, for always supporting me.

OTHER BOOKS BY
CYNTHIA EDEN

The Wizard's Spell
(Coming in early 2006)

The Vampire's Kiss

***

Cynthia Eden

ImaJinn
Books

MID-CONTINENT PUBLIC LIBRARY
Raytown Branch
6131 Raytown Road
Raytown, MO 64133

RT

MID-CONTINENT PUBLIC LIBRARY

3 0000 13106223 8

The sale of this book without its cover is unauthorized. If you purchased this book without a cover, you should be aware that it was reported to the publisher as "unsold and destroyed." Neither the author nor the publisher has received payment for the sale of this "stripped book."

THE VAMPIRE'S KISS
Published by ImaJinn Books

Copyright ©2005 by Cindy Roussos
Printed and bound in the United States of America. All rights reserved. No part of this book may be reproduced in any form or by any means (electronic, mechanical, photocopying, recording, or otherwise) without prior written permission of both the copyright holder and the above publisher of this book, except by a reviewer, who may quote brief passages in a review. For information, address: ImaJinn Books, P.O. Box 545, Canon City, CO 81215-0545; or call toll free 1-877-625-3592.

ISBN: 0-9759653-9-5

10 9 8 7 6 5 4 3 2 1

PUBLISHER'S NOTE:
This book is a work of fiction. Names, characters, places and incidents are products of the author's imagination or are used fictitiously. Any resemblance to actual events or locales or persons, living or dead, is entirely coincidental.

Books are available at quantity discounts when used to promote products or services. For information please write to: Marketing Division, ImaJinn Books, P.O. Box 545, Canon City, CO 81215-0545, or call toll free 1-877-625-3592.

Cover design by Patricia Lazarus

ImaJinn Books, a division of ImaJinn
P.O. Box 545, Canon City, CO 81215-0545
Toll Free: 1-877-625-3592
http://www.imajinnbooks.com

Prologue

The evil grows. I can feel its dark touch.
-Entry from the diary of Henry de Montfort,
September 2, 1068

"Mark!" She awoke screaming her twin brother's name.

She turned on her bedside lamp with hands that shook. Her gaze flew frantically around her bedroom, and her heart seemed to stop.

She didn't see her furniture. She didn't see the antique cherry dresser or chest. She didn't see the stacks of books that lined her shelves, shelves lovingly made by her grandfather's hands.

She just saw the blood.

And it was everywhere.

And she felt the evil. The overwhelming evil.

She closed her eyes, desperate to stop the vision.

A man's terror-filled scream echoed in her mind.

"No!" She shoved her covers aside and jumped from the bed.

In a flash, the vision ended.

She could see her room again. Cloaked in shadows, but recognizable nonetheless.

Her heartbeat pounded desperately in her ears. Her body shook with remembered fear.

Had it been a dream? Just a dream?

She shook her head. It couldn't have been a dream. It'd felt...too real.

She had a sudden desperate urge to call Mark. To hear his voice.

She reached for the phone.

A shrill ring froze her hand.

Her heart stopped.

The phone rang again, its cry eerily like the scream from her dream.

Her fingers shook as she lifted the receiver. "H-hello?"

As she listened to the caller, all of the blood drained from her face. Her body swayed and the phone dropped from her nerveless fingers.

Strange icy prickles shot across her skin. Lights flashed before her eyes.

Her body fell to the floor.

And she stumbled back into the dreams of a dead man.

One

Like a child, I fear the darkness.
-Entry from the diary of Henry de Montfort,
September 8, 1068

Savannah Daniels gathered her strength and pulled herself over the high granite wall. She slipped over its edge and fell to the ground, landing with a soft thud. Blood covered her body and her torn clothes.

It was a miracle that she'd made it up the mountain.

Her small rental car had died on her hours ago. Halfway up the treacherous mountain road, it had sputtered once and then stopped. Steam had burst from beneath the Toyota's hood. No amount of begging, pleading or cursing had been able to start the engine again.

She'd gotten out of the car, and she'd done the only thing that she could. She'd walked. For miles, she'd walked along the graveled road. Walked until her feet ached, until blisters grew on her heels and toes.

She'd kept walking, long after the graveled road had ended. She'd climbed under the barbed wire fence, ripping her clothes and the skin of her arms and back.

The stone wall had been her last hurdle. The last obstacle in her path.

She could see the house now, its imposing stone structure standing stark and strong against the mountain.

Thin streams of light shone from its high, Gothic windows. The light seemed to beckon her, promising her safety from the dark night, if only she would come inside.

For a moment, the howling of the wind quieted, and Savannah stared in silence at what lay before her.

She knew what she would find inside the walls of that house.

A monster.

A man.

A demon.

A savior.

For the past six months, she'd researched him carefully. She'd learned every detail that she could about

William Dark. Every horrifying detail.

Sometimes, she woke screaming in the night, his name upon her lips.

But the nightmares did not matter.

She needed William Dark. She needed the monster. She needed the man. And she would have him.

She approached the house slowly, almost timidly. Her tennis shoes crunched over the wet gravel. It had rained earlier in the day, and the air still smelled of the shower.

There was no sound in the courtyard. No birds chirping. No dogs barking. Not even the howl of the wind intruded on this quiet space.

She was the only intruder. Her stomach clenched, and she swallowed several times to relieve the tightness in her throat. Her heart pounded furiously. She wondered if he could hear the desperate beating.

From their perch high atop the house, two hideous gargoyles glared down at her, warning her away from their master. Savannah lifted her bruised chin in silent challenge. She had not let her friends dissuade her from her journey. She certainly would not be frightened off by two statues! Even if they did seem to stare down at her, their glittering eyes following her every move.

Finally, she stood before a tall, wooden door. A cross had been crudely etched into its surface. She stared at the spiritual sign, wondering at its presence. At its meaning in this place of darkness.

It didn't belong there.

Neither did she.

But she wasn't going to leave. Not until she'd gotten what she needed.

She took a deep breath.

The door opened before she could even lift her hand to knock against its hard surface. *He* opened the door. For a moment, she could only stare up at him in stunned surprise. Even in the night's shadow, she could tell that it was he.

He towered over her slender form. He was tall, easily over six feet, and his broad shoulders seemed to fill the doorframe. His long midnight hair was pulled back and clasped at the base of his neck. His eyes, a burning coal-black, seemed to glow as they stared piercingly into her own.

She'd seen a sketch of him before, of course. She'd known what he looked like. But seeing him up close was an entirely different matter.

She hadn't realized just how high and strong his cheekbones were, or how sensual his lips would be. His nose was perfectly straight, if a little sharp. His brow was high and elegant. He was an attractive man, even with the thin scar that sliced down his left cheek.

She knew how he had gotten that scar.

She knew everything about the man before her.

He was dressed in black, the color accentuating his tawny skin and making him look almost...sinister.

He stood within the shadows, watching her.

Finally, he spoke. "You are not welcome here." His voice was a purr, a seductive contrast to the harsh words. A slight English accent marked his formal words.

Savannah was not surprised by his abruptness. After all, it was the greeting that she'd expected. In a quick rush, she said, "I must speak with you, Mr. Dark." Her voice shook with intensity. He had to let her inside the house. He had to!

His head lifted slightly. Did curiosity flicker faintly in the depths of his black eyes? Savannah couldn't tell, not for certain.

"Must you?" he queried. His voice seemed to wrap around her, to sink into her.

She shook her head, clearing the sudden fog from her mind. "Let me come inside," Savannah entreated, trying in vain to stare around his shadowed body and glimpse the interior of the manor. "We have to talk. It's urgent."

He shook his head and stepped forward into a thin beam of light. "You are not welcome here," he repeated.

Savannah gathered her courage and stared at the man before her. "Please let me come inside. It's a matter of life or death."

A single black brow lifted. His gaze slowly traveled from the top of her head to the bottom of her sodden shoes. "You are a very stubborn woman, Ms.—"

"Daniels," She supplied in a rush. "My name is Savannah Daniels."

He nodded, as if he had already known her name.

"You may come inside, but only for a moment." He stepped back, opening the entranceway to his home.

She exhaled heavily. Sudden relief made her tired body tremble. He was letting her inside! Now, if only she could convince him to help her.

Her body brushed against his as she slipped into the house. Her shoulder casually touched his chest. For a moment, his black eyes flared red.

She hurriedly moved away and into the foyer. William lifted his arm and indicated an open door to the right. She nodded and stepped into the room.

A warm fire crackled in the fireplace. She immediately walked to it and lifted her hands, eager to feel the warmth. She was so cold. Had been cold, for so long. Ever since that night...

William continued to watch her, his stare hard and unflinching.

Savannah wondered what he saw when he looked at her. She glanced nervously down at herself. She knew she looked horrible. Her clothes and hair were a complete mess.

But even on a good day, she'd never considered herself to be a great beauty. Her hair was too curly, the color too red. True, it was thick and cut to fall lightly against her shoulders, but she'd always hated the bright color.

Her body was small and slender. In her heels, she stood at five foot five. She'd lost a lot of weight in the last year, so now she looked particularly delicate. Almost frail.

She exhaled heavily.

There was nothing she could do about her appearance. Besides, that didn't matter.

Her hands clenched into small fists, and she turned resolutely from the fire.

"I need your help." The words echoed in the great room.

William lounged in a large, cushioned chair. "My help? What is it exactly that you need me to do, Ms. Daniels?"

She swallowed and moved to take the chair opposite him. She'd known this wasn't going to be easy. She cleared her throat and looked deeply into the darkness of his eyes. "I need you to kill someone," she said simply, clearly.

He blinked. Once. Twice. "Excuse me?"

Savannah licked her lips. His eyes followed the nervous movement. "I need you to kill someone," she repeated, her gaze locked with his.

William laughed. He threw back his dark head and roared. His shoulders shook with mirth. Still smiling, he turned in his chair to study the young woman before him.

In truth, she was all flaming hair and eyes. She rather reminded him of a fairy. A small, lost little fairy.

It was a pity that she'd wandered into his realm.

Her face was a delicate oval. Her skin was incredibly translucent. Her nose was small, and her lips were temptingly full. Yet, it was her eyes that caught and held his attention. They were the greenest eyes that he had ever seen. Dark, deep, emerald eyes. Her rioting red curls contrasted richly with her eyes, giving her a strangely fey quality.

His gaze traveled down her body. Her breasts were small, gentle mounds that thrust proudly against her gray sweatshirt. Her nipples were pebbled slightly from the cold. Her hips were small, almost boyish, and her slender legs were encased in a pair of faded blue jeans.

The faint scent of blood clung to her body. The scent called softly to him, tempted him.

He took a deep breath and leaned back in his chair. One of his hands lifted to rub against the hard line of his jaw. What sort of game was the little fairy playing? Surely she did not think to tangle with one such as he...

"What makes you think I would kill someone?" he drawled, his voice soft. He watched her carefully, noting the slight tremor in her hands.

Her green eyes narrowed. "I know about you," she whispered, her fingers curling into the chair's armrest.

His body stilled. "What is it that you think you know?" The amusement of moments before was gone. Ice coated his words.

"I know your secret, Mr. Dark." Her voice was a hushed thread of sound.

William felt a sudden tension stretch through his body.

He studied the fairy very carefully. He considered reaching into the depths of her mind, but he discarded the notion almost immediately. He wanted to see what truths she would reveal on her own. Or what lies.

"I know who you are." She paused, and then said softly, "Or rather, I know *what* you are." Her full lips curled tentatively. "You might say that I'm something of an expert on you."

His own lips curved just slightly, though he knew that no trace of warmth filled his smile. "An expert? On me?" Rage filled him, but with an effort, he managed to keep his voice controlled as he asked, "Why am I so important to you? I assure you, my life is not that exciting."

She leaned forward. "On the contrary, your life is fascinating."

A sudden crash of thunder echoed in the distance.

"I am a man, no more, no less. My life is like any other."

She vehemently shook her head. "You are much more than a man, Mr. Dark, and we both know that." She took a deep breath. "I know *what* you are," she whispered. "I know."

His jaw clenched. "You know nothing." He stood abruptly. "It's time that you left."

She jumped from her chair and took a step toward him. "I'm not leaving. I need your help!"

He shook his head once. "I cannot help you, lady. I can't help anyone."

"I need you." Dark intensity filled her words and her gaze.

William frowned. He rose and walked slowly toward her. His fingers lifted and curled around her delicate chin. He stared down at her, a furrow between his brows. "You don't even know me."

"I know everything about you."

His head cocked to the side. "And what you know— it makes you think that I would kill someone?"

She swallowed. "Yes."

"You think I'm a killer?" he asked, just to be certain.

"Yes." Savannah's body tensed as she waited for his reaction.

He smiled. His fingers stroked the delicate line of her

jaw. "I think you're confused. Very, very confused. I'm not a killer. I'm just a man. A man who wants to be left alone." He released her and walked toward the crackling fire.

"You were a man once," she agreed. "But you're not any longer. You stopped being just a man almost a thousand years ago."

He turned and lunged toward her in a blur of speed. His right hand locked around the slender column of her throat. Her pulse pounded furiously beneath the cool touch of his fingers.

She spoke quickly, knowing she had not a moment to lose. The beast had been roused. "In 1038, you were born William de Montfort. In battle, you earned the name William the Dark. It was said that you earned that name because of your love for the dark arts. It was the evil magic you used then that made you into what you are now."

His fingers eased their tight hold and began to tenderly stroke the sensitive skin of her throat. "And what am I, Ms. Daniels?"

Her lashes lowered slowly and then lifted to meet his burning stare. His blood red stare. "You're a vampire."

His incisors extended, long and deadly. His eyes, those burning eyes, held her captive. His hand continued to stroke the column of her neck. "And you are a fool."

His head lowered, and she realized with numb shock that he was going to bite her. He was going to take her blood. Eagerly, she tilted her head back, offering herself to him.

His breath was hot against the tender skin of her throat. She waited, desperate to feel the plunge of his teeth as he drank from her. She just hoped that it didn't hurt too much...

She expected to feel the slashing cut of his teeth against her. Instead, she felt the rough velvet of his tongue as he licked her throbbing pulse. Slowly. Once. Twice. Her breathing hitched, and she heard herself moan.

His teeth scraped lightly against her skin. His tongue licked.

His scent surrounded her. Strong. Dark. The scent of the night.

You want this, don't you, little one? His voice purred seductively, although his lips did not move. *You came here for this, didn't you?* He began to gently suckle on her neck.

"Yes," she whispered, as her arms lifted to clutch his shoulders and pull him closer to her body. Her eyes were tightly closed.

William drew back slowly, wondering about the woman's motives, about her willingness to surrender to a monster.

Then he remembered what she'd said. "You wanted me to kill someone for you." It was a statement. What he had taken as a jest before suddenly seemed very serious. Who was this woman? And why did she seek the Angel of Death?

"Yes," she whispered again, refusing to open her eyes.

Look at me. The command came unbidden. The full force of his will was behind the order. He would know what the woman in his arms wanted, what dangers she presented to him. Then he would deal with her.

"Who do you want me to kill?"

Her lashes lifted slowly, languorously. Her breathing was ragged. Her chest rose and fell jerkily. "Me. I want you to kill me." Then her hands lifted and she buried them in his hair. She tightened her hold, silently urging his mouth back to her neck. Back to the place where her pulse pounded so frantically.

His eyes widened in shock. He, who had seen countless wars and deaths, was shocked by her statement. By her invitation.

Yet what shocked him more was how much he was tempted. For he desperately wanted to take the little fairy up on her offer. He wanted to take her blood...and her life.

With an effort, he forced himself to step back, to release her from his embrace. He stared at her, wondering why one so young and full of life would possibly want to surrender to the darkness. What demon had driven her to seek him out? "Why?" He asked as he moved back into the shadows of the room. "Why do you seek death?"

Her hands clenched and frustration flashed across her delicate features. "My motives shouldn't matter to you."

He cocked a dark brow. "They do." He'd never had someone just come to him, without compulsion, and offer blood. Offer life. He'd found that humans valued life too much to want to just give it away to a beast.

Her jaw clenched. "I *want* you to bite me."

"Yes." He nodded. "But I am not going to do it." He'd learned long ago to control his dark urges. And, even though she had come to him looking for death, he would not give it to her. The tattered remains of his conscience would not let him.

"You should leave now." He motioned toward the door.

She shook her head, sending her dark red curls flying. "I'm not leaving. I didn't come all this way just to have you refuse me." Her face seemed unnaturally pale in the flickering firelight. "I *can't* let you refuse me. I told you, I need your help."

"And I told you no. Now, it is time for you to leave."

Her chest rose and fell jerkily. "You have to help to me. If you don't, I'll tell everyone about you. I'll go to all the papers, all the news channels—"

He laughed softly, mockingly. "Come now. Do you really think they will believe you?" He shook his dark head. "If you go to them and say that I'm a vampire, they'll laugh at you." And quite possibly lock her up.

Her chin lifted. "They will believe me if I have proof."

"And what proof do you have?" he scoffed.

She smiled, showing even white teeth. "I have your brother's diary. Henry's diary. I translated it."

He tensed. The beast within him snarled in rage. "And where..." He clenched his back teeth and felt his incisors burn and lengthen. "...did you get that little prize?"

"It doesn't matter, does it?" She walked toward him. "I have his diary, and I'll show it to everyone that I can. Everyone. Eventually, someone *will* believe me. Your secret will be out." She stopped a foot away from him. "And, then, Mr. Dark, after hunting prey for a millennium, you'll be the one who is hunted."

"You really want death, don't you?" he asked, wonder in his voice.

"Death is just a means to an end," she replied, the expression in her eyes secretive.

He grabbed her shoulders roughly. "I don't like blackmail," he growled. He was so close to her that he could hear her heartbeat, that he could feel its desperate rhythm shaking through her body. And he could almost taste her.

"Neither do I." Genuine regret seemed to lace her words. "But I don't have a choice."

"Yes, you do. Leave now."

"No."

He looked deeply into her emerald gaze and saw both determination and fear. He tried to play on the fear. "If I do as you ask, you will feel pain like you can't imagine. Fear like you've never known. I will drain all of the blood from your beautiful body. I will drink from you until there is nothing left." He touched her cheek gently. "And then I will throw away your rotting corpse." His smile was chilling.

"I've felt fear before." Her words were calm, but her lips trembled. "I've felt pain. More pain that even *you* can imagine."

He was surprised by the anger that swept through him. The idea that someone, somewhere, had hurt this strange woman filled him with rage. A rage that had no reason. His fingers clenched around her shoulders. "Who hurt—"

She jerked back, away from him. "It doesn't matter right now."

It mattered. For some unknown reason, it mattered very much to him.

"Are you going to help me?" She asked again.

"You mean, am I going to kill you?" In truth, he found that he hungered for the taste of her blood. For her.

She took a deep breath. "Look, we're wasting time. I know how it works. I told you, I've done my research."

"Ah, yes...your research." His words mocked her.

"I know what has to be done," she said stubbornly, her bright gaze locked on his. "I know that I have to die in order to become..."

"Become what?" He asked as a dark suspicion wrapped its way around him. Surely she couldn't mean—

"Like you."

Two

Evil lives in this world. I have seen it.
-Entry from the diary of Henry de Montfort,
October 5, 1068

Silence filled the room.

Savannah held her breath, praying with all of her strength that she hadn't made a mistake by coming here, by coming to William.

He had been her last resort. Her only choice.

If she were to have her vengeance, then she would need him.

Finally, just when she thought the silence would never end, he spoke. His words were slow, considering. "So it isn't true death that you seek, is it, little one? You want the kiss, the kiss of immortality. The kiss of the vampire." He sounded almost disappointed.

"Yes, that's what I want." No, it wasn't really what she wanted, but it was what she had to have. She had to become like him, to become one the walking dead, if she were to complete her plans. Otherwise, all would be lost.

"You aren't so different, after all." He turned away dismissively and walked out of the room.

Her temples began to pound. She ignored the pain and hurried after him. "Wait! Stop!"

He was in the foyer. He pulled open the strong wooden door. The darkness from the night spilled into the room. It almost seemed as if the darkness were waiting for her, waiting to claim her.

"Good night, Ms. Daniels."

"No!" She slammed the door, shutting out the night. "You have to help me."

"I haven't helped any of those other poor fools who came to me over the years and asked for the kiss." A cynical smile curled his lips as he read the surprise on her face. "What? Did you think you were the first to discover my nature?"

Savannah felt a flush stain her cheeks. Yes, she had thought that she'd been the first. From the instant that she learned of William Dark's existence, she had felt a strange kinship with him. A special link had seemed to exist between them. But, perhaps that had just been in her mind, too.

"There have been at least a dozen others who have come to me over the centuries." William shrugged his broad shoulders. "They all stumbled upon the truth of my existence in one manner or another. And they all wanted the kiss. Men, women. Young and old. They didn't care what they would have to do once they were transformed. They didn't care about what they would become. They just wanted the kiss."

Savannah swallowed to ease her suddenly parched throat. Fear rolled through her. William was going to refuse her, as he'd done with others a dozen times before.

"I didn't change them. And I'm not going to change you."

"But if you don't, I'll—"

A gust of wind knocked the door open and flew through the foyer, sending Savannah's hair whipping around her face. "No threats!" William growled. "All of the others threatened me. First they begged, pleaded, and when that didn't work, they threatened. And do you know what I did to them?"

Staring into his swirling eyes, Savannah was afraid to ask about their fate.

"I could have killed them. I could have drained them dry or broken their necks. Then I wouldn't have had to worry about their sad attempts at blackmail."

Savannah winced.

"But I didn't do that," he said, his voice suddenly changing, lowering, flowing around her, through her, like rich wine. "I didn't have to kill them. And do you know why?"

"Why?" She whispered.

His head lowered toward hers. "Vampires have many powers. Both physical and mental."

Savannah knew all about the powers that vampires possessed. The superhuman strength, the psychic talents. It was said that some could fly. Some could shapeshift. And some could control the actions of humans with but a stray thought.

Mind control. A shudder racked her body.

He smiled. "That's right. I didn't have to kill them because I simply made them forget. As I will make you forget…"

His lips touched hers, a light, fleeting touch. A tingle shot through her body at the contact.

"That's the only kiss you'll be getting from me, sweet Savannah. Count yourself lucky for it."

He stepped back, and with one hand, he lifted her chin,

forcing her eyes to lock on his. "Now, it's time for you to go. Go back to your nice little world and forget me. Forget all about me and the kiss that you wanted."

As Savannah stared into his eyes, she felt as if her grip on the world was slipping away. The light in the foyer suddenly seemed incredibly dim.

Shadows surrounded William, and all she could see were his eyes, burning red.

"Forget, Savannah. Forget me. Forget the kiss."

A scream of denial trembled against her lips. A scream that was never voiced, for in the next instant, the darkness overwhelmed her and Savannah could remember no more.

***

He had no trouble taking her back to town, back to the small hotel room that she'd rented at the edge of the city.

When they'd gone down the mountain, he'd seen her car. It had sat, small and abandoned, on the old gravel drive. He would have to make arrangements for the car to be returned to her. In the mean time, he would plant an explanation for its absence in her mind.

He was very good at planting compulsions.

As they'd traveled, he'd cloaked their presence. No one would remember them. Even the few residents of town who had seen them would not actually be able to recall their presence.

It wasn't as if there had even been that many people out to see them. Tyler, North Carolina wasn't exactly the big city. There were a few shops and businesses along the main street, but most of the residents actually lived in nearby cabins. Nestled in the mountains, the city was occasionally visited by tourists hoping to get away from the rigors of big-city life. But even at the height of the tourist season, the town still only boasted a few thousand residents. It was a small town, quiet and secluded. Perfect for him.

With a wave of his hand, the door to Savannah's room flew open and he carried her inside. She was still unconscious, a result of the strong compulsion he'd given her. In repose, her features looked incredibly fragile. And incredibly lovely.

Her body felt good in his arms. Warm. Alive.

It had been years, too many years, since he'd felt the warmth of a woman against him. His body stirred with needs that he'd long thought dead.

Quickly, before he could change his mind, he placed her on the small bed. The springs squeaked softly as they took her weight.

For a moment, he hesitated, staring down at her. She looked so good. So pure. Why would one such as she coming looking for him?

He shook his head. It didn't matter. When she woke, she would have no memory of him.

But he would remember her.

He turned from the bed, from her, and forced himself to survey the room. Henry's diary was here. It had to be in the room.

He spotted her luggage sticking out of a small closet. He took a step toward it.

On the bed, Savannah stirred. She moaned and her thick lashes lifted.

William spun around in shock. Impossible! She couldn't be waking. She couldn't—

"William?" Her voice was thick, husky. It sent a shaft of desire burning though him.

He stared at her in wonder. She remembered him. She'd woken on her own, despite the compulsion, and she remembered him.

Impossible. How could she—

She licked her lips. Her head lifted and she met this gaze. "I remember you." She shook her head in confusion. "I thought you said I would forget."

She should have forgotten. *Never* before had someone resisted his compulsion.

She looked around the room. Her gaze fell on a small framed picture on the bedside table. A smiling man with dark hair and emerald eyes looked back at her.

A faint sheen of tears filled her eyes. "I still remember everything. Everything."

William sat down beside her on the bed. He cocked his head and studied her. "I was wrong. You're not like the others." He placed his hands on either side of her head.

Savannah felt a strange pressure. It was like she could feel him, from inside her mind. "Wh-what are you doing?"

He frowned and dropped his hands. "Your mind...it's different."

She bit her lip. Sadness filled her. "I'm more different than you can possibly know." Her hand reached for his.

William froze.

"I need you to help me. Please."

His gaze remained locked on her hand. "I've already told you, I can't."

"You *must* help me."

"Why?"

"Because you're the only one who can."

The faint light from the rising sun flickered through the window. William stood abruptly. "I have to go.

"William, I—"

"Meet me at midnight," he surprised her by saying. "At Jake's."

"Jake's?" Savannah had arrived in town just before sunset. She'd only had time to rent a room before heading off in search of William Dark.

"It's a bar on Miller Street. Just follow the sound of the music."

She nodded. "I'll be there." She looked nervously toward the window. "Is it safe for you to—"

He was gone. Just that fast, he'd vanished.

Savannah searched her room, but she could find no trace of him. He'd disappeared. Into thin air.

She walked slowly toward the bed. She couldn't believe that she'd done it. After all of those months of planning, she'd finally done it.

She sat down and reached for the picture. As always, the sight of her brother caused her chest to tighten with grief. "Soon, Mark. I promise. You'll have your vengeance. *Soon.*"

She gently put the frame back in its place, and with hands that trembled, she opened the nightstand drawer. She took out a small, unmarked plastic bottle.

She shook the bottle and two pills spilled into her palm.

She stared at the innocuous looking white pills. The doctors had prescribed them for her months ago. They were supposed to help her. Not make her better, for nothing could do that. But they were supposed to keep the pain away. And they did. Sometimes. Sometimes they completely stopped the pain. And sometimes they didn't do a damn thing.

Of course, they never stopped the nightmares. She didn't think anything could stop them.

***

He sat in the darkest corner of the bar, his back against the hard black wall, and he waited for her.

He ignored the crowd around him. The dancing. The laughter. It held no interest for him. The people in the bar, with their tight clothing and desperate eyes, didn't affect him.

But *she* did.

The moment that she stepped inside the dim bar, he felt her. In every inch of his body, he felt her.

And he hungered.

She wore a short black skirt that fell to mid-thigh. Her glorious legs immediately captured his attention. They were long and slender. Delicately muscled.

Her matching top dipped daringly low, revealing more than a hint of her cleavage. Her firm breasts pressed enticingly against her shirt's front, and he realized that he could see her nipples.

Every muscle in his body tightened. Strained. *Hungered.*

He was aware that others noticed her, too. Several men turned to watch her as she slowly made her way through the crowded bar. One fool even reached out and placed his hand upon her shoulder.

William studied the man carefully, memorizing his features. The fellow would pay for that careless touch.

Savannah smiled at the man, and William saw her murmur softly to him. The hand fell away from her body, and she once again began walking toward him.

William rose and went to meet her. He grabbed her arm and pulled her toward him.

"What do you think you are doing?" His voice was a low growl.

She lifted one delicate auburn brow. "Meeting you?"

His eyes narrowed. "Why are you dressed like that?"

"We're at a bar," she reminded him, a small smile playing around the corners of her mouth. "I wanted to fit in."

She wouldn't fit in. A woman like her would always stand out from the crowd. "Well, you're not fitting in. You're attracting more attention than we want." He hated the way the other men stared at her. He hated their lust-filled gazes.

And he hated even more that his own stare was filled with the same crazed need.

He steered her toward his waiting booth. At least the shadows would protect her from some of the prying eyes. Coming to Jake's had obviously been a mistake.

When she sat down, he followed her, moving his body close to hers.

Savannah reached into her bag and pulled out a brown package. "Here."

William frowned. "What is this?"

"Henry's diary."

His eyes widened in surprise.

She smiled. "I figured you should have it back."

He carefully unwrapped the precious gift. He peeled the paper away slowly and stared in wonder at the leather volume. His fingers delicately caressed the soft cover. He traced his family's crest and could have sworn that he actually felt heat, felt life, coming from the book. "Thank you."

"You're welcome." She frowned and looked around the bar. A band screamed lyrics from a lifted stage and a mass of bodies danced vigorously on the small dance floor. "Do you come here often?"

He almost smiled at her question. Almost, and then he remembered his purpose in bringing her to Jake's. Savannah had a lesson that she needed to learn. He carefully rewrapped the book and tucked it inside his coat pocket. He would explore that treasure later.

"I come here when I have a...need."

Her brow furrowed. "A need? I don't understand."

No, of course she didn't. But she would.

He leaned close to her, letting his breath fan against the delicate skin of her neck. The scent of lavender rose to tease his nostrils.

"Savannah," he breathed against her and had the pleasure of watching her shiver. "Look at those people. What do you see?"

She wet her lips and his gaze avidly followed that small, sensual movement. "I see..." He lifted his hand and rubbed it against her thigh. She jumped. "Ah...I see people dancing. Laughing. Having a good time."

"Really?" he purred. "That's not what I see." He leaned forward and lightly licked her neck. She gasped.

He loved the taste of her. So rich. So sweet. He wondered if her blood would taste the same.

And he knew, with sudden certainty, that he would have to find out. He wouldn't be able to let her go. Not without first having a taste. A taste of her.

"Wh-what do you see?" she asked softly, arching her neck.

He could read her need so easily. She wanted him to bite her. To sink his teeth into her delicate skin.

She still wanted the kiss.

He had to force her to change her mind.

Before he gave in to her need.

His need.

"I see food." His voice took on a harsh, grated edge. "I see blood."

She tried to jerk away from him. Effortlessly, he held her in place. "Look at them, Savannah. Look at them. Look at how fragile they are. How delicate. It's so easy to break them. So easy to kill them."

She lifted her chin and looked at him. Her eyes glistened with a faint sheen of tears. "You're trying to scare me." She shook her head once, almost sadly. "It's not going to work. You're not going to make me change my mind."

"We'll see," he growled and pulled her from the booth. She followed docilely, allowing him to lead her onto the crowded dance floor.

Bodies brushed against him as he passed. Scents flooded his nostrils. Cheap perfume. Booze. Sex.

He wondered if Savannah noticed the smells. He doubted it. His sense of smell was ten times stronger than a mortal's. As was his vision.

He stopped in the middle of the dance floor. Savannah stumbled into him.

"What—"

He paid her no attention. His eyes were locked on the man who'd touched her only moments before.

Like Savannah, he was young, probably in his late twenties. He had sandy hair and blue eyes. He had a long, lanky build, and a tattoo of a black snake circled his upper arm.

The guy was currently dancing with a scantily clad blonde. His hands were locked on her hips, and hers were tunneling through his hair.

William smiled. He would be perfect. And so would she.

"What are you doing?" Savannah asked, fear heavy in her voice. She tugged on his arm. "Let's go back to the booth."

"Not just yet," he murmured. Then he waited.

The guy looked up, seeming to sense William. Their gazes locked. William's eyes flared red. "Come with me," he commanded.

The man nodded, his face slack. He pulled away from the blonde and took a step toward William.

"Slade? What are you doin'?" The blonde grabbed his arm. "We ain't through dancin' yet!" She turned and noticed William. Her gaze flashed with sudden interest and she smiled flirtatiously. "Well, hi there, honey. You a friend of Slade's?"

"Not exactly," William murmured, turning the full force of his burning gaze upon her. "Why don't you come outside with us?"

She blinked once. Her features softened, her lips parted. "Okay."

"Stop it!" Savannah whispered. He could feel the tension humming through her body. "Stop playing with them."

He looked at her, letting her see the blood lust that swirled in the depths of his eyes. He hadn't fed that day, and the hunger was riding him hard. "I'm not playing."

He headed for the back door. Slade and his girl eagerly followed. He glanced over his shoulder. Savannah stood frozen on the dance floor, an expression of horror covering her lovely face.

Good. She should be horrified. Her horror would send her running back home. Away from him.

The thought didn't please him as much as it should have.

The crowd parted easily before him. In moments, he could see the back door, its metal surface gleaming dully in the poor florescent light. With one well-placed kick, he forced the door open, its hinges screeching in protest. He scanned the back alley. A stray black cat screeched and jumped behind a Dumpster.

He smiled, turned to face his victims, and motioned to Slade. "Come here."

Slade stumbled toward him, almost tripping in his haste.

"Don't do this," Savannah beseeched, walking slowly toward him. "Please, don't do this."

He was surprised that she'd followed him outside. He would have thought that she'd run from the bar. From him.

Apparently, it was going to take more to frighten her away.

He stared down at Slade, and the man eagerly tilted his head to the side, arching his neck. William felt his incisors burn and lengthen. He looked at Savannah, and he smiled, showing his razor sharp fangs.

"Don't worry, Savannah. It won't hurt him...much."

He lowered his head toward Slade's vulnerable throat.

"No!" Savannah screamed, shoving against his back. "Let him go!"

William snarled and tightened his grasp on Slade. He wasn't about to let his prey get away.

"Don't!" Savannah's eyes were wide and luminous. Her nails dug into his back. "Just let him go." She glanced quickly over at Slade's frozen companion. "Let them both go."

He shook his head. "I can't do that."

"Why?"

He turned his head and let her see his burning stare. Let her see the beast that was within him. "Because I'm hungry…"

Her lips trembled and her face became chalk-white. William expected her to run from the alley at any moment.

She took a deep breath. "I can't let you hurt him."

He arched a dark brow. "I have to feed." He smiled. "I need the blood."

She pushed Slade back and stepped protectively between his body and William's. Her gaze met his.

"Then take mine."

Three

My brother shares my secret, my torment.
He will walk with me in the shadows,
past the angels and past the devils.
He will walk with me through eternity.
-Entry from the diary of Henry de Montfort,
October 31, 1068

Lust flared through him at her bold offer. It was what he'd wanted, what he'd craved, since the first moment that he'd seen her.

To taste her. To drink from her.

It would be ecstasy to hold her body, to feel her breasts pressed against his chest. His body clenched at the thought.

It would be heaven. Or, at least, as close to heaven as he would ever get.

"Take my blood," her soft voice entreated, tempted.

The beast within him raged. He felt his control slipping.

He'd intended to only drink lightly from Slade, taking just enough blood to get through until the next full moon. He'd also wanted to frighten the man, to punish him for daring to touch Savannah.

And, he'd wanted to frighten Savannah, to force her to realize the reality of his existence. To force her to give up her crazed notion of becoming a vampire. Becoming like him.

But it seemed that his plan wasn't working. She wasn't acting as he'd anticipated. And his hunger was growing out of control.

"Leave," he growled, and Slade and his blonde companion fled down the alleyway. They wouldn't remember their encounter with him. He'd planted a strong compulsion in their minds.

Now, Savannah was a different story. His compulsion didn't work on her. She would remember their encounter tonight. She would remember every detail.

As the sound of fleeing footsteps echoed in the distance, they stared into each other's eyes.

The moonlight spilled over Savannah's features and wrapped her in a gentle glow. She looked almost otherworldly in the pale light. *Like an angel that had fallen down to earth.*

His gaze drifted over the garbage-filled alley. *Or to hell.*

"Are you going to do it?" she asked, her hand lifting to touch her throat.

He followed her movement, his keen stare noting the pulse that beat frantically at the base of her neck. He wanted to put his lips against that soft point. To press his tongue against her.

"I want you to do it," she whispered.

His control shattered. He grabbed her, pushing her against the rough brick wall. "Be careful what you ask for, sweet Savannah, because you just might get it."

And he did what he'd been hungering to do all night. He put his mouth on her, his lips claiming hers in a kiss of hunger, of need.

Her mouth was hot, tight, wet against his. Her tongue met his eagerly, and her arms wrapped tightly around his shoulders. She pulled him close against the heat of her body.

She was burning with heat, with life, and he had been cold, so cold, for such a long time.

His hand fisted in her hair, the soft strands easily sifting between his fingers. He tilted her head back, and she opened that delicious mouth of hers wider, letting him slide his tongue deep inside.

She tasted as he'd known she would. Sweet, and just a little bit wild. He couldn't get enough of her. He wanted more. More. All that she had to give.

His lower body was rock hard against her soft hips. He pushed gently, letting her feel his need. His hunger. He'd never wanted a woman this much. Never.

He didn't hear the sounds of the cars as they passed by on the main street. He didn't hear the laughter or the conversations from the bar. He forgot all about the dirty alley. His only thought, his only focus, was her.

He pulled his mouth slowly from hers, kissing her gently now, using his tongue to flick against her lips.

She moaned softly, and the yearning sound tore through him.

His lips moved slowly down her chin, then down farther, sliding around the curve of her neck. He licked her, tasting the salt on her skin. He could feel her pulse, could feel the vibration against his lips. He could smell her, the scent of lavender wrapping tightly around him. He sucked gently on her throat.

"Do it," she whispered, her voice a husky purr of seduction.

And he couldn't resist any longer. His teeth sank deep. She gasped, her body shaking in his arms.

With one hand, he held her head back, cradling her. With the other, he pulled her hips tightly against his own. His hips thrust against her. His lips drank from her.

Her blood was the sweetest he'd ever tasted. So pure. So good. He didn't know if he could ever get enough of that taste. He drank, taking deeply of her essence, loving the feel of her in his arms. Loving her taste.

She shuddered, her lashes slowly lowering. Her body began to slip, to sag slightly against him. He pulled back at once, his tongue licking away the drops of blood that trickled down her throat.

Need still burned through him. He wanted to strip away her clothes, to have her beautiful body bare before him. He wanted to sink himself into her, deep into her, until he could not tell where he ended and she began.

His body ached for her.

"Did you…" She paused and wet her lips. "…get what you wanted?" Her voice was thick, husky.

He stared down at her. "No, but I will…soon."

She frowned, and her body swayed against his. "William? I—" Her head fell back, and she slumped against him. He caught her easily in his arms, lifting her high up against his chest.

He cursed softly. He'd taken too much blood from her. She was a small woman, delicate. He should have used more care.

In truth, he never should have touched her. He'd given in to his need for Savannah, and now that need was raging inside of him. If he still had any conscience, he would let her go. He would send her far, far away from the monster that he'd become.

But his conscience had died a long time ago. It had died in a blood soaked field in France. It had died the moment he killed his brother.

His hands tightened around Savannah's still form.

She was the first thing that he'd wanted, that he'd needed, in over one thousand years.

And he didn't want to let her go.

***

Savannah awoke with a start, her brother's dying scream echoing in her mind.

Her breath panted out, hard and fast, and her heart pounded furiously against her breast.

"It's all right," a man's voice whispered from the darkness beside the bed. "You're safe."

Savannah froze. She knew that voice. "William?" She strained to see him in the shadows.

He stepped forward, and the moonlight from the open window spilled across his rough features.

She looked blankly around the unfamiliar room. "Where are we?" She shook her head, struggling to remember how she'd gotten to this place and into this bed.

"My home." His unnerving stare was locked upon her.

Savannah pushed back the bedcovers and hurriedly stood. Her body swayed. At once, William reached to steady her.

His hands wrapped around her arms. "Careful. Don't move too quickly."

Her body heated at his touch, and she looked away from him, glancing around the room. Trying to find something else, anything else, to focus upon.

Moonlight spilled through the windows and lit the room. She saw that the furniture was antique, heavy cherry wood. A large four poster bed was the center piece of the room. A silken white canopy clung to the top of the bed. A vanity table and mirror were located near the far wall. The mirror gleamed brightly. A silver brush and matching comb sat on the table's surface. Both looked as if they had never been used.

"How did I get here?" she asked curiously. "The last thing I remember was being in the alley…" Her brow furrowed as she struggled to remember those last few moments.

He seemed to stiffen. "I brought you here, after—"

"You bit me," she whispered, her hand rising to touch her throat. "I remember that you bit me! You took my blood." She raced toward the vanity mirror. She sat down heavily upon the cushioned chair and strained to see her neck in the mirror. Where was it? There…two small marks, tiny circles, upon her throat.

He walked up behind her, and she glanced at him, stunned. "I can see you," she murmured.

A dark brow lifted.

"In the mirror. I can see you."

He smiled. "Of course you can. Why wouldn't you be able to see me?"

"But…the legend says…"

He shook his dark head and bent to inspect her small wounds. "Forget the legend. Only half of it is true." He frowned.

"I'm sorry for hurting you."

Surprised, she stared at him.

His jaw clenched. "Despite what you think, I really *don't* enjoy hurting people."

She felt a hot blush hit her cheeks. He wasn't what she'd expected. In reality, she'd expected to be disgusted by him. Repulsed. After all, he was a killer, a vampire.

But when he'd touched her in the alley, she hadn't felt repulsed. She'd felt...desire.

When he'd kissed her, when he'd touched her, a fire had burned deep within her body. Despite all reason, she'd wanted him. She hadn't cared about where they were or who might see them. She hadn't cared about the dirt on the walls or the garbage on the ground. William was all she'd thought about.

And that knowledge shamed her to the depths of her being.

She had a promise to keep. She couldn't forget her vow, not for a moment.

"You've given me the first bite," she murmured, turning to face him, locking her gaze upon his. "Will you give me the other two?" She knew it took three bites to convert a human. Three bites and then a mixing of the blood.

"No." His voice was clipped. He moved away from her, heading toward the open balcony doors.

Savannah followed on his heels. "What do you mean, 'no?'" You have to!"

He stepped slowly onto the balcony, tilting his head back and staring up at the brilliant full moon. "I don't have to do anything." A warning.

A shiver skated up Savannah's spine at the steel laced in his tone. But she refused to back down. "Why did you give me the first bite if you didn't intend to transform me?" Her hands clenched into angry fists.

He turned to face her, and the moonlight seemed to shine in the depths of his eyes. "I wanted to taste you," he whispered, his voice a sensual purr. "I had to taste you."

She swallowed. She hadn't been expecting that answer.

Her surprise must have shown because a mask of anger swept across his face. "I can feel, Savannah. I can want, I can need, just like any man."

"But you're not a man," she blurted. He was more. So much more.

"Yet I have a man's needs." His eyes drifted slowly down

her body, lingering on the rounded curves of her breasts and hips. "A man's desires."

Heat pooled low in her belly. Her breath hitched.

He stepped toward her and lifted his hand to gently cup her cheek. "I want, just like any other man." His jaw clenched. "And I have found that I want you, very badly."

"So that's why you bit me," she concluded softly, her voice husky and quiet in the dying night. "Because you wanted me." The idea left her shaken.

William's hand dropped from her face. She suddenly felt very cold without his touch.

He walked to the edge of the balcony and stared down at the mountainside. "My wants, my needs, can be deadly."

"Not to me," she rushed to reassure him.

He glanced back over his shoulder. "Especially to you. And I am not willing to take the chance that I might put you in danger. I want you to leave at first light."

She moved to stand beside him. "I'm not leaving."

"You must!" He snarled, turning on her like a cornered animal. "If you stay, I'll take you. I need you like I've never needed anyone else in all my years of existence. I hunger for you. For your blood. For your body. For your very life."

Savannah lifted her chin. "I'm not afraid of you. Or of what you might do to me." She didn't have room in her heart for fear.

"I'll kill you," he said, his voice a tortured whisper. "I kill everyone who gets close to me."

"Then transform me. If you are so worried about me, then change me! Make me immortal!"

His face was a haggard mask. "You want me to condemn you to a life of darkness? Of endless hunger and death? Of loneliness? Because if you become like me, that is what you will get."

She took a deep breath and straightened her shoulders. It was time to lay her cards on the table. There was no choice. It was time for the truth. "And if I don't become like you, I'll die."

William froze. "What?" His eyes flashed fire.

"You heard me." Her words trembled faintly. "I'll die." She shook her head. "Why do you think I came to you? Why do you think I spent all of that time researching you? I'm dying, William. And your kiss is the only thing that can help me."

He grabbed her by the arms. "You're dying?"

She swallowed the lump in her throat. "The doctors say that I have six months, if I'm lucky."

"And if you're not?" His scar was a vivid white against his skin.

"Two months."

He swore viciously and closed his eyes.

"So, you see, I don't have anything to lose." She had to make him understand, had to make him listen. He must give her the kiss!

His eyes opened slowly and he stared down at her, his expression fierce. "What's wrong with you?"

She rubbed her throbbing temple with a tired hand. What wasn't wrong with her? She couldn't remember what it was like to feel healthy, strong. She'd spent the last five years of her life in and out of hospitals. Going through endless exams. Endless treatments. Nothing had helped her. Nothing could help her.

"I have a brain tumor." Her voice was perfectly calm. She'd gotten used to telling people. Her stomach didn't clench anymore. Her hands didn't shake.

"Surely the doctors can—"

She shook her head. "There's nothing they can do. They tried. Believe me, they tried, but…" She shrugged.

His eyes seemed to burn down at her. His face was like carved stone. Had her words affected him? Would he help her now?

"You understand, don't you? You understand why I must have the kiss?" She waited, hope flickering through her heart.

He turned from her and stared into the night. "No, I don't understand." He paused, seemingly lost in thought. "You said you didn't have anything else to lose. You're wrong. You still have your soul."

Unlike Savannah, William had lost his soul long ago. The moment Henry had taken his last, shuddering breath. The moment the blood had stopped flowing from the gaping hole in his chest, William's soul had died.

And he just couldn't bring himself to destroy Savannah's soul.

"So you're going to let me die?" Her voice was sharp, angry.

William felt his throat tighten at her words. Let her die? He shuddered at the thought. She had such strength, such passion within her.

He moved quickly, turning to capture her against his chest. "I'll help you. I'm rich. I can send you to the best doctor in the country—"

Her eyes flashed. "Didn't you hear me? The doctors can't help me! I'm dying, William. I will be dead before the year is out."

William knew that doctors could perform miracles these days. It wasn't like it had been in his time. Sickness could be cured. "With the right care—"

She laughed savagely. "The right care? They cut into my brain. They shaved my head, and they cut into my brain. Then they told me I was saved. That the cancer was gone." She took a deep breath. "Within two years, the tumor was back. And it was bigger than before. They made me endure their tests again. The therapy. The shots. Nothing worked. *Nothing.*" She looked deeply into his eyes. "The doctors can't help me. Only you can."

His jaw clenched against the pain he heard in her voice. Against the images her words aroused in his mind.

"Please." A whisper of sound. "Help me."

The moonlight caressed her skin, illuminating the two tears that trickled gently down her cheeks. He caught the tears on his fingers, stared wonderingly at them.

Savannah grabbed his hand. "William—*please.*"

She looked so beautiful in the moonlight. So pure. So alive.

Could he really just stand back and watch death take her?

Her gaze beseeched him, a silent echo to her plea. Her firm breasts pressed against his chest. The warmth from her body reached out to him, wrapped around him. The delicate scent of lavender rose once more to tease his nostrils.

"Please. I will do anything you want…"

His body stiffened as lust tore through him. "Be careful what you offer, sweet Savannah."

She shook her head and pressed ever closer to him. "No, name your price. If I have it, I'll give it to you, I swear!"

Need and hunger battled against his judgment.

"Anything," she whispered, her voice desperate.

"Why? *Why,* Savannah?"

She bit her lip and her lashes fell, cloaking her gaze from him. "Because of Mark."

"Who is Mark?" William asked softly, as an unfamiliar rage swept through him. "Your lover?" The words were a growl, and he knew his gaze pierced her.

"A dead man."

William frowned.

Savannah pulled away from William and rubbed her arms, telling herself that the chill she felt was caused by the night air and not the memory of her brother. "He's been gone almost a year now."

"I'm sorry." William's voice was solemn. "Death is never easy."

And he would know. Savannah nodded, accepting his sympathy. For months after Mark's death, she'd hated the empty words that her friends gave her. The empty condolences. They hadn't understood what she was going through. They hadn't understood what she felt.

He understood. She knew it. William understood her loss.

"What happened to him?"

"He was…killed." A scream echoed in her mind, and a flash of blood filled her vision.

William's gaze was intense. The moonlight seemed to reflect in his eyes and shine back at her. "How was he killed?"

She took a deep breath. "A vampire killed him. Him and his wife." They'd only been married for a little over a year. They'd gone to the family cabin in the woods, planning to have a nice, romantic weekend getaway.

"How do you know it was a vampire?"

"Mark and I were twins. We always had a special connection. And, when the second tumor came, something happened to me. It…changed me. Changed my mind. After that, Mark and I weren't just close emotionally, we were—" She broke off, not certain how to explain. "Sometimes, I could read his thoughts. Share his dreams. We were connected. More connected than I've ever been to another person." At first, the connection had been frightening, overwhelming. But, then, with each day that passed, she'd grown more accustomed to the feeling of sharing another's mind, another's thoughts.

William nodded once, accepting her words. "Were you connected to him the night that he died?"

She swallowed and looked down at her hands. They were clenched into tight fists. "I thought it was just a nightmare. I could see him, I could see Sharon, and they looked so happy." When she closed her eyes, she could still see them sitting by the fire, laughing, kissing.

"There was a knock at the door." Her voice was hollow,

wooden. "Mark had barely opened the door before…*it* attacked him." A shudder racked her body. "Its eyes, *his* eyes," she corrected, "were red, like they were on fire. He picked Mark up by the neck and threw him across the room." A scream echoed in her mind. "He killed Sharon. Before she could even stand up, she was dead. Blood soaked her neck. Her gown. The floor…"

Her temple began to pound. "By the time Mark realized what was happening, Sharon was gone. And then the creature turned on him…"

She couldn't, wouldn't, tell him of the horrors that Mark had endured. He'd been tortured, viciously tortured, before he had received the release of death. In the end, he'd begged his killer to end his torment. The man had laughed, seeming to enjoy Mark's pain, his anguish.

William didn't say a word. His eyes just watched her with unshakable intensity, as if he were looking into her very soul.

"When I woke up, I told myself that it was just a nightmare. That Mark was fine. Then the phone rang." A sad smile twisted her lips. "It was a police officer. He told me that my brother was dead. Mark's body had just been found at the cabin."

"I'm sorry, Savannah." His words were soft, sincere.

She barely heard him. Her gaze was turned inward, viewing a blood-filled scene that only she could see. "I went to the cabin. I drove there as fast as I could. There was blood everywhere. I saw Mark. And Sharon. It looked like they had been mauled by a wild animal."

William touched her arm, and she blinked, her eyes focusing on his dark visage. "But it wasn't an animal. It was a vampire."

"And you plan to go after him? To go after the vampire that killed your brother?" Disbelief was heavy in his voice.

"I *have* to." She couldn't rest until her brother was avenged. And she couldn't let that thing stay out there, killing innocent people.

A sad smile twisted William's sensual lips. "You haven't got a chance. There is no way that you can defeat a vampire. You don't have the strength."

A flush stained her cheeks at his dismissive words. "I don't have the strength now, but I will—if you transform me." Once she had the strength of an immortal, she could defeat the monster.

William stared down at her, his gaze hooded. "My poor, lost little fairy. You truly do not have any idea, do you? Even if

I transformed you, that doesn't mean you'll have the strength to defeat another vampire. A vampire's strength increases as he ages. You will be but a babe, while the creature that killed your brother—" He shrugged. "He could have the power of centuries."

Savannah paled. Her mind raced frantically. "*You* have the power of centuries." He'd been an immortal since the Battle of Hastings. He had to have immense power. "You can help me defeat him. You can teach me, show me what I need to know—"

"I could," he agreed slowly, his face giving nothing away, "but why would I?"

She gasped at his cold tone.

"It's time for you to leave." He turned away dismissively. "I'm sorry for your loss, but there is nothing that I can do for you." He walked back inside the house.

Savannah followed on his heels, leaving the balcony door open in her wake. "How can you turn me away?" she asked softly, confusion filling her. "I read Henry's diary. I know the kind of man that you are—"

He froze. "Don't you mean the kind of man that I *was?*" He glanced back over his shoulder and his eyes flashed red. "As you so astutely noted before, I'm not a man. I'm a vampire, a killer, just like the one who attacked your family." His razor sharp teeth gleamed as he smiled at her.

She refused to give in to the sudden fear that swept through her. She rushed toward him, grabbing his arms. "No, you're not. You're nothing like him. I read the diaries. I *know*." And she did know. She sensed it deep inside.

He pushed her back a step. "You know nothing." His words were little more than a growl. His hand lifted, caressing her throat lightly. "I could kill you now, and there would be nothing you could do to stop me."

"You won't kill me," she whispered. "You won't hurt me." Her gaze met his in an unblinking stare.

He stopped smiling. Hunger flashed across his face. Lust blazed in his eyes. "Won't I?"

Four

There is a price for the gift. A terrible price.
-Entry from the diary of Henry de Montfort,
November 5, 1068

Savannah's chin lifted and she met his gaze with a bold stare. "I'm not afraid of you."

"You should be. You should be terrified." The words were cold, flat.

"I'm not afraid of you," she repeated calmly. "But I think you're afraid of me."

He jerked back from her as if he'd been struck. "I fear nothing. No one."

"No, of course, the 'Dark Knight' would not admit to fear," she said, using the title he'd earned at William the Conqueror's side. "But not admitting it doesn't mean that it's not there. It doesn't mean that you don't feel the fear."

His lips twisted. "And why would I be afraid of you, little one?"

She lifted one brow. "I don't know, Dark Knight. Why are you?"

His eyes narrowed. Did a flush darken his cheeks? She couldn't tell, not for certain. The moonlight wasn't strong enough.

His arms lifted to wrap around her, to pull her against his chest. "I don't fear you," he muttered angrily. "But I do want you."

Her heart pounded. God help her, she wanted him, too.

"I want to drink from you, to taste the sweet nectar of your blood. I want to bury myself in you, to lock you to me," he growled. He bent, and licked the slender column of her throat. She shivered and molten heat pooled low in her belly.

"I want you, as I've never wanted another." He sounded angry, almost enraged, as he made the admission.

Her hands lifted to stroke the strong width of his arms, his shoulders. They felt like steel beneath her touch. His chest brushed against her breasts, bringing the peaks of her nipples to taut, aching life.

She gasped, stunned by the feelings flooding through her. Nothing in her limited experience had prepared her for this, for him.

His teeth scraped against her throat. Her neck arched, opening her more to him, to his touch.

With a growl, he pushed her away. His chest rose and fell in a quick, rapid rhythm. He stared at her, hunger clear on his face.

Need blazed through her body. Savannah clenched her hands into fists, fighting the urge to go to him, to wrap her hands around him.

"You want my kiss." A beast stared at her from behind the face of a man. "And you want my strength to aid in your quest."

"Yes," she whispered, wondering at the sudden change in him.

"How far will you go," he queried softly, "in order to obtain your justice?"

"I told you, I'll do anything." And she would. She would go to any lengths to seek justice for her brother.

He smiled, and for just an instant, a flicker of fear licked through her. "I'll give you what you want, sweet Savannah. I'll see to it that you get the justice that you crave and the kiss that you need so badly." He paused. "And in return..." His gaze roved hungrily over her body.

She swallowed and lifted her chin. "In return?"

"I want you."

Her heart seemed to freeze at the low, harsh words. "I don't understand."

"If I give you the kiss, then I want you. I want you to stay with me. To become my companion. My mate."

Her eyes widened. Surely he couldn't mean it. She laughed, the sound high and nervous. "You can't be serious. You—"

"I've never been more serious." His jaw was tightly clenched. "If you want your justice, you will have to pay a price."

"You mean I would have to sell myself," she snapped. She couldn't believe the proposition that he was offering. Why? Why would he do it? "I thought you said you hated blackmail."

He lifted one dark brow. His lips curved mockingly. "Ah, but this isn't blackmail. It's a bargain."

So this was what it felt like to sell your soul to the devil. Savannah stared into William's swirling eyes and knew that she had no choice. "For how long?"

He froze. "Excuse me?" The words seemed strangled from him.

"How long will I have to stay with you?" She asked, her cheeks flushing.

He took two steps toward her. His hand lifted and gently caressed her cheek. "Why, forever, of course."

Forever. Her skin seemed to burn at his touch. "And what would I have to do as your...companion?" She couldn't bring herself to say the word mate.

He traced the delicate outline of her lips with one tapered finger. "You'd be my lover. You'd share my home, my bed."

"I'd be your whore," she said softly, feeling a wave of shame and anger wash through her.

"No!"

Her gaze flew to his face. She wondered at the rage she saw there.

He took a deep breath, apparently struggling for control. "You'd be my mate."

She swallowed, startled by his intensity. "Why me? You could have anyone that you wanted." And she knew it was true. William was compelling, mysterious. Surely he could have any woman without having to promise immortality.

"I want you," he said simply. "I don't want anyone else."

She frowned, surprised by his answer.

William swore and glanced toward the open balcony door. "Dawn comes. I must leave." He stepped back, staring down at her confused expression. "Take the day to think about my offer. When darkness falls, I will come for you."

She nodded and watched silently as he strode across the room. He stopped at the door and turned back to face her. "If you aren't here when I rise, I'll know what your choice was and I'll understand. But if you are here..." His gaze narrowed, and he continued roughly, "If you are still here, then you'll be mine. Forever."

The door slammed behind him, and the sound echoed in Savannah's heart.

***

He was a fool.

Why had he made that ridiculous offer to her?

William lay on his bed, secure in the tunnels under his home, and wondered at the madness that had swept through him. What had driven him to make that devil's bargain with Savannah?

He could still see the anger that had flared in her eyes, still read the rage that had swept across her expressive face.

He sighed and shifted on the bed, frustration sweeping though him. Was she still there? Was she in the house above him? Or had she already fled from him?

A low growl rumbled in his throat. He hated being trapped in the tunnels. But they were his only option. His gaze scanned the room quickly, and he wondered what Savannah would think of his resting place.

The main room was large, with granite flooring that he'd imported from Italy. Bookshelves lined the walls of the room, and two oversized chairs were arranged in the far corner. His bed was in the middle of the room. Like the one in Savannah's room, it was a huge four-poster made of rich cherry wood.

She probably thought that he slept in a coffin. And, in truth, he had when he'd first become a vampire. The coffin had protected him from the harsh rays of the sun.

But he'd moved on since then. He'd learned much in the centuries of his vampire existence. He'd mastered his strength. He'd learned to hunt. He'd learned to survive.

And he had learned to be alone.

Then Savannah had walked into his world. He wondered what it would be like to share the bed with her. To lay her down on the satin sheets and take her.

He closed his eyes, trying to block the vision from his mind. But in the darkness, the image continued to torment him. He could see her so clearly. Her silken mane of hair, spread on his pillow. The pale column of her thighs, spread for him.

And he knew why he'd made his offer to her. Because he wanted her, craved her, with a desire that was raging out of control.

His body began to grow slack. His time of sleep was upon him. He couldn't fight the dawn. None of his kind could.

Before the darkness claimed him, his last thought was of Savannah. Would she still be there when he awoke?

***

She needed her pills.

Savannah paced her room like a caged lion. With each step that she took, the throbbing in her head seemed to increase.

It was always worse in the mornings. She didn't know why, but her head always ached more in the early hours of the day.

She gritted her teeth against the pain.

She wanted to scream, to rage against the agony that was tearing her mind apart.

But screaming wouldn't do any good. She'd learned that long ago. Neither would begging, or pleading.

She turned on her heel and headed toward the door. She had to get out. She couldn't stay here a moment longer.

She twisted the knob and pulled the wooden door open with a quick jerk. She glanced down the deserted hall, wondering where William was. She knew that he was sleeping. His kind had to sleep during the day.

She walked slowly down the long hall, gazing curiously around her. Paintings lined the walls. Some were of castles, crumbling castles from long ago. Others were of blood-soaked battlefields. Who had painted them? William?

She was at the top of the stairs now. Her hand locked tightly on the banister, and she began to walk down the steps. Halfway down, a sudden wave of dizziness washed over her.

She held on to the banister with all of her strength, praying that the wave would pass soon, fearing that she'd fall, and tumble to her death.

Time seemed to stop as she held onto the wooden rail. Splinters bit into her palms. Black dots danced before her eyes.

She took several deep, gasping breaths. And she willed the sickness to pass. Slowly, the trembling left her body. The dizziness faded. And the darkness vanished.

She crept slowly down the remaining stairs. That had been too close. She had to get her pills.

A phone sat on a table at the base of the stairs. She picked up the receiver and dialed information.

"Yes, hello. What city? Um, Tyler, North Carolina. Yes, I need the number for a cab company. What? Thanks."

Savannah disconnected the call and quickly punched the number for the cab. A gruff voice answered on the second ring.

"Mel's Cabs."

"Yes, I need for a cab to come and pick me up." She rubbed her temple and glanced around the shadowed foyer. "As soon as possible."

"Where are you, Ma'am?"

Savannah rattled off William's address.

A soft whistle blew over the line. "Up on the mountain, huh? It'll be at least an hour before I can get anyone up there."

Savannah's lips tightened. "Fine. Just tell your driver to hurry, okay?" The sooner she got back to her hotel room, the better it would be for her.

"Will do, Ma'am."

Savannah sighed and replaced the receiver. She glanced around, wondering how she could possibly occupy her time until the cab arrived. She didn't want to go back to her room. She couldn't risk another dizzy spell that might send her stumbling down the stairs.

A door to her right stood open, and a soft light shone from within. It was the same room that she'd entered the first night she'd met William. She crept slowly toward the room.

No fire burned in the fireplace. The light came from a small lamp in the corner. She walked toward the lamp. And she saw the diary. Henry's diary. It rested on the table closest to the lamp.

She picked it up, her fingers running lightly over the engraved crest. She traced the shield, and the detailed design of a hawk that lined its surface. This diary had led her to William.

She sighed. What was she to do about William? Could she really agree to his bargain?

She thought of her brother and the screams that still echoed in her mind. Could she allow her brother's killer to go unpunished?

Still holding the diary, she sat down in one of the high-backed chairs in the corner. Her fingers continued to trace the crest.

What should she do?

***

Two hours later, she was back at the Traveler's Inn.

The hotel room looked exactly as she'd left it. She locked the door behind her and hurried toward the nightstand drawer. She pulled open the drawer and grabbed her pills. She swallowed two quickly, not even taking the time to get a glass of water.

She stared down at the bottle, hating it, hating her reliance on the wretched pills. She couldn't even go for a single day without them.

What would it be like to be strong? To be free of the pain? Free of the terrible need for those little white pills?

William could give her that freedom.

Her fingers clenched around the pill bottle.

A loud knock sounded at her door. She jerked around. The knock sounded again. Her door shook slightly.

She carefully replaced the pills and walked slowly toward the door. She leaned forward, peering through the peephole.

A man stood on the other side of her door. His features

were tense, almost angry. As she stared at him, he lifted his hand and pounded again.

"Ms. Daniels? I know you're in there. Please, open the door. I have to speak with you."

She frowned. How did this stranger know her name?

"Please, Ms. Daniels. I have some information for you regarding your brother's killer."

Her eyes widened and she stepped quickly back from the door. She hurried to the closet and pulled a small, locked box from its darkened interior. She punched in the lock's combination, and, with a soft click, the box opened.

A gleaming black handgun rested inside.

She lifted the gun, and with hands that were rock steady, she loaded the bullets. She checked the safety, making certain the mechanism was in place. She stood, holding the gun at her side, and walked carefully toward the door.

She opened the door a tiny bit, barely two inches, keeping the golden top lock in place. "Who are you?"

"My name's Jack Donovan." A soft, southern drawl accented his words. He had dark hair, perhaps a shade lighter than William's, and smooth, handsome features. Savannah surveyed him quickly. He was tall, probably six-two or six-three. His body was muscled, fit. She judged that he was in his early thirties, maybe a little younger.

He was dressed casually, in loose jeans and a black pullover. Both of his hands were lifted in the air, as if he wanted to prove to her that he was no threat.

Savannah didn't open the door another inch. She didn't trust this man, this Jack Donovan. There was something about him that put her on edge.

"How do you know who I am, Jack Donovan?" She asked softly, her gaze firmly locked on his.

His blue eyes held her stare. "I'm a private investigator." He took a deep breath. "I've been following you."

"What?"

He glanced quickly over his shoulder. "Look, I really don't want to discuss this outside, Okay? Let me in, and I'll tell you as much as I can."

Savannah hesitated. She didn't know him, and she sure as hell didn't trust him. "I don't think so."

A door slammed down the hall. Jack swore softly. "Lady, you're in danger. You're going to get yourself killed!"

She lifted one brow. "I'm dying. What's the difference?" Her smile mocked him. If he'd been investigating her, then he had to know about her condition.

A muscle jerked along the column of his jaw. "The difference is the way that you go. Easy, lying in a hospital bed. Or screaming in agony as all the blood is drained from your body."

Her smile vanished.

"Let me come in." His gaze was intent. "We can help each other if you will just let me in."

Her fingers tightened around the handle of the gun. It felt cold, heavy. Reassuring. "All right, you can come inside. But only for a moment."

He nodded and again glanced over his shoulder.

Savannah hoped she wasn't making a mistake. She would hate to have to kill Mr. Jack Donovan. She pulled open the lock and stepped back. He hurried inside.

Savannah silently watched him as he headed toward the center of the room. She shut the door, turning the lock to keep out any more visitors. Then she lifted the gun. She pulled back the safety. The soft click seemed to echo in the room.

Jack spun around, eyes wide. "Hold on!" He lifted his hands, palms out. "I'm not here to hurt you!"

Savannah aimed the gun straight at his heart. She'd learned to shoot long ago, back when she'd been a carefree girl. Long before illness had ravaged her body and her mind. Her father had taught her, and she remembered well the lessons she'd learned. Besides, as close as she was to him, there was no way she could possibly miss.

"What do you want?" Her voice was cool.

He gulped, his gaze locked on the gun. "Look, just put that thing down—"

A small smile twisted her lips. "I don't think so, Mr. Donovan. Now, who hired you?"

A sheen of perspiration appeared on his forehead. "I can't tell you that."

She cocked the hammer of the gun. "That's not the answer I was hoping to hear."

His eyes widened. "I can't tell you, okay? Part of my contract with my client was that I would keep his identity completely secret."

"How do I know that you're even a real detective?"

Savannah mused. She was a bit surprised at herself. She'd never actually held anyone at gunpoint before. She thought she was doing a pretty good job of it.

His hands began to lower.

"Ah-ah! Keep your hands up!" She couldn't risk him pulling a weapon on her.

"I'm just going to get my ID, okay? I'm just going to reach into my back pocket—"

Her body stiffened, going instantly to high alert.

Jack moved slowly. Inch by careful inch, he removed his wallet. He flipped it open and held it up for her to examine. "My detective's license is in here."

She squinted, trying in vain to read the small card. "Throw it to me."

His mouth tightened, but he threw the wallet across the room. It landed at her feet.

She carefully bent and picked up the wallet, scanning the ID. "This could be fake."

"It isn't."

"Why were you hired to follow me?"

"It seems that both you and my employer share a common enemy." His gaze was hooded, watchful.

Her stomach clenched. She put the safety back on the gun, but she did not lower the weapon. Her palms were starting to sweat. "What do you mean?"

"I know you're after your brother's killer."

Savannah said nothing, neither confirming nor denying his words.

"My employer's brother was killed, too," Jack said softly, his gaze watching her, waiting for her response.

Savannah lowered her gun. "How was he killed?"

"Can't you guess?" He waited a beat and then said, "All of the blood was drained from his body."

Savannah swallowed. The fingers of her left hand lifted and rubbed lightly against the two small marks on her neck. Jake frowned at the gesture, and Savannah dropped her hand instantly, swinging her hair forward to cover the wounds. "And your...employer...how did he find out about me?"

"He read about your brother in the paper, about the way he died. And he knew the same killer had committed both crimes."

"But how did he find out about *me?*" Savannah repeated her question, her tone fierce.

"He did some research, and he hired me." Jack shrugged. "Your name was mentioned in a few of the newspaper clippings that I found. Once I knew your name, it wasn't hard to track you."

"How do you know that I am going after the killer?" How could a stranger have known her plans? She'd only confided her intentions to her closest friends.

He blinked, as if surprised by her question. "I knew that you were going after him because you came here."

"What?"

"You came to Tyler. You came to the killer's town. That's how I knew what you were planning."

She stared blankly at him.

"Didn't you know?" he asked softly. Then he swore at the expression on her face. "Hell, you had no idea! You were just stumbling around in the dark."

What was he talking about? The killer wasn't in Tyler. She would know. She would feel him. "You're wrong. You—"

"You've been to his house, lady," he snapped. "You've been to the bastard's house!"

She shook her head. He was wrong. It wasn't—

"William Dark. He murdered your brother. He's the killer!"

Five

The evil lives, even in my dreams.
-Entry from the diary of Henry de Montfort,
November 15, 1068

"You're wrong," Savannah said instantly. "William's not the killer."

"Yes, he is." Jack was adamant. "I'm sorry, but he's the one who murdered your brother." His gaze was filled with quiet pity.

Savannah clenched her jaw. "I know William. He wouldn't—"

"He was in Washington at the time of your brother's murder." Jack's words stunned her into silence. "Did you know that, Ms. Daniels?"

No, she hadn't known. But she'd be damned if she'd admit that fact to this stranger. "It's a free country. A man can travel wherever he wants."

"True. But William Dark was also in Panama City when my client's brother was killed. And he was in Atlanta when a young prostitute was rushed to the hospital. She was suffering from severe blood loss." He shook his head. "The EMTs thought she'd die before they could get her to the emergency room. But she made it. Barely. And she was able to give a description of her attacker to the police."

Savannah's heart thudded dully. "What...what did she say the man looked like?"

Jack never took his eyes off her as he recited the description. "A male, approximately six foot two, one hundred and ninety pounds. He was in his late twenties. He had long black hair that he kept pulled back at the nape of his neck. Sound familiar?"

Savannah refused to answer him.

Jack continued, "She couldn't remember exactly what happened to her during the attack. The last thing she saw was the man. He grabbed her, and then everything went black."

Savannah swallowed. "You think that man was William?"

"No." Jack shook his head once. "I *know* it was him. He fits the description perfectly. And he was in each city at the time of the attacks. He's the one that the police are after. I know it's him!"

"You don't know anything," Savannah whispered, glancing down at the gun she still clutched in her right hand. "Now, I want you to leave."

"Lady, are you listening to me? He's a killer!" He took a step toward her.

Her head snapped up. "No," she said clearly. "He's not." Savannah unlocked the door and stepped to the side. "Like I said, it's time for you to leave."

Jack didn't move. He stared at her, eyes blazing. "You're putting yourself in danger. Don't you understand what he's capable of?"

"I understand him very well." And she did. She knew William. She knew what he was really like. "You're wrong about him. He's not the one you're after." She believed that, with every bit of her heart. She believed in William's innocence.

Jack walked toward the door. He paused, staring down at her. "For your sake, I pray you're right." He pulled a worn business card from his wallet. "But if you're wrong, call me. It doesn't matter what time it is. Call me, and I'll come to you."

Savannah took the card. A faint frown marred her forehead. "You're planning to stay in town?"

"I'll be around," he said vaguely. "Remember, just call me. Don't let him hurt you. Don't let William do to you what he did to the others."

"William didn't do anything to the others." Her voice was firm. "You're wrong about him."

"We'll see." His gaze roamed over her face. "We'll see." He walked out of the room, slamming the door behind him.

Savannah locked her door and hurried to the bedside phone. She wanted to find out more information about that detective.

She punched in the number and waited impatiently for the call to be answered. One ring. Two. Thr—

"Hello?" A crisp feminine voice answered.

Savannah smiled at the sound of her friend Mary's voice. "Hey, Mary. It's me."

"Savannah? Savannah!" Her shriek was loud and clear. "I've been worried sick about you, woman! Why didn't you call me sooner?"

Savannah winced at the reprimand. "I'm sorry. Things have just been moving really fast here. I meant to call you the moment I got into town." Had that really been just two days ago? She took a deep breath. "Mary, I met him."

"Him? You mean William? You met William?" Mary sounded both incredibly thrilled and incredibly frightened.

Savannah sat on the edge of the bed and stretched her legs out in front of her. She was still wearing her outfit from the night before. And her high-heels were killing her. She toed them off and let her feet sink into the worn carpet. "Yeah, I met William."

"And?"

Savannah closed her eyes. "He's everything that I thought he'd be." And he was.

"Savannah…" Mary definitely sounded worried now. "I know you think you know this guy, that you understand him because of that book you read—"

Savannah frowned. "It was a diary, Mary. A diary that you gave to me."

"Yeah, well, when I gave it to you, I had no idea it would lead to this!"

Savannah had known. From the moment that her hands had touched that diary, she'd known it would lead her to William.

"Is he really a…um…" Mary's words stumbled to a halt. Savannah was certain that a dull flush was staining Mary's cheeks at that moment.

"A vampire?" Savannah queried softly.

"Yes…"

"What do you think?"

Mary didn't answer.

A door slammed in the background and laughter drifted softly across the line. Mary swore. "Damn. My roommate is back. I'd better go."

"Wait! I need a favor."

"What do you want me to do?"

Savanna's lips twisted. That was Mary. Always willing to help. "I need you to check someone out for me. Can you do one of those Internet searches again?"

"Sure. Who do you need me to research?" Mary was a true hacker. She'd graduated from college with a degree in information technology at the age of nineteen. Give the woman a computer, and there was nothing that she couldn't do with it. She'd found William for Savannah. She could easily find out information on Jack Donovan.

"His name's Jack Donovan. He said he was a private detective."

Silence hummed on the line. "You don't believe him?" Mary finally asked, her voice soft. She was obviously afraid that her roommate might overhear her words.

"I don't know. I want you to find out for me. Find out everything that you can."

"Sure. Is there a number where I can reach you?"

"I'm staying at the Traveler's Inn, room 718. I'll be here until nightfall." Then she would have to go back to William.

"Okay. It might take me some time to track this guy, but I'll call you as soon as I know something."

"Thanks, Mary. Thanks for all of your help."

"Anytime, Vannie," Mary said using Savannah's old nickname. "Anytime. You just be careful, okay?"

"I'm always careful." And she was, usually.

"Don't forget your meds."

As if she could. "I'll remember." Mary always reminded Savannah to take her meds. No matter where they were, or what they were doing, Mary always reminded her.

It was good to have a friend like Mary. Someone she could rely on, someone she would trust with her secrets.

"I'll talk to you soon."

"Bye, Vannie."

As she replaced the receiver, Savannah's stomach rumbled loudly, reminding her that she hadn't eaten since the day before. And then she'd only had time for a quick bite.

She glanced at the bedside clock. It was just a little past noon. She would have plenty of time to grab lunch, pack, and return to William's by nightfall.

She stood and stretched her tired muscles. Maybe she would even be able to fit a small nap into her schedule. She couldn't afford to let her strength wane, not while she was finally so close to her goal.

She glanced down at her clothes. First things first. While her outfit may have been appropriate for a place like Jake's, she would *definitely* stand out if she tried to walk in the diner wearing these clothes.

Savannah headed resolutely toward the shower. She'd clean up, and then she'd eat. And, maybe, while she was at the diner, she could get one of the locals to tell her a bit more about William. Maybe.

***

William's body lay perfectly still. His chest did not rise.

His heart did not beat.

His mind, shadowed by the cobwebs of his deep sleep, flickered faintly. Unease moved though him.

Something was coming. Someone. He could feel it.

He could feel the evil. So close. Too close.

***

"Hi, honey!" A tall, matronly woman with steel gray hair appeared at Savannah's table. "What can I get for you?" Her pencil was poised above a small, white pad.

"Ah…" Savannah floundered. The woman's quick appearance had startled her. "Do you have any specials?"

The waitress, whose nametag identified as Pat, smiled. "Hon, we always have specials." She jerked her head toward the kitchen. "Today's lunch special is the tuna sandwich combo. You'll get the sandwich, the fries and some coleslaw, all for five dollars."

Savannah snagged a menu from the center of the table. She had never been fond of tuna fish. She scanned down the list of sandwiches. "I think I'll just take the club combo, with a Sprite, please."

Pat scribbled quickly. "Sure thing, hon. Anything else I can get for you?"

Savannah smiled vaguely. "Not right now, but thanks."

"Be right back with your order." With a swish of her hips, Pat turned and vanished through the swinging kitchen doors.

There were only a handful of other customers in the diner. Two truckers sat at the counter, and a man in a deputy's uniform was drinking coffee in the back corner.

Savannah sighed. Everything about the place just seemed so incredibly normal to her. The soft country music playing on the jukebox. The old-fashioned checkered table cloths that decorated the tables. Everything was so amazingly normal.

Who would have ever guessed that a place like this would be home to a vampire?

"You aren't from around here, are you?"

Savannah's head jerked up, and she found herself staring into the deputy's warm brown gaze.

"Ah, no. No, I'm not." What did he want?

"I didn't think so." He continued to stare down at her. "I'm one of the deputies here in Tyler. My name's John. John Sykes."

Savannah offered her hand. "Savannah Daniels."

His grip was firm, but not overwhelming. "And what brings you to our town, Ms. Daniels?"

"I'm visiting a friend," she replied immediately, sensing her chance to push for more information about William. "Perhaps you know him."

"I know everybody in this town. In a place the size of Tyler, it's real easy to get to know your neighbors."

"I'm sure it is," she murmured with a polite smile.

"What's your friend's name?"

It was the opportunity that she'd been waiting for. "His name's William Dark. He lives up on the mountain."

The deputy's eyes widened. He let out a low whistle. "You're in town to see William Dark? Are you sure about that?" He sounded like he questioned her sanity.

Savannah stiffened. "I think I know who I'm visiting," she said, her tone dripping with ice.

John flushed. "It's just that, well, Mr. Dark isn't exactly the type to have visitors, you know?"

That wasn't surprising. "Surely he's had other friends come to town."

John shook his head. "Not that I know of."

"What, exactly, do you know about him?" Savannah held her breath, waiting anxiously for his response.

"Very little." John shrugged. "I heard that his grandfather bought the property on the mountain back in the twenties. And I remember seeing William's dad in town some, back when I was a kid. Course, his dad wasn't much for talking either. And I think he must have used the property here as kind of a retreat." His gaze clouded as he struggled to remember. "Yeah, he came here in the summers. Every summer, until I was about eight or nine."

"When did William move to town?" Savannah asked quietly. She found it fascinating that William would pretend to be his own father, his own grandfather. He had created a thin veil of deception to fool the townsfolk so that he could keep his mountain hideaway.

"He moved here about six or seven years ago. I heard that he inherited the property when his old man died."

Six or seven years. Where had he been before that? What had he been doing? Had he truly been alone for all of those years? All of those centuries? The idea was jarring, chilling. No wonder he wanted a companion.

John frowned at Savannah, sudden suspicion sweeping across his features. "But you should know all this, shouldn't you? Since you're here to visit him…"

"We're…newly acquainted." Yeah, they'd only met two days ago. That definitely qualified as newly acquainted. "There's still a lot we don't know about each other." And that was the problem.

"Hmmm." John didn't look convinced. "Where did you say you were from, ma'am?"

"I didn't. But I'm from Washington. Seattle, Washington."

"You sure did come a long way to visit your friend."

"Yes, I did." She wasn't going to give the deputy any more information.

"Here you go, hon!" Pat appeared, carrying a large plate in one hand and a drink in the other. "One club combo, just like you ordered."

"Thanks."

Pat smiled at the deputy. "Want another coffee?"

He shook his head. "Nah. I got to be getting back on duty." He glanced back at Savannah. "Nice to meet you, Ms. Daniels. I'm sure that I'll see you again."

As he walked away, Savannah wondered why, despite his friendly smile, the words had sounded almost…threatening.

***

By the time Savannah returned to her hotel room, it took all of the meager energy she had to unlock her door.

The sudden wave of exhaustion had come upon her as she finished her meal. She'd been forced to push her half-eaten sandwich away and hurry from the diner.

It was another side effect of her medicine. Severe drowsiness. In her case, severe was definitely the word of choice.

Of course, the fact that she'd no rest the night before only aggravated her condition.

She fumbled with the lock, barely fitting the key inside. All of her muscles felt heavy. Her eyelids kept lowering, her chin sliding down. She took a series of deep, quick breaths, trying to force her body to stay awake.

The key turned in the lock and Savannah stumbled inside her room. She leaned against the cool wood of the door, giving her body a moment to rest. With hands that trembled, she turned the lock on the door handle.

The bed looked so far away. She was so tired. Tired of the exhaustion that plagued her body. Tired of the pain. When would it all end?

She took a step forward. Her leg seemed to buckle. She staggered, struggling for balance. One more step. Two more. She could feel the base of the bed against her knees, and she fell on the bed, her body bouncing lightly. The old springs squeaked in protest.

She stopped fighting the exhaustion and closed her eyes. She would rest, just for an hour or two. The rest would give her enough strength to make it through the rest of the day.

She just needed to sleep for a little while…

***

William's body twitched.

Evil. The word screamed through his mind, but not a sound passed from his lips.

He could feel the presence. Feel its darkness.

So close.

***

She was at the cabin. She could see the sparkling wood. She could smell the crisp scent of a winter fire.

Everything was just as she remembered. The table that her father had made the summer of her sixteenth birthday sat in the corner. Her mother's painting hung over the mantle.

A cheerful fire burned, the flames dancing.

She walked toward the fire, wanting to feel its warmth. Needing so desperately to banish the cold that was sweeping through her.

She looked around, surprised to find herself alone. She'd thought for certain that Mark would be there. Or Sharon.

She felt something wet and sticky touch her bare foot. She glanced down, frowning. Was that water? It seemed to be flowing straight out of the fire.

How could water come from fire?

She bent down, touching the liquid with one fingertip. She held up her hand, straining to see in the flickering fire light.

Her fingertip was red—blood red.

She gasped and jumped back, trying to escape from the

cool touch of the blood. The pool seemed to follow her, moving like a snake on the floor.

The sound of laughter, light and mocking, froze Savannah.

"I've been waiting for you." The words were soft, purring, lightly accented.

Her gaze flew frantically around the room. "Who's there?" She strained to see in the shadows.

"Don't you know?" He whispered. "Don't you know who I am?"

Her heart pounded. "No. No, I don't know you."

"Of course you do, my dear." He laughed again, softly. "You know me very well. Better than any lovers I've ever had. After all, you've shared a kill with me."

"What?" Her feet were becoming soaked in the blood.

"You were here with me. I could feel you. You were here while I fed." His voice drifted from the shadows, seeming to surround her.

What was he talking about?

Mark. Her memory returned in a blinding rush. Mark had died. He'd died here, in the cabin. She'd seen it. She'd—

"That's right," he purred. "Your dear sweet brother. I'm afraid I had to drain him dry."

A cool touch drifted across the back of her arm. Savannah jerked forward, a scream rising in her throat. She turned quickly, hoping to see the face of the killer who stalked her.

No one was there.

His words continued to whisper from the darkness. "But you know what I did, don't you, Savannah? You were there that night. I felt you. I felt your fear. Your anger."

Her hair was lifted gently. A cool breeze blew against the nape of her neck. Savannah trembled.

"Your fear made me strong." The voice was louder now, closer. "It made me hungry."

The flames of the fire raged, snapping out from the fireplace like greedy hands. Savannah felt the heat burn across her skin. Then, in a flash, the fire died.

The room was plunged into darkness.

Something brushed against her leg. Savannah bit her lip, choking back a scream. She knew it wasn't real. The cabin. The voice. None of it was real. It was just another dream. Another nightmare.

His hand grabbed hers, locking tightly around her wrist, crushing the skin and bones in a powerful grip.

It just felt so damn real!

"Tell me, Savannah." His breath whispered across her face. "Did you enjoy it? Did you enjoy watching them die? Did you enjoy it as much as I did?"

She tried to jerk away, but he held her fast. She kicked him, once, twice, but he just laughed at her. "Let me go!"

"Never." He brought her hand up to his lips and kissed the skin on the back of her hand. She could feel the edge of his teeth against her. The sharp edge of his teeth. His fangs.

"Who are you?" She whispered.

"Don't you know?" He turned her hand over, and his teeth scraped against her palm.

Savannah gasped at the sudden flash of pain. The skin split open in two long, narrow slits, and blood oozed onto her palm.

It didn't make any sense. Dreams weren't supposed to hurt. Why did she feel the pain? Why? Why couldn't she just wake up?

She shook her head frantically. "This isn't real. It's just a dream."

His eyes began to glow. An eerie red glow. She couldn't see his face. Or his body. Just his eyes.

"Oh, it's more than a dream. Much more."

It was hell. Being trapped with him, having him touch her, was pure hell for Savannah. Wake up, she ordered herself. Wake up!

"You're not going anywhere, my dear." He licked the blood on her palm. She shuddered. "I have plans for you..."

She had to wake up. She had to!

The red glow of his eyes burned down on her.

True terror burst in her heart. She couldn't get away from him. She couldn't wake up. She was trapped, alone—

"That's it, fear me. Give me that fear. It feels so good..."

"Savannah!" William shouted her name. "Savannah!"

A snarl escaped from her captor, and he shoved her away.

Savannah slipped, falling down into the pool of blood. She still couldn't see anything. She couldn't see William. Or the killer. "William! William, where are you?"

"He can't help you," a deep voice snarled from above her. "He'll only destroy you."

"No!" She scrambled to her feet. "William! Where are you?"

"Savannah! Don't be afraid." His warm voice drifted to her. "I won't let him hurt you." He sounded closer.

She took a deep breath. She didn't understand what was happening. How had William gotten into her dream?

Fire burst once again from the smoking logs, sending light flashing into the room.

William stood in the doorway, rage etched on his face. And, by the fire, another man stood, a man as tall as William and with midnight hair. His arm was thrown over his face, as if to protect him from the fire.

The stranger turned toward William, placing his back before Savannah.

William stiffened when he saw the man's face.

"So, we finally meet again." A low laugh, vicious and cruel, slipped past his lips. "Hello, brother."

Savannah gasped. No, it couldn't be—

***

"No!" Savannah awoke, screaming. Her heart pounded furiously, the sound echoing like a drum in her ears.

The cabin was gone. She was back in her hotel room.

Had it all just been a dream? A horrible nightmare?

She lifted her hand, trying to brush the hair back from her eyes.

She became aware of the pain then. Of the throbbing ache. She turned on the light and stared down at her hand in disbelief. A dark black bruise circled the skin of her wrist.

Savannah's eyes widened. Slowly, she turned her hand over.

Two thin scratches marred the skin of her palm.

And, for just a second, she heard the echo of laughter in her mind. Low, vicious laughter.

Six

Every man has secrets. Dark, dangerous secrets.
-Entry from the diary of Henry de Montfort,
November 25, 1068

The moment the sun set, William's eyes flashed open. He jumped from the bed in a movement so quick it was little more than a blur.

Rage consumed him. How dare that bastard attack Savannah? How dare he? He would destroy him, once and for all.

He cocked his head, listening intently for any sounds in the manor above him. His acute hearing picked up nothing.

Where was Savannah? Why wasn't she in the house?

He sent his mind out, freeing his psychic power, as he searched for her. He could find no trace of her, no trace of the telltale warmth that usually characterized her presence.

He sighed. She was gone. She'd made her choice.

He walked slowly through the tunnel, up the winding staircase and into the house. He traveled through each room, checking carefully just in case he'd missed her. Just in case she was there.

The house was empty.

He stood in the great room, and with a wave of his hand, he sent the fire blazing. He stared into the flames, not really seeing them. Instead, he saw her.

Savannah. With her fiery mane of curls and beautiful eyes. Her passion. Her strength.

He couldn't blame her for leaving. His hands clenched. He understood, really. Why would she want to tie herself to a monster?

He lifted his hand toward the flame. He could feel the warmth on his cold skin. It reminded him of Savannah. For a brief time, she'd brought warmth back into his cold existence. For too brief a time…

He closed his eyes. And heard the sound of an approaching car in the distance. Was it her? Was she coming to him?

His mind sought hers. He felt her instantly. Her warmth. The soothing touch of her spirit. The feel of her almost drove him to his knees.

He took a step forward and then stopped. She would have to come to him. It must be her decision.

So he waited, listening to the quiet purr of the car's motor, to the crunch of gravel beneath the tires.

Slowly, ever so slowly, the car neared the house. He could hear them, hear the driver, an older man with a New York accent, talking to Savannah. He heard her soft, quiet responses.

The car stopped at his gate. His mind flashed, and the heavy iron doors swung open instantly. He felt the driver's surprise, felt the man's fear.

William heard Savannah open her door and step out of the car. He heard her as she began to walk toward the house. He heard her as her heart began to pound, louder, harder. Then she was at the door.

His muscles strained, but he didn't move. She must come to him. *She must!* Even though he longed to go to her.

Her hand knocked against the wooden door, her knuckles scraping lightly. The wind howled, sending the door crashing open. Savannah gasped, the sound traveling easily to him.

So close. She was so close now. Barely twenty feet away from him. He could smell her. Lavender. He could almost taste her.

She took a deep breath, the sound a mere whisper. And she stepped forward. Her tennis shoes squeaked softly on the wooden floor. One step. Another. Closer. Another step. So close. His entire focus was on her.

She stood at the threshold of the great room. He turned slowly, hungry for the sight of her.

Her eyes, bright and clear, met his. She didn't say a word.

She was *here*. He'd told what would happen if she was at the house. *"If you're still here, then you'll be mine. Forever."* The words whispered through his mind.

Savannah dropped a small duffel bag onto the floor. Then she rubbed her hands down the front of her jeans.

William's gaze followed her nervous movement.

"I've chosen," she said softly.

The husky timbre of her voice sent desire shooting through him. He wanted to go to her, to take her into his arms and crush her against him. Instead, he waited, barely moving, desperately needing her to say the words that would bind them together.

"You have to transform me, and you have to help me get justice for my brother and his wife." She licked her lips and took a quick breath. "In return, I'll be your companion, forever."

His companion. His body tightened. "Forever is a long time, Savannah. How do I know that you won't change your mind?" That she wouldn't leave him one day, leave him as his brother had left him centuries ago? Could he trust her? He hadn't trusted another person since his transformation.

Her chin lifted. "I give you my word. I'll stay with you."

"As my mate?" he pressed, a muscle clenching along his jaw.

She flushed. "Yes…"

He walked toward her, taking his time, studying the emotions that flashed across her face. Anger. Fear. He stopped barely an inch away from her. His hands lifted, curling around her and pulling her against him. "A kiss," he whispered, "to seal the bargain."

Her lips trembled, then parted. He lowered his head and locked his mouth upon hers.

She was as sweet as he remembered. The taste of her was so pure, so rich. His tongue slid past her lips, sliding gently into the warmth of her mouth. She met him eagerly, leaning forward into his touch, his kiss.

He swirled his tongue against hers and tasted her, lightly, softly, as if she were a fine wine. And, like a wine, he knew that he could all too easily get drunk from the taste of her.

His arms wrapped around her, pulling her tightly against him. She felt so good. So soft and yielding.

He slid his hands under the edge of her shirt. Her back was smooth, incredibly soft. His fingers caressed her spine, moving lightly up the edge of her back. She felt so delicate, so fragile. Yet she met his kiss with a passionate force that stunned him.

His hand slipped around the edge of her shirt, moving to rest just below the curve of her breast. He wanted to cup her in his hand, to feel her nipple tighten against his fingers. He wanted to take her into his mouth. To suck her. To lick her.

His fingers traced a light pattern on the top of her lacy bra. Her nipple tightened in response. He growled.

Savannah wrenched herself away from him. She took a step back, breathing heavily.

His jaw clenched. He could feel his teeth, burning sharply against his gums. The beast had been roused. "Backing out of our bargain already?" His voice was guttural.

Savannah's eyes were wide, deep pools of mystery. She

swallowed once and shook her head. "Before we go any further, I have to know…"

"What?" What did she need to know? Didn't she already know all of his secrets? What more could she possibly want? Must he lay bare before her? Anger burned through him. He grabbed her arm and pulled her body back against his, forcing her to feel the lust that burned him. "Our bargain is set, sweet fairy. There is no going back now."

"I know," she said, her voice low, almost sad. Her gaze met his. "I don't want to go back."

He held onto his control, refusing to give the beast within his freedom. William took a deep, shuddering breath. He would have Savannah. Soon.

He studied her carefully, searching her face. "What is it that you want to know?"

She held her hand up, her palm facing him. Two thin red scratches ran the length of her hand. William stiffened at the sight.

"What happened to me today? It wasn't a dream." Her hand clenched. "Dreams don't hurt you."

Some dreams did. It was a lesson that William had learned long ago.

"Tell me what happened," Savannah demanded. "I need to know. I *have* to know."

And she had the right to know. He knew that she did. But he didn't want to tell her. He didn't want to see the anger, the hatred, that he knew would mark her beautiful face. He didn't want to risk losing her.

"Tell me, William! Tell me." Her eyes seemed to flash at him.

He had no choice. "It was more than a dream."

She watched him, her very silence urging him onward.

He took a deep breath and stepped away from her. He walked toward the fire. "More than a dream, but less than reality."

"I don't understand." She sounded very calm. He'd expected her to rage, to scream. Perhaps that would come later.

"The…creature that was in your dream—" He broke off, not certain how to explain. "He—he has certain powers."

"What kind of powers?"

"He is a creature of the night. He can control the shadows, the mists—"

"I wasn't in the shadows." Savannah snapped. "I was in my hotel room, in broad daylight."

William turned to face her. "There are shadows everywhere. They are in dark alleyways, deserted parks. Even in the minds of humans." In fact, shadows were most often found in the mind. They lived, they grew, hiding in the darkness of the mind.

Savannah ran a frustrated hand through her disheveled hair. "I don't understand. Stop with the stupid riddles and just *tell me* what happened."

"I am telling you." His voice was as soft as hers was loud. "You have to open your mind; you have to listen to me."

She gritted her teeth. "Fine. He controls shadows. Shadows that are in my head."

"Everyone has shadows." It was one of man's greatest weaknesses. "Shadows of fear, of anger. Shadows that lie in the darkness of the human mind, waiting to grow. Waiting to spread."

She frowned. "I still don't—"

"It's your fear. Your anger. It draws him. And it gives him strength." It gave the creature strength, and it made Savannah weak. He would have to teach her to shield her mind, to protect herself.

"Strength to enter my mind?"

"Strength to enter your very soul." He had to make her understand her peril. "As long as you have the fear, he can enter your mind. He can get to you. He can feel you." He touched her injured hand. "He can make you feel him."

"He said that he'd felt me before." She spoke softly, her gaze hooded. "That he knew I'd been there when he'd…when he'd—" She broke off abruptly, apparently unable to continue.

But William knew what she was going to say, and he finished for her, murmuring softly, "When he killed your brother."

Her eyes welled with tears. "Yes," she whispered. A tear slid down her cheek, but she wiped it away with a quick swipe of her hand. "He said he felt me when he killed Mark." Horror was etched on her face.

"Your mind is strong, Savannah. He's drawn to it. To you." But William would be damned if he'd let the bastard get his hands on Savannah. She was *his*. The bargain had been made.

Her brow furrowed. "You know him, don't you?"

William tensed. It was the question that he'd feared. He thought about lying, about denying the truth. At least for just a little while longer. But, as he stared into her somber gaze, he could offer her only the truth. "Yes. Yes, I know him."

"Who is he?"

He lowered his lashes, veiling his gaze. How would she react? Would his words drive her away? Would their bargain be broken so easily? He spoke softly, "He's a killer. A murderer who has been feeding on the blood of the innocent for hundreds of years."

"We have to stop him," she said, her hands clenched. "We can't let him hurt anyone else."

William nodded. Too many people had already died.

Savannah's eyes narrowed. "There's something else, isn't there? Something you're not telling me."

Surprise shot through him. How had she known? He'd grown amazingly adept at hiding his feelings. "Yes, there's more."

"Tell me."

She stood before him, looking for all the world as if a strong wind would blow her down. But her gaze was filled with such strength, such courage. It was time for the truth. "His name is Geoffrey."

"Geoffrey," she repeated the name softly. A smile of satisfaction curved her lips.

William could read her so easily. She had a focus now, a name. Before, she'd only had shadows. A monster waiting in the darkness. Now she had a name, a target for her anger, her hate.

Her gaze sharpened upon him. "How do you know him?" She asked.

"He's my half-brother."

"What?"

He steeled himself for her rage. For her rejection. "Geoffrey de Montfort is my half-brother."

She shook her head in vehement denial. "No. No, that can't be."

"You read the diary," he reminded her brutally. "You know that I had two brothers. Henry and Geoffrey. One golden like the day, and the other with a soul as dark as the night itself."

"But how—"

"How is he alive? How is he here, now, to kill?" William's lips twisted. "He's my blood. He shares the same curse that I do." They were bound by their heritage. Bound to walk the earth, to feel the eternal hunger.

Suspicion filled her stare. "You knew," she whispered. "You knew he was killing, didn't you? That's why you were in Panama City and in Atlanta. You knew what he was doing!"

How had she known about Panama City and Atlanta? He thought that he'd covered his presence well in those cities. Yes, he'd known that Geoffrey was out of control, that he was out to kill, to destroy everyone that he could. "I knew." Simple, flat.

"And you didn't stop him?" She shoved against him, pushing with all of her strength against his chest. He didn't move. "Why didn't you stop him, you bastard? Why?" She shoved him again.

William caught her hands, easily holding them within his grasp. He opened his mouth to reply, but closed it instead. He should have stopped Geoffrey. He should have stopped him years ago. He was responsible for the evil that his brother had wrought.

"He killed Mark. He killed Sharon, and God knows how many other people! If you knew what he was doing, why didn't you stop him?"

He'd tried. He'd tried to stop Geoffrey. He'd tried to stop him on that bloody battlefield in France. They'd fought for hours, until their bones were broken, until their strength was all but gone. He'd had the stake against Geoffrey's heart. He'd been seconds away from ending his brother's life. And then he'd looked into his brother's eyes...

And seen Henry staring back at him.

For a moment, he'd lost his focus, his strength.

A moment was all the time that Geoffrey had needed. Geoffrey had knocked William aside and fled as fast as he could.

William had been tracking his brother since then, following him around the globe. Finding dead bodies in every city, but never arriving in time to stop his brother.

"I was too late," he finally told Savannah. "Each time, I was too late." The memory of Geoffrey's victims burned him. He could still see them, see their blank eyes and white bodies. See the fear etched on their frozen faces.

Those faces would haunt him for eternity.

"Each time?" Savannah swallowed. Her lips trembled faintly. "Do you mean you were there? When he was killing, you were there?"

Ah. There it was. The fear. The revulsion. He'd known it

would come. He turned from her, not wanting to face that look, not wanting to see her condemning gaze. "You have to understand. He's as old as I am, as strong as I am. I've been tracking him for centuries. Whenever I would get close, when I thought that I had him, he'd slip away. And there would be another trail of blood for me to follow." William knew that Geoffrey had deliberately left many of his kills for him to find. It was yet another way his brother enjoyed tormenting him.

"We have to stop him." Her voice was soft, but firm. "We can't let him hurt anyone else." She touched his shoulder lightly.

William spun around. He couldn't believe that she would want to speak to him, much less touch him, after knowing the truth.

"We have to stop him," she repeated softly, staring up at him with a solemn gaze.

"We will." It was a vow. William would not rest until Geoffrey had been destroyed.

A faint line marred her brow. "Will you be able to do it?"

He nodded. He would do whatever was necessary to stop Geoffrey.

"Are you certain?" Savannah asked. "Will you be able to destroy your brother?"

A wave of sadness washed through him. He'd done it before. "I'll do what must be done." And he meant it. There was no way that he would allow Savannah to be hurt by his brother.

She touched his cheek. Her fingers felt soft against him. "You've had so much sorrow in your life. So much pain," she said.

He said nothing. No one had ever offered him sympathy before. No one had cared.

"I'm sorry, William."

She was sorry? His brother was terrorizing her, had killed her family, and she was apologizing to him?

"I wish…" A sad smile curved her lips. "I wish your life had been different."

For a thousand years, he'd prayed for a different life. But God had long ago turned his back on him. "Don't waste your time wishing. You can't change what is." He stepped back from her, suddenly needing to have some space between them. Needing to escape from the sympathy, from the pity, he saw in her eyes.

"I'll help you. I'll transform you and teach you everything

that you need to know about a vampire's strength. We'll find Geoffrey, and we'll destroy him. You have my promise." His gaze traveled over her body, down from her beautiful face to her high, firm breasts. Slowly, so slowly, his gaze lowered, dropping to her slender hips and her long, long legs. "In return, I want what you've promised me." He didn't want her sympathy. He wanted her body, hot and needy, straining against his. "I want you." Now. In front of the blazing fire.

Savannah lifted her chin. "I've given my word. I won't back down."

He smiled, showing his fangs. "Good. Then let's begin…"

Seven

William has been sent on a devil's mission.
I pray he returns to me in time...
-Entry from the diary of Henry de Montfort,
November 30, 1068

Savannah wouldn't give him the satisfaction of seeing her fear. She hid her trembling hands behind her body and faced him, her stare direct. "I'm ready."

He laughed softly, the sound dark and sensuous. The sound wrapped around her, sliding through her. She took a deep breath.

He began to walk around her, inching his body ever closer to hers. She could smell him. The scent of man. Of dark nights and mystery.

He was studying her, his hot stare traveling over every inch of her body.

"You're not ready," he whispered, moving to stand directly behind her. She could feel his breath tickling the delicate skin of her neck. He leaned forward, putting his mouth next to her ear. "Not yet. But you will be."

He pulled her hair to the side, exposing the skin of her throat. He blew gently against her nape, and a shiver slid through her body. She closed her eyes, trying to shut him out, to block her own rioting emotions. Was he going to do it now? Was he going to claim her body now?

She felt his lips, moving lightly against her skin. His tongue, licking her neck ever so delicately. She moaned, the sound slipping past her lips before she could stop it.

His arm, a band of steel, circled her waist and pulled her back against the hard cradle of his body. She could feel him, feel the rigid length of his desire pressing against her hip.

She took a deep breath, and arched against him.

This time, he was the one who moaned. The sound was low, ragged, full of need.

"Sweet Savannah," he whispered, licking her vulnerable throat. "I want to taste you, all of you."

His hand moved under her shirt, pushing the soft cotton aside as he stoked the skin of her stomach. "You're so soft. Like silk."

His fingers felt rough, yet his touch was incredibly gentle. His hand lifted, moving up her rib cage and toward the rise of her breasts.

Heat pooled low in her belly. Her nipples tightened in anticipation. And she knew that she'd never wanted anyone the way she wanted William.

His hand cradled her breast, lightly teasing the nipple through the lacy covering of her bra. His other arm locked her hips against his, and he pushed against her. His tongue continued to stroke her throat. Long, sensuous licks of his tongue flicked against her skin. She felt the edge of his incisors press against her.

Her eyes flew open, and she stared into the fire. The flames burned, strong and bright. Like the desire that raged through her.

He growled, spinning her around in a quick move that left her gasping for breath. He stared down at her. His eyes were black, deep pools of black desire. She could see the edge of his fangs. White, gleaming.

"Take off your shirt," he ordered, his gaze locked on her face.

Before, with her back to him, it had been different. She'd been lost to his touch, to the magic of the feelings flowing through her. Now, standing face-to-face with him, she felt suddenly awkward, shy.

But she wouldn't back down. Her hands shook as she reached for the bottom of her shirt. She pulled it up quickly, and then she tossed the garment onto a nearby chair. She took a deep breath, feeling the warmth of the fire against her skin. She looked up, staring into his swirling gaze.

What would he think of her? She knew her breasts were small, that her skin was too pale. He'd undoubtedly been with dozens of women. Beautiful women with perfect bodies. She would never measure up to them.

His stare dropped, and he stared at the lacy black bra she wore. It was small, just scraps of lace. He licked his lips.

Savannah swallowed.

"Now your jeans," he said, his voice guttural. His cheeks were flushed and his jaw was clenched.

Savannah kicked off her shoes and pushed off her socks. She took a deep breath, and her fingers lifted to the button at her waist. She fumbled, struggling with the clasp. Her hands shook as she slowly slid down the zipper. In seconds, she'd pushed the jeans away, and she stood before him, clad only in the thin black lace of her bra and panties.

He stared at her, his gaze traveling over her like a physical touch. "You're beautiful. Every inch of you."

He stepped toward her. His hands lifted, locking around her waist. He pulled her against him, against the rough fabric of his shirt and pants. She gasped, her skin feeling hypersensitive.

He lowered his head, and his lips locked on hers. His tongue pushed boldly into her mouth. She met him full force, kissing him with all of the desire she had.

She felt her bra drop to the floor, and she wondered when he'd unhooked it. Then his hands were on her body, and she stopped thinking at all.

His fingers plucked at her nipples, squeezing and releasing the tight buds. Her knees shook, and she leaned into his touch. His head lowered, and he began to lick and suckle his way down her body. His tongue felt like rough silk.

He lowered her onto the hard wooden floor. It felt cold against her back. But she didn't care. His lips were locked on her nipple, and he was licking her, suckling her hungrily.

She moaned. Never had she felt such need. She lifted her lower body, arching against him. She felt so empty. She needed him, needed him to fill the emptiness inside of her.

She felt his pants against the tender skin of her thighs. She wanted to feel *him*.

"Your clothes," she gasped. "Take off your clothes. I want to—"

Before she could finish the sentence, his clothes melted away. Her eyes widened in shock. How had he—

He spread her legs, positioning his body carefully against her. His mouth continued to lick her breasts, to stroke and arouse. His hand slid down, over the curve of her stomach and then to the curling patch of red hair at the juncture of her thighs. He parted her tender folds, and his fingers began to stroke her. A choked cry slipped past her lips.

He growled, and his mouth suckled harder.

One of his fingers moved to her opening. Her hips moved frantically. She could feel the tension tightening through her body. She needed him, needed him desperately. Her head thrashed.

His finger slid inside.

She gasped.

He lifted his head, staring down at her with eyes that glowed red.

"You're wet for me, Savannah. I can feel your need."

His finger stroked deeper, moving in and out of her body in

a light rhythm.

It wasn't enough. Her body shook. She needed more. She needed him.

"William!" She shuddered, pressing her body against his hand.

"You're so tight." He licked the curve of her breast. "But you'll take me, won't you? You'll take me into your beautiful body."

His thumb pressed against her, and the tension in her body mounted. Heat flashed through her, and she strained, desperate for a release from the savage hunger sweeping through her.

She'd never felt such need. Her body ached, throbbed. She was struggling desperately for relief, an ease to the pounding need that swept through her. "I can't—I can't—" Savannah didn't know what she needed, what would stop the fire that burned her.

William knew. He moved, pressing his erection against her moist opening. "Look at me," he growled. The tip of his shaft penetrated her. "Look at me!"

Her gaze snapped to meet his. His face was carved in harsh lines of need. Of hunger.

"There's no going back, Savannah."

He thrust against her, a strong, deep thrust that pushed him fully into her body. Savannah cried out at the unexpected pain.

He froze and stared at her, his expression shocked. He held his body still within her. Sweat broke out on his brow.

Savannah's body slowly relaxed around him as the burning pain faded to a slow throb. "It's all right," she whispered. "I'm okay now." She moved her hips slightly against his.

His control shattered. A low growl rumbled in his throat, the sound like that of a wild beast. His hands lifted her, positioning her legs around his waist and holding her body tightly against his. He thrust into her, deep and hard. Again and again.

And her need returned. Desire tore through her. With every thrust of his hips, he sent her higher, closer to the edge of burning pleasure. She could feel him all around her. In her. So strong.

He moved her hips, pushing deeper into her than ever before. Savannah's body tightened. His hand slid between their bodies and he touched her, just one touch.

She exploded. Pleasure roared through her body. She screamed his name.

He kept thrusting against her. Deeper. Harder. He lowered his head. She felt his breath against her neck. Felt the scrape of his teeth.

Impossibly, she felt her body struggling for another release. The tension within her wound tighter. Tighter.

His teeth plunged into her neck. Burning pleasure ripped through her. He thrust into her one more time and spilled himself into her, his body shuddering.

The cord of tension snapped. Her body convulsed in a climax so intense she sobbed. Lights flashed before her eyes and then faded to darkness.

Complete darkness.

***

Her neck felt sore.

Savannah frowned, feeling the pain dimly. Why was her neck sore? What had—

Her eyelids snapped open.

William was frowning down at her. His hair had come free of its tie, and the dark mass hung loosely around his bare shoulders. He looked fierce. Dangerous. But then again, he always looked dangerous. There was no hiding the true nature of the beast.

She tried to sit up, but he put his hands on her shoulders, holding her easily in place. "Don't move." There was a trace of gruffness in his tone. "Your body's weak."

She nodded. Her limbs felt heavy and a deep lethargy filled her.

"It's from the blood loss." His assessing gaze traveled over her. "I took too much from you. I should have used more care—" His jaw clenched, and the scar on his cheek seemed to whiten even more. He looked up, gazing into the flames. "There's no excuse. I'm sorry, Savannah."

There was such sadness in his words. She didn't want William to be sad. He'd had enough pain in his life. "I wanted you to do it. You know that." She'd wanted him to do everything. Wanted him to claim her body. To take her blood.

"I should have had more control." His hands clenched around her shoulders. She flinched at the painful grip, and his hold immediately eased.

"I didn't have much control, either." Her lips curved in a wan smile.

He searched her face. "Why didn't you tell me?"

"Tell you?" She swallowed, trying to ease the dryness in her throat. "Tell you what?"

"That you'd never been with a man. That it was your first time." The words fell heavily into the quiet room.

She took a deep breath and pushed herself into a sitting position. His hands fell away from her shoulders. "You didn't ask," she muttered, feeling a flush stain her cheeks. So she'd never had sex before. Big deal. Why was he making such an issue over it?

"You should have told me," he murmured, his gaze falling to rest on the gentle rise of her breasts. "Things would have been different. I could have made it better for you—"

It got better? Savannah didn't know if she could survive a "better."

"William, I didn't want anything different. I just wanted you." And that was the truth. She hadn't cared about their bargain. She'd only thought of him. And of the need that he stirred within her.

His hand reached out and he began to caress her breast. "Why did you wait? Why didn't you find some nice human and have sex long ago?"

Her nipple tightened. Just a touch and already her body was burning again. She took a deep breath, trying to focus on his words. "Why did I wait?" She laughed softly, a light, bitter laugh. "At first, I was too sick to care. After all, when you're dying, making love is very low on your list of priorities. I was in and out of the hospitals. Sick from the therapy, the surgery, the medicine. I didn't have the energy to waste on a relationship."

She thought about the way it felt when William claimed her. Thought about the pleasure. The need. Yes, it was true that she hadn't cared enough about making love to experiment. But if she'd known what she was missing...

His hand cupped her breast and Savannah bit back a sharp moan.

Oh, if she'd known...

But then again, making love with someone else wouldn't have been the same. There was no one else like William. No one.

Already, her body was heating, her muscles clenching, as a new hunger swept over her.

"You're so responsive." His eyes began to smolder. He stared down at her, his features tense. His hand slid down her stomach, to the cradle of her thighs. "I want you again," he said, his voice guttural. "I need to feel you, wrapped around me, squeezing me—" His fingers slipped inside her.

Savannah gasped at the mix of pleasure and pain that ripped through her.

William froze. "Savannah?"

She licked her lips. "I-I'm a little sore." But she had a feeling that he could make her forget all about the pain.

He swore, the words eloquent and harsh. His fingers slowly withdrew from her, easing out of her passageway. "Of course, you are. I'm sorry. I—" His jaw clenched. "I don't seem to have control around you."

Her heart pounded at his heated expression. She realized she didn't want him to have control. She wanted him to need her, to want her, desperately. No one had ever wanted her like that before. No one.

He locked one of his arms around her shoulders and slid his other arm under the curve of her knees. He lifted her easily, cradling her against his chest. He stared down at her, his gaze intent. "I'll take care of you, Savannah."

She gently traced the line of his scar. A scar his brother had given him on a bloody battlefield. "And I'll take care of you."

He blinked, as if startled.

Savannah smiled and rested her head against his broad shoulder. William didn't realize it, but she knew that he needed her. Just as much as she needed him.

He walked through the house, carrying her easily. His arms were tight around her, secure. And she felt so safe in his arms. Being there, being with him, felt right.

In moments, he was standing on the back deck. Savannah glanced around curiously. A huge wooden deck extended along the entire length of the house. A large hot tub sat in the middle of the deck. The night sky shone down on them, the glitter of a thousand stars lighting the area. Savannah shivered, feeling the cool touch of the air upon her skin.

William eased Savannah to her feet, and his arm braced her against him. He bent down, quickly turning on the tub. A stream of bubbles erupted.

"This will help you. It'll ease the soreness."

The steam from the water began to rise, drifting like a ghost in the night. The soft sound of the bubbling water relaxed her. William helped her into the tub, and she sighed at the feel of the water. She sat down slowly, letting the warmth of the water envelope her.

William moved in beside her, his gaze watchful.

She leaned back, resting her head against the edge of the tub. The water felt good against her skin. But not as good as William.

"Better?" His hand rested on her thigh.

Savannah nodded, not trusting herself to speak.

He moved closer to her, his muscled leg sliding against her. His arm slipped behind her neck, cushioning her head.

He sat with her for an endless time, seemingly content to just stare into the night. Savannah didn't speak. The moment seemed strangely special. The two of them, sitting in the quiet of the night. There was no death here. No monster waiting to attack. Just them.

She heard the distant cry of an owl, a sad, mournful cry. William shifted against her, pulling her closer to his body.

He was so strong. His body was full of thick, steely muscles that had been hidden behind his clothes. Now, naked, he looked like the warrior he'd been so long ago. The warrior that he still was.

She looked at him carefully, studying him from under the veil of her lashes. What had his life been like? What all had he seen and done in his thousand years?

She had done little in her life. She'd only just graduated from high school when the first tumor had been discovered. After that, her life had been a blur of hospitals and surgeries. She'd wanted to go to college. To study art in Europe. But she'd never had the chance.

"I can feel you, Savannah. Your sadness." His voice rumbled against her. "What troubles you?"

"How can you tell—" She stopped as realization dawned. Of course, he knew. He'd given her the second bite. They were linked now. The second bite gave a vampire enormous power over his victim. According to the legend, he would be able to read her thoughts now. If he wanted, he could completely access her mind, no matter how far away she was from him.

She would never be able to escape him now.

"No," he said softly. "You won't." His arms tightened around her.

"I don't like you being in my mind," she told him, her gaze fixed on the bubbling water. She didn't want him, or anyone, to know all of her emotions, all of her thoughts.

"Why not?" There was a hard edge to his words. "You've been in mine for days."

Her head snapped up, and she stared at him, stunned. "Wh-what do you mean?"

His stare was locked on her, fierce with intensity. "From the first moment that I saw you, you've been all that I could think about. Waking. Sleeping. You've been there. In my mind. Driving me crazy."

She swallowed.

"I thought about you all the time. About the things that I wanted to do to you." His stare burned her. "I wanted you, naked, beneath me. Holding me so tight that I couldn't tell where you ended and I began."

Need ripped through her. She'd thought she was too tired to respond anymore. But with just a few words, he had desire stirring within her again.

"You want me, too, don't you?" William murmured, lifting his hand to caress her breast beneath the churning water. "I can feel your desire." And it was true. He could feel it. Her passion. Her need. It inflamed him. He wanted her. Now. Wanted to feel her body clenching around his. Wanted to hear her moaning his name. Her desire was a temptation he couldn't resist. His head lowered. "I want to taste it. Taste you."

His lips captured hers. She met him eagerly, her moist lips parting instantly for the thrust of his tongue. His body was rock hard, throbbing for her. He had to have her again. He had to.

His hands cupped her breasts. Perfect breasts. They fit into his hands like they were made for him. She moaned, and he drank the sound eagerly from her lips.

He parted her thighs, pushing his hips between them. The broad tip of his penis pushed against her opening, eager to return to the paradise of her body.

His right hand slid between their bodies. He found her core, teased her, pushed lightly against her button of desire. Her legs strained against him.

"You're so beautiful," he whispered. And she was. He'd never seen anyone so perfect. Her eyes were bright, flashing with desire. Her cheeks flushed a light pink. Her lips were parted and moist, just waiting for his kiss. The starlight shone down on her, lighting her delicate skin with a gentle glow. She was so beautiful that he ached just looking at her.

Her nails dug into his back. Her hips pushed against him. The bloodlust rose within him. The beast, hungry for her, roared its need. Just a taste. Just one more taste...

His head lowered to her throat. He licked her. Once, twice. She was so sweet. So damn sweet. And he just needed a taste.

His incisors burned. He could feel them stretching. All it would take would be one bite. Just one bite. And she would be his forever.

He scraped her neck, opening his mouth wider. He caught her delicate skin with the edge of his teeth.

"William," she whispered, her voice soft, full of need.

He froze. The beast within him howled. The man struggled for control.

She wasn't strong enough. Her body wouldn't survive the third bite. Not now. He'd taken too much from her earlier. The blood loss had made her too weak.

His body shook with the effort of maintaining control. He couldn't do it. Not now. He couldn't drink from her. If he did, he would kill her.

His head lifted slowly, painfully, away from her neck. He stared down at her, taking deep, gulping breaths. He had to stay in control. He couldn't risk hurting her.

She lifted her hands, curving them around his shoulders and then sliding them down his chest. Her fingers brushed against his chest hair, rubbing against his nipples. Her scent wrapped around him, stirring his need, and her hips pressed against him, pushing the tip of his penis inside of her tight opening just a little more.

He shuddered. "So damn good," he whispered, his voice a savage growl. He lifted her smooth, soft legs and wrapped them around his waist.

He couldn't wait any longer. He thrust, deep and strong, into her welcoming warmth. They both gasped.

She was so tight. He could feel her body squeezing him, gently milking him. He moved slowly at first, trying to give her body a chance to grow accustomed to the feel of him. But then she moved, pushing her hips up against his. And he was lost.

He pulled back and then thrust deep. Again and again. His jaw clenched. Sweat beaded his brow. Deeper. He had to get deeper.

"Come on, Savannah. Come for me. Give me more. Give me—" *Everything*, he finished silently. He wanted everything that she had to give.

He felt her clench around him, heard her choked scream and felt the ripples of her release.

Her climax sent him over the edge. He thrust deep one more time and erupted. Pleasure slammed through him. His entire body shook in blissful release. He felt consumed by her, by the pleasure that ripped through him.

When the tide finally ended, his head dropped to her shoulder. His body shook slightly. His breathing was ragged. His heart pounded.

The water bubbled around them.

He kissed her smooth skin.

For the first time in over nine hundred years, he felt at peace. And it was because of her.

She lifted her hand, brushing it lightly through his wet hair.

He moved, shifting his body up. He captured her hand within his. His vision was strong. Even in the starlight, he could see the two red lines that marred her palm. He pulled her hand toward his mouth, licking the lines with gentle care.

She stared at him, her gaze direct, searching. She was his mate. This woman with the emerald eyes and sad mouth. She was his. And he would protect her with his life.

He withdrew slowly from her body, hating the separation from her warmth, but knowing that she needed time to rest. He had plans for her. And he had to make certain that she kept her strength. After all, it was going to be a long night.

***

"I spoke to her today." Jack didn't bother to identify himself. He knew that his employer would recognize his voice.

"And what did Ms. Daniels have to say?" The voice was cultured, slightly accented.

Jack had never been able to pinpoint the accent. Sometimes it sounded English. Sometimes French. He could never be certain. "She didn't believe me, said William wasn't the killer."

"But he is." His employer's tone never changed. He spoke calmly, politely. "She must be made to see that. William Dark is a killer."

Jack took a deep breath. He knew his boss wasn't going to like this next bit of news, but he had to tell him. "She went to William."

Silence.

Jack glanced quickly around his small hotel room. It was a floor below Savannah's. All the furniture was the same. Small, sagging bed. Old color television that only picked up five channels. Scratched dresser and desk.

He was really getting tired of staying in places like this. Getting tired of chasing people that didn't want to be caught.

"I didn't hear you, Jack. Tell me again. What did Ms. Daniels do?"

Jack sighed and ran a hand through his already disheveled hair. "She went to him. I followed her. She left a little after dusk and took a cab up to his place." She'd also taken a small duffel bag, so he knew that she planned to stay the night with William. She planned to stay, even though Jack had warned her away. "Dammit! I thought she'd have more sense. I thought she'd understand. That bastard killed her brother."

"Some people just don't know what's good for them."

That was the truth. Savannah Daniels had put her life in danger, but she didn't seem to care. She'd stood before him, stubbornly declaring William's innocence. She'd ignored Jack's evidence, trusting completely in a man he knew to be a killer.

"Do you want me to keep following her?" Jack asked, trying to rub out the tension in his neck.

"Actually, I think I'll handle Ms. Daniels from now on."

Jack frowned. He suddenly went on high alert. Handle her? What did he mean by that? "What are you talking about?"

"No need for you to worry, Jack. I'll keep an eye on Ms. Daniels from now on."

For some reason, those calm words sent a chill skating down Jack's spine. "But I'm here. In Tyler. I can keep an eye out, make certain she's safe—"

"Your job's finished, Jack. Go back home. Go back to that cute little school teacher that's waiting on you."

Jack's fingers tightened around the receiver. How had he known about Kelly?

His employer continued talking, his voice as smooth as silk. "Don't worry, Jack. I promise you, I'll take special care of Ms. Daniels."

The line went dead, and Jack suddenly realized that he had just a made a terrible, terrible mistake.

A mistake that might just cost an innocent woman her life.

Eight

William is my only hope, my last salvation.
-Entry from the diary of Henry de Montfort,
December 2, 1068

William took Savannah back upstairs just before dawn. He cradled her gently against his chest, holding her like the precious gift that she was. And he thought of the passion they'd shared...

He'd held her through the night. He'd heard her sweet moans, felt the clenching of her muscles that signaled her climax. He'd held her, heard her choked cry when she'd come beneath him. Heard her cry his name. He'd made love to her countless times. And every moment, he'd had to fight the beast inside, to fight the urge to take more of her precious blood. But she wasn't ready for the final exchange yet. He would have to wait.

He stared down at her sleeping face. She was so beautiful. She had no idea of the power that she already wielded. She could get him to do anything she wanted with but a crook of her slender finger.

He knew it was dangerous to let her get so close. She would make him weak, vulnerable. And he couldn't afford to be vulnerable, not with Geoffrey hunting.

He placed her gently onto her bed, pulling the covers over her naked body. She didn't stir. He'd worn her out. He knew he should have restrained himself, but his need, his desire for her, had been too strong. And each time he'd reached for her, she'd met him with equal passion.

He stroked her cheek. She was his weakness. He knew that, and he would have to guard her well.

He kissed her lips, a light, whisper touch. He wouldn't let Geoffrey touch her, not even in her dreams. He would stand guard for her, making certain that her sleep was peaceful.

After all, she was his mate. *His.*

He walked slowly down the stairs and into the great room, almost as if he'd been drawn there. He stood at the threshold, staring at Henry's diary. He moved silently across the room and lifted his hands to pick up the diary, but then he stopped. He couldn't do it. Not yet. He couldn't read Henry's words, see his brother's last thoughts.

He was responsible for his brother's death. His brother's

blood would always be on his hands.

He clenched his fists. No, his hands couldn't touch the diary. Couldn't open its precious pages. Not yet. He closed his eyes and saw his brother's face.

Forgive me, Henry.

***

Savannah awoke, alone. She squinted, her eyes slowly adjusting to the sunlight that streamed through the glass doors of the balcony.

She glanced around the expansive room, recognizing the furnishings. She knew this room. She'd been there yesterday. William had brought her there after he'd taken her blood in that horrible alley.

William.

She stretched slowly, feeling small aches all over her body.

She'd never known that lovemaking would feel that way. So intense. So consuming. She'd expected to enjoy being with William, but she hadn't expected for the pleasure to literally overwhelm her.

She blushed as she remembered the things they'd done. The things she'd done. And she knew that she couldn't wait to see him again. To once more feel the magic of his touch. It wasn't about the bargain. It was about him.

Death had surrounded her for so long, and he made her feel alive.

She sat up, wondering what time it was. She knew William was down below, resting in his room. He'd told that he would rise at sunset.

How many more hours until sunset? How much longer until she saw him again?

Her clothes were neatly folded on the settee at the end of the bed. William must have brought them, perhaps when he'd carried her upstairs. She slipped on her jeans and her rumpled pullover and walked toward the balcony. With a soft push, she opened the doors and let in the sunlight and the crisp mountain air. The scent of pine tickled her nose.

She looked up, trying to gauge the sun's location. It was already starting to sink into the western sky. In another hour or two, it would be dusk.

And William would rise.

She couldn't believe that she'd slept so long. She usually rose early, especially since she'd started having the dreams.

Turning from the balcony, she stepped back into her room. It was such a beautiful day, and she knew she wouldn't see many more sunlit days. Soon, she would only see the night, so she'd better enjoy the light while she still could.

Her shoes were arranged on the floor beside the settee. She hurriedly put them on, then combed her hair and secured her mane in a loose bun at the back of her head.

She walked back out onto the balcony. The forest stood before her, the pine trees swaying gently. She moved toward them eagerly, a slight bounce in her step.

Birds chirped a soft melody. A light, happy melody. Her lips curved faintly as she caught sight of a cardinal soaring near the treetops. At that moment, she realized that something was missing. For the first time in over five months, she hadn't awoken with her usual headache. Instead, she felt strong, refreshed.

Alive.

She smiled, contented. She felt good. For the first time in so very long, she felt good.

She walked along an old trail, strolling easily through the woods. She wondered how long the tress had been there. Some of them were old and twisted. Stretching high into the sky.

It was so beautiful on the mountain. So peaceful. So—

A twig snapped, the sound echoing like a shot. She spun around, her hand rising instinctively to her throat. She couldn't see anyone. "Is someone there?"

The forest was eerily still. Even the birds were silent.

Savannah frowned. Maybe it had been an animal. A raccoon. Then again, maybe it had been something else. *Someone else.*

She took a step back, her eyes scanning the thatch of woods. She couldn't shake the feeling that someone was there, watching her.

Her heart pounded. She retreated another step and stumbled into something. Into *someone.* A hand grabbed her shoulder, and she spun around, kicking out with her right foot. He grunted, his arms shooting out to catch her body in a tight grip.

She opened her mouth to scream, and his hand slammed down over her lips, silencing her before she could even make a sound.

"I'm not here to hurt you," he whispered, his voice fierce. "I came to help."

Savannah blinked, staring up in shock at the man before

her.

Jack Donovan stared down at her, his jaw clenched. "I promise I'm here to help you."

She shoved his hand away from her mouth. "Sure you are." Her gaze was full of suspicion as she studied him.

He took a deep breath. "Look, lady, I think you're in serious danger."

She crossed her arms over her chest. She really wasn't in the mood to listen to him attack William again. "I told you William wasn't involved. He didn't kill anyone!"

Jack didn't respond.

Savannah glared at him. He'd followed her into the woods, terrified her, and now he was still blaming William for the murders—even though she'd told him that William was innocent. She pushed past him, heading back to the house. She wouldn't listen to any more of his lies.

"Wait!" He hurried to catch up to her. "Dammit, would you just stop?"

She kept going.

He grabbed her elbow. "Please, stop and listen to me."

She jerked her arm free. "I don't want to hear anything you have to say. Why don't you just go back to town?" And get the hell away from her.

"I can't leave you here."

She glanced back over her shoulder, a sneer curving her lips. "Sure you can. Just get back into your car, crank it up, and drive down the mountain. I'll be fine."

"No! You don't understand—" He ran an agitated hand through his hair. "I'm trying to help you!" There was an almost desperate edge to his words

It was the desperation that stopped her. She turned back to stare at him, her eyes narrowed. "William isn't the killer, Mr. Donovan. I told you that already. I'm not in any danger from him."

"It's not William that I'm worried about," Jack said.

"What?"

Jack looked around the woods, his gaze darting frantically to the left and right. The setting sun sent dark shadows drifting through the forest. "Look, can we go inside? We really need to talk."

Savannah hesitated.

"I'm not going to hurt you," he promised. "I only want to

help."

"What about your client?"

A muscle flexed in his jaw. "I'm not working for him anymore."

Savannah's brows snapped together. "Then what are you doing here?"

"I told you, I'm here to help you."

"Why?"

His lips thinned into a small line. "Because I think I've just arranged your murder."

* * *

William could feel her. Something was wrong. She was afraid.

He lay perfectly still on the bed. Not a single muscle moved. Yet his mind raged.

Something had happened. Savannah was in danger.

The evil was growing closer once more.

* * *

Savannah locked the balcony door behind Jack. "Okay. We're inside. Now say that again."

He exhaled heavily and dropped into a nearby chair. "I've screwed up."

"How?" He was starting to scare her, and she didn't like to be scared. She clenched her hands. "What have you done?"

He leaned his head back and closed his eyes. "Remember when I told you that my client's brother had been killed?"

"Yes." His words still echoed in her mind. *All of the blood was drained from his body.* Her neck tingled.

"I called a buddy of mine on the Panama City force. He gave me the victim's name. Peter Gilbert." Savannah paced, listening intently to his words as he continued, "That matched up with what I'd been told. My buddy confirmed the victim had one brother, a man named Jonathan."

"And Jonathan was your client?"

"Jonathan Gilbert was the name my client gave me," Jack replied carefully.

Savannah stopped pacing. "The name that he gave you? Are you telling me that wasn't his real name?"

He shook his head wearily. "No. It wasn't his real name. I spoke to the real Jonathan Gilbert late last night. He didn't know me. He had no idea that I was even working on his brother's case."

Savannah felt icy tendrils close over her heart. "If you weren't working for Jonathan, then, who, exactly, was your client? Who hired you to follow me?"

Jack met her blazing stare without flinching. "I don't know."

"What?"

Jack flushed. "I never met him in person. I talked to him on the phone and via the Internet. He wired money directly to my account." He shrugged. "He sent me files to back up his story. I had no reason to doubt his identity."

"You're telling me that someone hired you to follow me around the country, and you have no idea who that person is?"

He nodded, his cheeks staining a dark red.

Great. Just great. The detective had no clue.

Unfortunately, Savannah had an idea who his client was. Deep inside, she knew. But she prayed that she was wrong. She rubbed her arms and began to pace around the room. "You said that you'd set up my murder. What did you mean by that?"

"Yes," William drawled from the open doorway. "Tell us how you arranged for her to die."

Jack jumped from the chair as if he'd been scalded. "Who—" He turned, catching sight of William's furious visage. His eyes widened.

William stalked toward him with the slow, unrelenting stride of a hunter. A hunter that has scented true prey. A faint sheen of red glowed from the depths of his black eyes.

Savannah hurriedly placed herself between the two men. William looked like he could easily kill Jack in that moment. "William, I can explain—"

William never took his gaze off Jack. "I want *him* to explain. I want *him* to tell me why I shouldn't do the world a favor and just kill him right now." His accent was heavier.

Savannah touched his arm lightly. "I'll tell you why. Because you aren't a killer."

"Yes, he is." Jack moved to stand beside her, trying to push her behind him.

When Jack's hand closed around her arm, a low growl emitted from William's throat. Savannah thought she could see the edge of his teeth.

"Step back," she whispered to Jack, knowing that he was in serious danger.

"No way." Jack was obviously terrified, but he stood his ground. "I know about him. William Dark is a cold-blooded murderer, and I'm not going to let him kill you!"

A cold wind swept through the room. Goose bumps rose along Savannah's arms. William stared at Jack and smiled.

His canines were long. Lethal. And his eyes were blood red. True fear swept through Savannah in that moment.

"No!" She screamed and took a step forward, breaking free of Jack's restraining hold.

"Are you crazy?" Jack snapped, "He's going to kill us!"

No, William wasn't going to kill her. She knew that he would never hurt her. But Jack was a different story. "William, calm down. It's not what you think. He's a detective. He's been following me—"

Rage swept across his face. She could feel his anger, beating against her mind. Uh-oh. She'd definitely said the wrong thing.

Jack foolishly grabbed her again, pulling her back toward the balcony doors.

William just watched them, his gaze burning, swirling with deadly intent.

"We're getting out of here," Jack said, reaching for the balcony door. He turned the knob, shoving the glass door open.

A gust of wind slammed the door shut before he could take a single step.

"You're not going anywhere." William took a slow step forward. His hands were at his sides, relaxed, loose. But his nails were lengthening into razor sharp claws. "Now step away from Savannah or I'll rip out your throat."

Savannah knew he meant it. She wondered if Jack realized he was seconds away from his death.

Jack froze. And he seemed to look at William for the first time. To really look at him. Jack's eyes widened in horror. "Jesus Christ, what the hell are you?"

William smiled again, showing his wickedly sharp teeth. "I'm death."

No. She wasn't going to let William hurt Jack. Just because the man had been duped didn't mean he deserved to be attacked. "William," she said, deliberately injecting a calm, soothing note in her voice, "we need to talk. There's been a misunderstanding."

"Misunderstanding?" Jack shook his head. His eyes were huge. "Lady, you've got to be kidding me. That guy's some kind of a monster!" His fingers bit into her arm, causing a sharp gasp of pain to slip from her lips.

In the next second, Jack was the one gasping in pain.

William had moved in a blur, launching his body across the room. He ripped Jack's hand from Savannah, effortlessly squeezing bones and tendons.

"You need to leave the room *now,* Savannah." William's focus was on his prey.

Savannah shook her head. She took a step forward and shoved William back. He snarled, turning that terrifying stare onto her. She watched his eyes flash. Red. Black. Red.

"Listen to me," she entreated, her stare fierce. "I know you think he was trying to hurt me, but it wasn't like that. He came here to help me." She had to make him believe her. She couldn't have Jack's blood on her hands, too.

William touched her cheek. His eyes closed and he took two deep breaths. When his lashes lifted, his midnight stare was back. "You risk too much," he whispered, bending his head to press his lips quickly against hers.

She smiled, relief sweeping through her. He'd beaten the beast, at least for the moment. Her arms wrapped tightly around him. "I risked nothing. I know you'd never hurt me." And she did. She trusted him, completely.

He swept her against his body, holding her close. She could feel the faint tremble that swept through him.

Jack rattled the doorknob.

William's head jerked up. "You're not trying to leave so soon, are you?" His arms slowly released Savannah. She stood by his side.

Jack's hand jerked away from the knob. "Uh, no. I was just, uh, making sure the door was still locked."

All things considered, Savannah thought Jack was showing amazing composure. He'd almost been killed by a vampire, yet he wasn't screaming in fear. His hands shook, but he pushed them behind his back as he faced William.

"Who are you?" William demanded.

"Jack Donovan." His voice wasn't quite steady, but he managed to meet William's probing stare.

"And you were hired to follow Savannah."

Jack nodded.

"Why?"

Jack looked beseechingly at Savannah. She said, "Jack knows that I'm after the man who murdered my brother. He was trying to find the killer, too."

"So he trailed you." William shook his head in disgust.

"How long have you been following her?"

"Since she left Seattle."

"Tell me who hired you."

Savannah heard the compulsion in William's voice.

Jack answered immediately. "I don't know. He said his name was Jonathan Gilbert. He told me his brother had been killed by the same person that attacked Mark Daniels. He hired me to follow Savannah. He said she would lead me to the killer."

Savannah sat on the edge of the bed. "He never met his client. They just talked on the phone and exchanged messages on the Internet."

"How much did you tell him?" William asked, using that same soft, compelling tone.

"Everything," Jack said, his voice flat. "I told him every move that she made. Who she talked to. Where she was staying. When she came to visit you."

William swore and turned to look at Savannah. "He's going to be coming for you."

"Wait just a minute!" Jack held up his hand. "What are you saying? That my client—"

"Is the one who butchered those people," William finished. "And, thanks to you, he now knows exactly where he can find Savannah."

Savannah stared down at her right palm. The scratches were barely visible now. *He's going to be coming for you.* Her fingers clenched into a fist.

"Let's not jump to conclusions—" Jack began.

"You know I'm right," William interrupted, his tone brisk. "Don't deny it. That's why you're here. Deep down, you know who he is. You know what he's capable of." He paused a beat. "You know what he's going to do."

Jack's shoulders slumped. He suddenly looked very, pale. "We need to call the cops." His voice was hoarse. "If you're right, if that guy's the killer, we have to get the hell out here."

"No," Savannah said softly, firmly. "The police can't help us." And they couldn't. She'd learned that lesson already. The only one who could help her was William.

"Of course, they can!" Jack's voice was stronger. Fiercer. "They've got guns. If this guy comes after you, they can stop him. They can shoot him!"

"A gun won't stop him," Savannah said. If only it were that easy. "You can't kill him with a gun."

Jack stopped pacing. "Lady, you can kill anything with a gun. Trust me. I was on the force for ten years. A bullet in the heart will stop any killer in his tracks."

William moved closer to Savannah. His legs brushed against the side of the bed. "But it won't stop a vampire."

"A vamp—" Jack's eyes widened in disbelief. "What are you talking about, man? Are you crazy or some—" He broke off, his mouth falling open in disbelief.

William stared back at him, his eyes glowing blood red, his gleaming incisors a dark threat.

"Shit." Jack's body seemed to tremble. "Shit," he repeated. "This can't be happening. You can't be a—"

"He is," Savannah said. "William's a vampire."

"Your eyes! Your teeth!" Jake began to breathe heavily. "You're a freaking vampire!"

William's lips twitched. "You're certainly observant, Detective."

Savannah frowned at Jack, vaguely concerned. He sounded like he might be having an asthma attack. "Are you all right?"

"Fine." He gasped. "Just." Gasp. "Great." He breathed deeply, inhaling and exhaling. He looked a bit like a fish that had been jerked out of his nice, comfortable home in the water. "I don't believe this," he whispered. "I don't believe this!"

"Believe it." William's eyes glowed.

"But vampires aren't real."

"Trust me." William smiled, showing his fangs. "I'm very real."

Jack's body swayed.

Uh-oh. Savannah bit her lip. It looked like the good detective might pass out at any moment. "Jack? Are you sure you're all right?"

"Dandy. Just freakin' dandy." He closed his eyes and exhaled. He stood there a moment, not saying a word, just breathing. In. Out. In. Out.

Savannah frowned.

His eyes snapped open. He pointed at William. "You're a vampire."

"Guilty." Mocking, cold.

Jack's lips thinned. "And the guy out there killing people, he's a vampire, too?"

Savannah thought he appeared to have his focus back now. Good. Maybe he could help them, after all. "That's why all of the blood was drained from the victims. He was feeding."

Jack asked, "I've been talking to a vampire? My client was a vampire?"

"Yes," she said.

Jack squared his shoulders. His breathing was still erratic, but he appeared to be regaining control. "You're right. The cops can't help."

Savannah looked up at William. "When do you think he'll come?" She wanted to be ready. She *had* to be ready.

William didn't immediately reply. He cocked his head to the side, almost as if he were listening to something. Or someone.

"William?"

He shook his head, his gaze focusing on her. "Soon. He'll come as soon as he can."

"We have to be ready."

"Ready?" Jack shook his head. "We'll be ready when we get the hell out of here."

"No," William disagreed softly. "Savannah's safer here than she would be anywhere else."

Jack looked doubtful. "No offense, but, I got to her. And if I could get to her, then I am damn sure *he* could get to her."

William stiffened. He peered down at Savannah. "How, exactly, did the good detective get to you?"

It was Jack who answered. "It wasn't hard. She was alone, walking in the woods. If I'd been the killer, she would be dead now."

Savannah shot to her feet. She ran toward Jack, pushing her finger against his chest. "You're lucky that *you're* not dead!" It infuriated her that he thought she was so defenseless. She could protect herself.

He grabbed her hand. "Come on, Savannah. You're not strong enough—"

His words ended on a yell as Savannah pulled his arm forward and effortlessly flipped him to the floor.

"My mistake," he managed, staring up at the ceiling. "You might not have been dead, after all."

"I'm a black belt," she told him, her eyes fierce. "I can take care of myself." She'd learned, over the protests of her doctors, to defend herself. She had wanted to prove to them, to her family, and to herself, that she could be strong. That she was strong.

William's fingers came up, wrapping lightly around her throat. His breath blew gently against her skin. "I'm impressed," he murmured "But I'm afraid that your skills won't be enough to stop Geoffrey."

She knew that. She could send Jack crashing to the floor, but she wasn't physically strong enough to defeat a vampire. Not yet.

But when she had the third bite, she would be.

Jack pushed himself to his feet. He winced, rubbing his back. "I don't know who I'm more afraid of," he said, staring at Savannah. "You and your boyfriend or the killer."

"It's not us you should fear," William said. "Geoffrey is going to come after you, too. He's not going to let you live. You know too much."

Jack paled. "Kelly," he whispered.

Savannah frowned. "Who?"

He swore, running a shaking hand through his hair. "Kelly Taylor. My fiancé. He knows about her. The bastard mentioned her name the last time we talked."

Savanna's stomach clenched. Geoffrey wouldn't have mentioned the woman's name unless—

"He's going to kill her." Jack looked sick. "He's going to kill my Kelly, isn't he?"

"Go to her." William ordered, his eyes unfocused, staring within. "Take her out of the country. Take her as far away as you can."

"But you said he'll follow."

"No," Savannah whispered, knowing she spoke the truth. "He's going to come after me first." And he would. Jack and his Kelly would be a bonus. Geoffrey would first attack her and William.

But they would be ready for him. They would stop him.

"Go. Protect your woman." With a wave of his hand, William sent the balcony doors crashing open. He looked down at Savannah. "And I'll protect mine."

Nine

There is no place to hide. The devil sees all.
-Entry from the diary of Henry de Montfort,
December 5, 1068

He hadn't liked seeing the other man near her. The beast within had raged, demanding he punish the man who'd dared touch what belonged to *him*. He'd only been able to maintain his control because of her. *Savannah*.

She stared at him now, her eyes deep emerald pools of mystery. What was she thinking? Was she afraid of Geoffrey? She had to know that he would protect her.

He took her hand within his own, marveling at the delicacy of her bones. "There is nothing to fear. Geoffrey will not hurt you." He would make certain that Geoffrey never hurt her again.

"What about Jack? Will he be safe?" Worry clouded her gaze.

"We'll stop Geoffrey," William promised. "We won't let him hurt Jack. We won't let him hurt anyone else."

"Are you going to give me the kiss tonight?" Savannah asked suddenly.

William hesitated. He wanted, more than anything else, to give her his kiss. He wanted to transform her, to make her his mate for all eternity. But he couldn't, not yet. He could feel the weakness emanating from her.

If he tried to convert her now, he couldn't guarantee that she would survive. It was a chance he wasn't willing to take.

"Not yet," he said softly. "Not yet."

"When?" It was a demand.

He walked toward the door. "When you're strong enough. Now, come with me, I have something for you."

She didn't move. "You could try saying please, you know. It's considered proper manners."

He stopped at the door and glanced back over his shoulder. His eyes met hers. "*Please* come with me."

Her full lips curved. "That wasn't so hard, was it?" She walked toward him, and he could have sworn that he saw a sparkle of mischief dance in her eyes. "You have to remember that you aren't on a battlefield anymore. You can't just boss people around."

"I'll remember that," he murmured, inhaling her sweet scent

as her body brushed past his. Need slammed through him, sudden and sharp. He wanted to taste her, to slip his tongue into the warmth of her mouth. It had been hours since he'd last held her. Since he'd felt her shuddering in his arms.

"What do you want to show me?" She walked down the hall, oblivious to the struggle going on inside him.

He took a deep breath, grabbed his self-control with both hands, and followed her. "You'll see. It's a surprise." After he'd left Savannah in her bed, he'd gone out to pick up the items for her. He'd raced against the sun, determined to return home with her supplies.

He followed her down the stairs, and when she turned to enter the great room, he captured her wrist and pulled her down the narrow hallway.

"I don't think I've ever come this way," she said.

He knew that she hadn't explored his home. He wished she would. She could go anywhere she wanted. After all, it was to be her home, too. He didn't want her to feel like a guest. He wanted her to feel like she belonged.

Like she was home.

He tried to make her understand. "My home is yours. Feel free to explore to your heart's content."

They approached a white swinging door. William pushed the door open and ushered Savannah inside.

"What—" Her eyes widened in delight at the sight of the gleaming kitchen.

The kitchen was huge. There were two double ovens, a gleaming chrome refrigerator and freezer, and an assortment of gadgets on the marble countertops. A large island sat in the middle of the room. And, toward the back of the room, a cozy table for two had already been set.

She opened the refrigerator, gazing in surprise at the assortment of food inside.

She frowned, still leaning inside the open door. "I don't understand. I didn't think you needed food." She closed the door slowly, staring up at him.

"I don't." He could survive on blood alone. Many of his kind chose to do that. "The food is for you. I picked it up before dawn."

She blinked and a red flush stained her cheeks. "You got all of this for me?"

He shifted, suddenly uncomfortable. "You need to eat," he

muttered. "You have to regain your strength."

She waved her hand to indicate the appliances. "What about all of those? Where did they—"

"I said that I didn't have to eat. Not that I couldn't." After five hundred years, he'd begun to long for the taste of something other than blood. He'd discovered that he could still eat human food, as long as he ate in moderation. "I don't eat often, but I do eat." He shrugged. "Besides, if someone were to come to the house and see that I didn't have a kitchen...let's just say that might raise a few questions."

A wry smile lit her face. "I could see where that might pose a problem." She opened the refrigerator and reached inside, pulling out ham and turkey. "I think I'll have a sandwich." She looked at him inquiringly.

He took a step back. "No. I have something." He motioned to the table where a thick glass was filled with a blood-red liquid.

Savannah swallowed. "I'm guessing that's not wine."

He almost smiled. "No, it's not."

She squared her shoulders and turned back to her food. She grabbed a loaf of bread and began creating her sandwich. When she was finished, she walked to the small table, carrying her plate carefully. Her gaze drifted to his drink.

William sat down. His brows lifted. "Would you rather I not drink now?"

She took a deep breath. "No, go ahead." Her smile was weak.

William moved his glass to the side, putting his hands in front of him. He wanted Savannah to eat first. He knew she needed the energy the food could provide, and he was afraid that if she saw him drink, she wouldn't be able to eat.

"Tell me about your life," he said, deliberately pitching his voice low. He knew a compulsion wouldn't work on her, but he still might be able to use his powers to soothe her.

Her fingers toyed with the table cloth. "What do you want to know?" She wasn't touching her sandwich. Or the glass of orange juice that he'd set out for her.

"Anything." Everything. Every detail of her life. "I know you lived in Seattle. Did you like it there?"

Her shoulders seemed to relax. "Oh, yes. I mean, it rained all the time, but I like the rain. Everyone there was always so busy. The city seemed to be alive with people."

"Have you ever lived anywhere else?"

She shook her head. "No. I was born and raised there. My

mother was from the south, though. From Georgia. That's why she named me Savannah." She picked up her sandwich and took a small bite.

"I haven't heard you mention your parents before," he murmured, his gaze sharp.

Sadness swept across her face. "My parents are dead. They were killed in a car accident a little over four years ago."

"I'm sorry, Savannah." That would have left just her and her brother.

"Mark took care of me," Savannah said, seeming to read his mind. "He's the one who took me to the hospital each time. He held my hand. He told me everything would be all right." She bit her lip. "But it wasn't all right. The cancer just came back. And then he died."

He ached for her, for all the pain that she had endured in her short life. He wished that he could take it all away from her. The burden that her slender shoulders carried was far too heavy.

"His death wasn't your fault, Savannah." He could see into her mind, her heart. The second exchange had linked them, and he could read her all too easily.

"Wasn't it?" She wasn't eating anymore. One bite, that's all she'd had.

"You can't believe it was your fault!" he said in disbelief. "Geoffrey killed him. And Geoffrey is the one who will pay, I promise you. Stop blaming yourself. There's nothing to be gained from it." He reached for her hand. "Haven't you punished yourself enough?"

She stared at their locked hands. "I should have helped him. He helped me, protected me, for years. I should have done something for him."

"You will do something." His fingers tightened. "You'll give him justice. And you'll stop Geoffrey from ever hurting anyone else."

She nodded. "Yes, I will." Her free hand reached for the sandwich.

He made certain that she ate it all, and then one more. He deliberately kept the conversation light, telling her of the different countries he'd traveled to, of the wonders he'd seen.

When he mentioned Italy, her face seemed to light up. "I've always wanted to go to Italy," she said, reaching for her juice. "Is it as beautiful as I've heard?"

He stared at her. "More."

She sighed, swirling her drink. "I wanted to be an artist, back when I thought the world was mine and I could do anything, be anything, that I wanted." Her lips twisted, seeming to mock her youthful dreams. "I planned to go to Europe. I wanted to see the Sistine Chapel. I wanted to paint the canals of Venice. Silly, isn't it?"

"No, it's not silly at all." He tried to think back, to see what dreams he'd had as a youth. All he could remember was blood and death and battles that never ended.

He reached for his glass. "We must plan a trip to Italy."

Her breath caught. "Truly? Do you mean that?" He could hear the hope and excitement in her voice.

"Of course." He smiled. "After all, we'll have plenty of time."

She seemed to absorb his words. "I guess we will." She shook her head. "It's strange. For so long, I've known that my time here was short. Limited. And now, to know that I won't die—" She smiled, her eyes shimmering. "It just doesn't seem real."

He drank from his glass, and the blood slid down his throat. He knew his eyes flared red at the delicious taste.

Savannah stopped smiling. "And then sometimes it seems all too real." She looked away, staring fixedly at the large freezer in the back of the room.

William finished his drink, never taking his gaze from her. "Would you rather I took the blood from a living man? That I tore open his throat and drank his blood?"

"Of course not!" Her gaze flew back to him. "How can you even ask that?"

He held up his empty glass. "I use this so I don't have to hunt. So I don't have to go out every night and drink from someone." So he didn't have to stare into his victim's eyes.

A faint line marred her forehead. "But you were going to drink from Slade—"

He carefully set his glass down on the tabletop. "At least once every full moon, I must have fresh blood. If I don't, my strength weakens." But when he fed, he held himself tightly in check, always aware that if his control broke, he could easily kill his prey.

"So I will need fresh blood, too." Her face looked very pale, very delicate.

"Yes. You'll have to drink in order to survive." He waited a beat then asked, "Will you be able to do it?"

Her gaze darted to the empty glass and then to his lips, which he knew would be blood red. She set her shoulders and lifted her chin. "I'll do what I have to do. I might not like it, but I'll do it."

William smiled, relief sweeping through him. "Don't worry. I'll show you how to take the blood. You won't hurt those you drink from, and with a small compulsion, you can make your victim forget the entire encounter."

"I'll have a lot to learn, won't I?"

"I'll teach you. I'll teach you everything that you need to know." And he would. He would make certain that Savannah fully understand her new powers. He pushed his chair back, stood, and walked toward a heavy metal door on the far side of the room. He pulled a large, silver key out of his pocket and inserted it into the lock.

Savannah moved to stand behind him. "What's in there?"

"Your first lesson."

Savannah stepped forward, only to come up short at the sight of a long, winding staircase. She peered down, trying to see the bottom. She saw nothing but darkness. "What's down there?"

"Why don't you go down and find out?" His words challenged her, and his hands pushed gently against the small of her back.

She didn't like the sound of that. She began to climb slowly down the stairs. They creaked beneath her, the sound strangely like a woman's moan.

She could feel William behind her—feel the warmth of his body, the kiss of his breath against her hair. She felt so acutely attuned to him that she could swear that she even heard his heart beating.

The stairs ended in front of another large, metal door. She glanced over her shoulder. She didn't know if she wanted to see this. Her stomach clenched as dread grew heavy within her.

William handed her the silver key. "Go on, Savannah," he urged. "Open the door."

Feeling like Pandora, she hesitantly inserted the key into the lock and heard a soft click as the key slid into place. Her palms were sweaty as she turned the knob and pushed the door open.

She walked slowly over the threshold and into a long, twisting tunnel. The tunnel was lit by a series of small lights.

She didn't ask William any questions. She just walked, wondering what would be waiting for her at the end of the tunnel.

In moments, she had her answer. Another door. Wooden this time, not metal. There was no lock upon its old, scarred surface.

She pushed it open, not waiting for William. A deep curiosity was beginning to burn inside her. What would she find in the room? A coffin? She closed her eyes for a moment, and then she stepped inside.

At first, she saw only darkness. Then, in a flash, a dozen white candles lit, illuminating the room.

And then she saw a large, Victorian bed like the one in her room. The covers were rumpled, as if someone had recently risen. She swallowed, pulling her eyes from the bed and forcing her gaze to travel over the rest of the room. There was a bookshelf in the back corner. It was stuffed with an assortment of books—hardbacks, paperbacks, classics and contemporary thrillers. The jackets were well-worn, the spines creased as if they'd all been read often.

Two chairs sat near the bookshelf. They were old-fashioned, high-backed chairs. A small table sat between them, and a lamp rested on top of its carved surface.

There was no sign of a coffin, and she let out a small sign of relief.

"So, this is where you sleep during the day?" It wasn't what she'd expected. The room, with its soft lighting and inviting bed, was cozy and welcoming. Not at all what she'd expected of William. *Not what she'd expected of a vampire.*

He shut the door, and the sound seemed to echo through the underground tunnels.

"Yes," he said. "I'm safe down here. The sun can't touch me, and the doors keep my enemies out."

She thought of the long tunnels and the curving stairs. "We're inside the mountain, aren't we?"

He nodded. "It took me years to build this place."

"You built it?" She was impressed. For one man to have done so much work...

"I needed a safe place to rest," he said with a small shrug. "So I did what had to be done."

She couldn't believe it. To dig inside the mountain. One man. "How is it possible? How could—"

He laughed. "Ah, Savannah. Already you forget. I have the strength of ten mortal men. And I can move and work, ten times faster than an average human. It wasn't hard for me to build this place. In fact, I've created over a dozen similar safe houses all around the world."

The strength of ten mortal men. She shook her head, dazed.

"I didn't realize you were so strong." The words sounded silly to her ears, but they were the truth. She hadn't fully understood the true extent of William's power. Each time he'd touched her, he'd been gentle, considerate. She hadn't realized he could literally crush her bones if he chose to do so.

The physical strength is only the beginning. His words whispered through her mind, yet he did not say a word.

She stilled. How could—

We're linked, Savannah. Joined in a way that few can ever truly understand. Wherever you go, whatever you do, I'll be with you. In you.

She felt his touch upon her, a light stroke against her brow. Yet he stood a good ten feet away from her.

When he spoke, his voice was clear and his words were frightening. "I can do just about anything. My mind is incredibly strong."

"You can move objects," she said, thinking of all the open doors and his vanishing clothes. "You can read minds. Control minds."

"Yes."

That kind of power stunned her. "How is that possible?"

"The gifts come with the dark kiss." He held his hand up, silently urging her to come to him.

Savannah took a step back. "You said before that you couldn't control me." She vividly remembered their encounter in her hotel room. "But that was before the second exchange."

His expression never altered.

"I know you can get inside my mind. You've proven that. But can you control my thoughts?" Fear almost choked her. She couldn't stand being under someone else's control.

His hand dropped back to his side. He stood in front of the bed, staring across at her. She could actually feel the heat of his touch. "I don't know," he said. "I haven't tried to control you again." He frowned, apparently concentrating intently.

"What? What is it?" Her heart seemed to freeze.

He shook his head. "No good. I told you before, your mind is different."

"You can't control me?" Could he hear the hope in her voice?

"If I could, you'd be standing in front of me right now, naked and begging me to make love to you."

She blinked.

"Since you haven't moved, I'm going to have to assume that

my attempt to bend you to my will failed." The words were light, but his stare was that of a hungry predator. "So I guess I'll just have to try another method of persuasion."

She was stunned. Surely he didn't mean... "You want to make love to me? Now?" Her heart began to pound. A moment ago, she'd been afraid. Now, with just a look, a heated glance, need slammed through her.

He stalked toward her. "Yes."

She looked up at him. His cheeks were flushed, his pupils dilated.

He wrapped his arms around her, pulling her body flush against his. She could feel his arousal pressing against her. Hot. Strong.

Heat began to pool between her legs. How was it possible? How could she go from fearing him to needing him all within mere moments?

He kissed her, his mouth feeding on hers. She didn't hesitate. She kissed him back, her tongue sliding against his, causing a low growl to sound from the depths of his throat.

He pulled back, moving his mouth down the slender column of her neck. She felt the rough silk of his tongue sliding against her skin. She closed her eyes, her breath coming hard and fast. She fought to hold on to her reason, which was quickly disappearing into a whirlpool of desire. "Are you sure," she paused, wetting her lips, "that you're not controlling me?"

His head lifted and his gaze locked on hers. Anger flashed across his face. "What do you think?"

Her fingers clenched around the muscular width of his arms. "I think I need you more than I've ever needed anyone else. I think I want you so much that I can hardly breathe because the hunger is so sharp." She could feel her body trembling. "I've never been like this before. This isn't *me!*" And it wasn't. She was always cool, always controlled. All of her emotions, her feelings, were held carefully in check. Now she felt wild, reckless. Her body was too hot. Her clothes too confining.

William's face softened. His fingers rubbed lightly over her sensitive lips. "Poor Savannah. You don't completely understand what's happening yet, do you?" His hands soothed her hair back with gentle care. "I feel it, too. The hunger. The need. I am as captive to it as you."

Her eyes widened.

"I want you," he whispered, his breath feathering over her.

"I want you more than anything else on earth. You're a fire within me. I see you, and I hunger. *I need.*"

Her lips trembled. Her body yearned.

"I'm not controlling you," he continued, his voice husky. "I wouldn't do that to you."

She believed him. Her lips parted to speak.

William stepped back and her arms fell weakly to her sides. She felt cold, empty, without him.

With a wave of his hand, William sent the wooden door swinging open. "You can leave. You can go upstairs and sleep alone. You don't have to be with me tonight. The choice is yours."

She thought about leaving. About returning to her quiet, empty room. And she thought about him.

She took a step forward, wrapping her arms around him. "I want you, William. *You.*" Her will was her own. As was her desire.

William scooped her up in his arms, carrying her easily toward the bed. The lights from the candles seemed to flare brighter.

He held her tightly, pressing her against the strength of his chest. She could feel his heart pounding beneath her fingers. She could feel the tremor of desire that slid over his body.

He placed her in the middle of the bed. Before she could even blink, he'd removed both their clothes. He stood, naked and strong, surveying her in the flickering candlelight. His gaze was intent, almost worshipful as it fell upon her.

"You are the most perfect thing I've ever seen." He touched her breast gently. Her nipple hardened. She arched into his touch.

He closed his eyes and took a deep breath. When his lashes lifted, she could see a faint red circle around his pupils. "I won't be able to go slowly, not tonight." The words were guttural.

She reached for him, her arms sliding down his chest. Down to the curling mass of hair at the juncture of his thighs. She touched him, marveling at the strength and heat of his desire. Her fingers closed around him, squeezing lightly. He growled. She leaned forward, her tongue sliding to taste the tip of his shaft.

"I don't care," she whispered. "I just want you." She took him into her mouth.

His fingers fisted in her hair. His eyes closed, and he shuddered against her.

She kissed him. She licked him. He felt so strong. So hot. So—

"Enough!" He pushed her back onto the bedcovers. His body

slid on top of hers, and he pushed her thighs apart.

She lifted her hips, eager to feel him once more.

His mouth claimed hers, his kiss full of passion. Hunger. He thrust into her, and Savannah moaned as pleasure shot through her.

His hands locked around her hips, and he lifted her, moving her in time with his powerful thrusts. Her head thrashed against the pillows. She heard someone crying, moaning, but she didn't realize the noises were coming from her.

William's face was intent. His eyes blood red. His fingers were clenched so tightly around her hips that she knew they would leave marks. But she didn't care. The pleasure was building. Closer. Closer. Her body tightened. Tensed.

William surged into her. She exploded as waves of pleasure slammed through her. She screamed his name.

He stiffened against her, his body going as taut as a wire. He closed his eyes, his teeth clenched. And he whispered her name.

They rode the climax together, the pleasure so intense it was almost painful. Their bodies were locked together. Their hearts beat as one.

For a timeless moment, they were one.

***

"How did you become a vampire?"

William flinched at her question, his hand clenching around her arm. He'd been enjoying the aftermath of their lovemaking, enjoying the feel of her in his arms.

"William?"

Reality was intruding into his world, and he didn't want it. He didn't want to talk about his past. Not now. Not while they were still together. Not while the scent of lavender hung in the air. Not while he still touched her.

He leaned forward and kissed her softly, a caress of the lips. And she had such wonderful lips. Full. Tempting.

He pulled her closer, cradling her body against his. He wanted to hold her. To—

She pushed against his chest. "William." She swallowed, and he could see the need in her eyes. A need that she was struggling to control. "Tell me. Tell me what happened."

He sighed and ran his hand through his loosened mane of hair. "I thought you already knew. What was it you said that first day?" He frowned a moment, thinking. "Ah, yes, something along the lines of becoming a vampire because of my love of the 'dark arts?'"

She shook her head once, a quick motion. She pulled the sheet up over those soft, delicious breasts and stared at him, her lips pressed into a thin line. "That wasn't true."

He lifted one brow. "And how do you know that?" His love of the dark arts was a legend that had begun before he even reached manhood.

"You're not evil, William." Simple words. Honest words. He could see the sincerity on her face, hear it in her voice.

Those simple words pierced him to the core. "There are those who would disagree with you," he said, his jaw clenching. Sometimes, when he slept, he could still hear the whispers of the villagers. He could still see the fear and revulsion that filled their gazes. "They called me the Devil's bastard." The words slipped out without violation.

She gasped, her face paling. "Who said that?"

He remembered the little boy, not more than ten years old. The old hag. The blacksmith. "Everyone said it. They whispered it each time that I passed them. Every person on my father's land thought I was cursed. And they hated me."

"I don't understand." Savannah shook her head in confusion. "Why? Why would they say that about you? Why would they hate you?"

He sighed. "Because I was my father's son."

Confusion and disbelief filled her gaze. "That's crazy! Your father wasn't—"

He held up his hand, halting her speech. "Their stories were wrong, of course. My father wasn't the Devil. Although at times he certainly acted the part." His father, Baron Guy de Montfort, had been a cruel, sadistic warrior. He'd had no place in his life for weakness or sentiment of any sort. He'd tolerated William. He'd ignored Geoffrey. And he'd despised Henry.

"My father was obsessed with power," William told her. "He wanted control, absolute control of everyone and everything. He was a strong man. He commanded a vast army with a steel grip. No one could go against my father's might and survive. *No one.* The villagers said that he'd traded his soul to the Devil in order to get his power."

"Had he?" Savannah asked.

"My father never had a soul." Cold, harsh words. "He never cared about anyone, certainly not me or my brothers." Geoffrey had grown to be a man exactly like his father. Hungry only for blood and power.

Savannah sat quietly, her gaze fixed upon him.

He began to stroke her arm lightly. He wasn't even aware of the gesture. "By the time I reached manhood, my father's strength had started to wane, and he hated it." He could still hear the sound of his father's angry screams. Guy had been enraged by his body's betrayal, by the onset of the weakness in his limbs. "He began to shake. To have spasms. He couldn't lead his armies anymore. He became desperate."

William swallowed, seeing only the past. "He couldn't stand what was happening to him. So he began to...seek out the counsel of others. Doctors." He paused, and then he said, "Witches. Seers."

"What did he find out?" she whispered.

"He found out that he could live forever." William remembered his father's wicked glee. "He found out that he could transform himself into a new being. An immortal."

"Your father became a vampire?" Her shock was clear.

William shook his head. "No. You see, he wasn't sure the ritual would work. He wanted someone else to go through the change first, just in case something happened. Just in case his famed seer was wrong."

"Dear God," she whispered. "He made you do it, didn't he?"

He nodded, his jaw clenched. The scar on his cheek was a vivid white. "He imprisoned Henry. He never cared for him. He thought Henry was weak. Henry hated our father. He couldn't stomach his evil. He wouldn't march with Guy in battle, and Guy viewed his actions as a betrayal. He told me that the punishment for betrayal was death.

"He tortured Henry. Kept him captive for days without my knowledge. Then, when he was barely alive, Guy brought him to me. I was training with my men, and Guy dragged Henry's battered body into the courtyard. Henry was hardly recognizable. He told me that Henry was dying. That if I wanted to save him, I would seek out a dark creature. A vampire. And I would take his power."

She stroked his cheek gently. "Oh, William. I'm so sorry."

His eyes flashed at her. "I don't need your pity, Savannah."

She flinched and dropped her hand.

His jaw clenched. He knew he'd hurt her. But he wasn't used to someone caring about him; he wasn't used to someone trying to comfort him.

He took her hand in his, a silent apology. After a moment, he kept talking, needing to tell the story, the whole story. To finally tell the dark story to someone. No, needing to tell *her*. "I followed the seer's instructions, and I found the vampire. It was a man." He shook his head, remembering his first sight of the vampire. "He looked barely eighteen. I thought he was just a lad. I remember that he had blond hair and light blue eyes." Sad eyes. Eyes that had seen too much of the world. Eyes that had seen too much death. "I told him about Henry, I told him that he had to transform me."

"And he agreed."

William nodded. "He looked into my mind and gave me the gift."

She licked her lips. "And then you returned home."

"I returned to hell," he corrected softly. "I returned to find my father's butchered body. Geoffrey had killed him. Gutted him. And left his body waiting for me."

She closed her eyes. "What about Henry?"

"You read the diary. Don't you know?"

"No." Her shoulders lifted and fell. The sheet dipped slightly. "The entries ended with your father's death. On the eve of the New Year. Henry noted that you went to seek out the vampire, but he never said what happened when you returned." Her lashes lifted, and she met his gaze. "When I read the diary, I suspected that you'd gotten the gift. I just…knew." She swallowed. "I got my friend Mary to research you. Mary's a whiz with computers. She found a reference to a man named William Dark in 1101. And then again in 1290. And in 1670…All of the descriptions of William were the same."

She lifted her hand and touched his scar. "This scar. It was mentioned every time. So I knew, I *knew* that you'd become…"

"A vampire," he finished softly.

She nodded. "But I didn't know what had happened to your family. To Geoffrey, to Henry—"

"Geoffrey found out about my father's plans, and he went in search of the vampire on his own."

"Was he trying to save Henry?"

"I don't know," William said. And he didn't. He didn't know if Geoffrey's original motivation had been Henry or if he'd just wanted the power of an immortal. "Geoffrey was always hard, cruel. He thought nothing of slicing off the hand of a peasant who touched him. And my father encouraged such acts."

"Why did he kill his own father?" Savannah shook her head. "Why would he do that?"

"Because Guy de Montfort wasn't his father. Geoffrey was my half-brother, Savannah. We had the same mother, but our fathers were different."

"Who was his father?"

He rose from the bed and began to stalk around the room, barely aware of his nudity. "Guy's brother. A year after I was born, my mother became pregnant with his child. Guy killed his brother as soon as he found out. My mother died of a fever shortly after the baby was born." William had always secretly thought her death was an act of kindness from God. She had been spared from facing Guy's deadly wrath.

"So your father took Geoffrey in and raised him?"

"At that time, a man couldn't have too many sons. All leaders needed men to follow them, sons to lead their armies. He told the world that Geoffrey was his, and he used him, just as he used Henry and me." He stopped, gripping the bedpost. "I don't know why Geoffrey finally killed him. Maybe it was because of what Guy did to Henry. Geoffrey always seemed to…care for Henry. At least in his own, sick, twisted way. I think my father's attack just drove him over the edge."

"And he sought out the vampire." He could almost see the wheels turning in her mind as she explored possibilities. "And you returned home." She paused a beat, and then she said, "And you found Henry."

"Henry knew what I'd become. I saw it in his eyes." He could still remember the fear he'd seen in his brother's gaze. "He was barely hanging on. He'd been attacked again, and left to die. He was choking on his blood." He clenched his teeth, wanting to finish the dark tale and be done with the past.

Savannah stared at him, an uncanny knowledge in her emerald gaze. "You tried to change him anyway, didn't you?"

He nodded. "He was my brother," he said simply, knowing she, of all people, would understand. "He'd known that I'd gone for the dark gift. I tried to convert him, to give him my blood. And, I think, I think it had begun to work—"

"What happened?"

"We were attacked. Word of my father's death had reached his enemies. They stormed our holding, killing everyone in their path. Knights, servants. It made no difference. They showed my people the same cruelty that my father had so often shown them."

The screams echoed in his mind. He could hear the sound of shattering wood. See the swords swinging toward him. "Soldiers found Henry and me. They attacked us. I fought them, killed them. But when I turned back to Henry—"

Sorrow flashed across her expressive face. "He was dead."

He nodded and swallowed against the painful memory. Pain that was trying to choke him. "One of the swords hit him in the chest. There was blood everywhere." He'd pulled the sword from Henry's chest and stood, numb, staring down at the still form of his brother. "I waited too long to transform him. He died, because of me."

She jumped from the bed, dropping the sheet and running to his side. "Don't say that, William! It's not true. You did everything that you could to save Henry."

"If I'd only gotten back to him sooner, if I'd only transformed him sooner—" The past had haunted him for so long. If only things had been different...

She grabbed his arms, forcing him to turn and face her. "Listen to me! It wasn't your fault. You did everything in your power to help Henry. You can't keep blaming yourself for his death! You can't!" She paused then softly said, "Henry wouldn't blame you."

Wouldn't he? "Geoffrey blames me."

"What?"

He opened his mouth to reply, then frowned, feeling the slight change in the atmosphere. A chill of warning skated down his spine. Dawn was coming.

He pulled away from her, ignoring her questioning stare and padded to the bookcase.

"William?" Savannah stared blankly after him. "What are you doing?" Surely he wasn't just going to drop a bombshell like that on her and walk away!

He pulled a black box from the top shelf. He opened the lid and removed a silver key, a key exactly like the one he'd used to unlock all of the metal doors in the tunnels.

He walked back to her. "I want you to keep this," he said. "It will allow you to come and go as you please from the tunnels."

She took the key from him. It felt cold, heavy, in her hand. "But what about Geoffrey—"

He touched her cheek gently. "That's another story. One that will have to be saved for another time. Dawn is coming." He pointed to the key. "I want you to feel free to explore the house during the day. No room is blocked to you. I only ask that you stay inside." His eyes were deep, swirling pools. "It's safer inside."

She was touched by his concern. "I won't leave," she promised, curling her fingers around the key.

"You'll be safe during the day," he told her. "Geoffrey will have to rest then. He won't be able to touch you."

"What about my dreams?" She asked softly, with a shiver of remembered apprehension. "It was during the day when he entered my dreams before."

He touched her cheek. A light, fleeting touch. "I'll guard you. Now that you've had the second bite, I can link with you. I'll make certain he doesn't slip into your mind."

Relief swept through her.

William's head lifted, his eyes narrowing. "The sun is rising." His voice was clipped. "You must go."

"No, I want to stay with you." And she did. She didn't want to return to an empty room. She wanted to stay with William.

A muscle flexed along the plane of his jaw.

She touched his shoulder. "What is it?"

He didn't look at her. "When the dawn comes, the change will come."

"The change?"

His fingers clenched. "My body will shut down. I won't breathe. My heart won't beat." He finally glanced at her tense features. "It will be as if I'm dead."

"I know what happens when you sleep, William," she told him gently. "I know you have to conserve your strength during the daylight hours." She'd read about the vampire's need for complete stillness. The sun was fierce, draining to a creature of the night. During the day, all vampires shut down their physical bodies. Their minds remained strong, tangled in the dream world, but their bodies were forced to lay motionless.

"Then you know why you must leave."

Savannah shook her head. "No, I don't. I want to stay with you." She knew she was being stubborn, but she didn't really care. She wanted to prove to him that she wasn't afraid. She could handle him, all of him.

His lips pressed against hers. Hard. Fast. "Then stay." His fingers curled around hers. "Stay with me through the dawn."

She smiled at him. And, just for an instant, his lips curved in response.

They lay back in the bed, curled in one another's arms.

It felt good being there with him. Right.

"Sleep, Savannah." William's voice was soft. His arms were strong around her.

Savannah closed her eyes, feeling safe, completely protected. She slipped into the haunting mists of sleep with a gentle sigh. Moments later, when the sun rose, she was already in the land of dreams and didn't feel the sudden tense coldness of William's body against hers.

At first, her dreams were happy. She was with William. They were dancing under a star-filled night sky. She was so happy. But then he pulled back, and his body seemed to waver before her eyes. She reached for him, but he vanished.

There were woods around her. Twisted trees. She ran, searching for William.

But it wasn't William that she found. In the shadowy world of her dreams, she saw her friend Mary. Her long black hair billowed in the breeze as she stood looking down into a flowing river.

A smile curved Savannah's lips as she ran to greet her.

Mary stepped forward, into the river. A flash of lightning lit the night sky. The water churned, and Mary stumbled, falling to her knees.

Savannah realized the water was black. As black as the night itself.

The hungry waves seemed to surround Mary, pulling her deeper and deeper into its cold embrace.

Savannah ran as fast as she could, desperate to get to Mary. Her bare feet pounded on the dank earth. Her heat pounded in her chest.

She was close. So close. Just a few more feet—

Mary turned, her pale face a mask of fear.

Her arms reached out to Savannah.

And Savannah heard the echo of a scream.

Ten

My brother has a taste for death.
-Entry from the diary of Henry de Montfort,
December 11, 1068

The sun had not yet risen in Seattle. Night's darkness still clung to the empty city streets. The shadows of the night cloaked him as he watched her.

He could see her so clearly through the thin glass of the window. Her black hair was pulled back into a careless ponytail. Her face, tense with concentration, peered at the computer screen. Her thin shoulders were hunched over, her fingers typing frantically on the keyboard.

He touched the pane of glass, feeling its cool surface against his hand. He was so close to her.

He inhaled deeply, scenting the night air. He could smell sweat, blood, and the faint odor of burning leaves and garbage. But he could detect no trace of her. Not yet.

She was rubbing her forehead, obviously tired. She'd been at that computer of hers for over four hours. He knew because he'd been watching her all night. Watching. And waiting.

Over the years he'd learned the value of patience. He could wait endlessly for his prey. She'd been easy to track. Almost too easy. Would she be easy to kill? Would she scream? Would she fight him?

He'd always enjoyed a good fight. He hoped that she wouldn't let him down.

She stood up and turned off her machine. He saw her walk to the closet and grab a black leather jacket. He smiled, his teeth glinting in the faint street light. She was coming to him.

He moved away from the window and back into the shadows.

The front door opened with a soft squeak. He heard the jingle of her keys as she carefully locked up the house. She appeared to be such a cautious little thing, locking her doors like a good little girl. As if that would save her.

Her back was to him as she bent over the lock. It would be so easy to go her, to take her now. She would never even know what had happened.

But that wouldn't be any fun. So he waited. Silent. Watchful.

She walked down the stone steps, her padded shoes making no sound against the concrete. When she reached the sidewalk, she paused, her gaze sweeping around the area. He knew she wouldn't see him. He was far too adept at cloaking his presence.

She walked down the sidewalk.

Where was she going at such a late hour? Hadn't her mother ever told her that the night could be dangerous?

He crept behind her, inhaling her scent. He could smell her shampoo. It reminded him of apples. He'd always loved apples.

She still had her keys in her hand. They were clenched between her fingers. He almost smiled at her pitiful weapon. He could hear her heart, pounding fiercely in her breast, and he could almost taste her blood, flowing richly through her veins. Sweet, sweet blood. Oh, how he loved the taste...

He crept closer, trailing her by mere inches.

She never turned around. The street was completely empty. All of the houses were dark. No one could see her. Or him. He reached out, touching her neck gently.

She screamed and jerked around, trying to scratch him with her keys.

He laughed as the keys cut into his face.

His arms wrapped around her, pulling her flush against him. He yanked the keys from her and hurled them to the ground.

"Hello, pretty lady," he whispered, his eyes blood red. "I've been waiting for you."

Her eyes widened in horrified recognition. She opened her mouth to scream again.

He clamped his hand over her mouth. "Shhh, love. We don't want to wake the neighbors, now, do we?" He smiled, letting her see his teeth.

He could smell the rich, heady aroma of her fear. He loved the taste of fear. "Hold still, love." He licked her throat and felt her tremble.

Tears leaked from the corners of her eyes. He'd always hated a woman's tears. They were weak. Useless. "Are you afraid to die?" He asked her, his voice tender.

He felt her slow nod.

"That's too bad," he murmured. And he sank his teeth into her throat.

***

"Mary!" Savannah jerked awake, her heart pounding. She'd seen her friend so clearly, struggling in the dark waters of the river. Screaming. Asking for her help.

A cold knot of dread formed in the pit of her stomach. Something was wrong. Terribly wrong.

Beside her, William's body was eerily still. She touched him, her fingers feathering over his bare shoulders. His skin was so cold, and he wasn't breathing. He wasn't moving.

"William?"

He didn't answer, but then, she hadn't really expected him to. He wouldn't, couldn't, rise until dusk.

Fear was growing within her. She was terrified that something had happened to Mary.

She slid from the bed, wondering what time it was. How long had she slept? How long had she dreamt of a black river that churned with hate?

She slipped on her clothes and grabbed her key. She had to call Mary. She had to make certain that her friend was all right.

She ran through the tunnels and up the stairs. Her legs burned, but she pushed herself, moving as fast as she could. She burst into the kitchen and ran across the room. She sent the door swinging back with a hard shove of her hand and raced down the hallway, her bare feet pounding on the cold wooden floor. She grabbed the phone and quickly dialed Mary's apartment number.

The phone rang. Once. Twice.

Savannah began to pray.

Three times. Mary usually answered her phone on the second ring. She'd always said she just couldn't wait to find out who was calling.

Four rings. Still no answer.

Savannah's hand grew slick around the receiver. Why wasn't Mary answering? Where was she?

"Hello?" The voice was female, soft and husky.

Savannah's knees sagged. "Mary?"

"No." A deep sigh. "Mary's in the hospital."

The hospital? The room seemed to spin. Savannah slid to the floor, clutching the phone with all of her strength. She recognized the voice of Mary's roommate. "Sarah, it's Savannah. Is Mary all right? What happened?"

There was a tense pause. "She's not all right, Savannah. The doctors don't think she's going to make it."

Savannah could hear the pain in Sarah's voice. "What happened?" She felt numb.

"She was in a car accident. They found her at the end of the street. She drove her car straight into a tree," Sarah said. "It was just before dawn. What the hell was she doing out at that time? Why was she driving?" Tears choked her voice.

Savannah's lips trembled. "What hospital is she at?"

"Mercy's Heart. Look, Savannah, if you want to see Mary, you'd better get here, fast. I don't think she's got much time."

You'd better get here, fast. "I-I can't. I can't leave—" She'd promised William. *I only ask that you stay inside.* His words echoed in her mind. *It's safer inside.*

"You *have* to come." Sarah's voice was urgent. "She's...she's dying. The doctors say it's a matter of days, maybe hours."

A tear slid down Savannah's cheek. Not Mary. Dear God, no, not Mary.

"Savannah? Are you there?"

"Yes." A whisper.

"You *have* to come. You have to see her before, before—"

Before it was too late. Before she died. "I'll be there." There was no choice. "I'll be there as soon as I can," Savannah said, her voice husky. William would understand. He would know that she'd had to go, that she'd had to see Mary.

Oh, God, Mary.

She swallowed, tasting tears and pain. Nothing would stop her from seeing Mary again. Nothing.

***

William felt her pain. It beat against him, pounding into his mind.

He tried to reach out, to touch her, but he found only emptiness.

He could hear her voice. Hear her tears.

What was wrong? What had happened?

Savannah. The cry echoed in his mind.

***

Savannah barely remembered the car ride down the mountain. The frantic dash through the airport was but a hazy memory. As she sat on the plane, gazing out of the window at the vast land below, she could only remember Mary. Her dear friend. Her best friend.

Why? Why had Mary been hurt? Had it been just a simple accident? Why had Mary been out so late? What had she been doing?

Something wasn't right. Savannah could feel it. There was more to the story. More to Mary's "accident."

Had Geoffrey gone after Mary? Was he the cause of her injuries? Guilt almost smothered Savannah at the thought. Had she led the killer to her friend's door?

She prayed that Mary would still be alive. That she would recover. She prayed and she begged, hoping God would hear her desperate calls. Her fingers were locked tightly together. Her shoulders hunched forward. Her temples throbbed in a steady, pounding rhythm. She was terrified.

As the miles rushed by, a fleeting thought whispered through her mind. She wished William were with her.

***

William awoke to find himself alone in the bed.

He knew Savannah was gone even before he took his first breath. He could feel her absence. Feel the emptiness of the house.

And he could feel the echoes of her pain.

Something had happened. Something that had forced her to leave the shelter of his home.

His heart clenched. She was out there, in the night. Alone. Geoffrey would be waiting for her. Waiting for his perfect kill.

He tore through the tunnels, reaching the ground level of the house in mere seconds. His entire focus was on Savannah. He had to get to her. He had to find her. Before it was too late.

He went to her room. He knew she wouldn't be there, but he found himself compelled to climb the narrow flight of stairs and hurry toward the dark room. He had to see for himself. He had to see—

The room was empty. But he could still smell her. The faint scent of lavender clung to the sheets, the pillows.

He didn't bother to turn on a light. He could see just as well in darkness as he could in light. There was a note on her bed, propped lightly against the pillow. It was short, brief, terrifying.

I'm sorry, William. I have to go back to Seattle. My friend Mary has been in a terrible accident. I have to see her.

Don't worry about me. I'll be safe. And I will return as soon as I can. I promise.

She hadn't signed the note, she hadn't needed to.

He crumpled the letter in his fist. She wouldn't be coming back. Not if Geoffrey had his way. He knew that Savannah was walking into a trap. Geoffrey had attacked her friend in order to draw her out into the open. It was a tactic that his brother had used nine hundred years ago. It had worked then, and William was very much afraid that it would work now.

He had to get to Savannah before Geoffrey did.

He sent the balcony doors crashing open with a wave of his hand and ran straight into the night. He leapt high into the air, his body shifting, transforming. He had many dark gifts. And he would use them all to save Savannah.

The man disappeared. In his place, a large, menacing hawk took to the skies.

He would find her. There was no other choice.

Savannah.

***

She hated hospitals. Hated the scents, the sounds, and the overwhelming whiteness of the rooms. Hospitals were cold, stark, places of death and despair. She'd spent too many years of her life inside the icy walls of a hospital. She'd hoped to never step foot past the sliding glass doors again.

She couldn't believe that Mary was here. That she might be dying. Not Mary. She was too strong. Too good.

Her friend was in the intensive care unit. Her body was tied to a dozen different tubes and machines. Constant beeps emitted from the machinery. Visitors weren't supposed to be in the room with her. But Savannah had known the nurse on duty from her many visits to Mercy's Heart. Patty O'Connor was a sweet, matronly woman in her late fifties who had taken good care of Savannah during her long hospital stays. She and Patty had become friends during those many hours. Patty had agreed to let Savannah sneak back and visit with Mary, but she'd told her that she could only stay for a few moments.

Tears clouded her eyes as she stared down at her friend. Mary's face was covered in bruises and cuts. Both of her legs were broken. Patty had said that her friend had also suffered a concussion, two broken ribs, and a crushed pelvis. Her left lung had been punctured. By the time the paramedics got to Mary, her lung had already begun to fill with fluid.

Mary had lost a lot of blood. Too much. The doctors had frantically pumped the precious liquid back into her body. It was truly a miracle that she was still alive. Unfortunately, the doctors weren't sure just how much longer she would be able to hold on.

Savannah cradled Mary's hand, her fingers rubbing lightly

over its back. "Mary, it's Savannah." She swallowed, trying to clear the lump from her throat. "Can you hear me?"

There was no response. The machines continued to beep. The liquids continued to feed into Mary's body.

"Please, Mary. You've got to fight. You can't leave yet. You just can't." But as she gazed at Mary's pale, still face, she was desperately afraid that Mary would, indeed, leave her soon.

Her fingers tightened around Mary's. "How many times did you hold my hand when I was in a hospital bed? How many times did you tell me that I couldn't give up? Do you remember that, Mary? You and Mark. You both kept telling me not to give up. You told me to fight."

Tears filled her eyes. "Well, now I'm telling you. You've got to fight, Mary. You have to live!"

Did Mary's lashes flicker faintly? Savannah continued talking, her voice feverish with intensity. "You can hear me, can't you, Mary? I know you can. Stay with me, Mary. Stay with me! I know you're tired and that you hurt, and all you want to do is to slip away and let the pain stop. I know, because I've been there. I just wanted to close my eyes and make it all stop. But I didn't. I kept fighting. I wanted to live. And you want to live, too. I know you do. You want to get married. Have kids. Cute little kids that you can teach to hack computers. You want to go to Spain. You want to run with the bulls. You want to do so much. But if you don't fight, you won't be able to do anything."

She felt Mary's fingers jerk against her.

Savannah leaned forward, hope lighting her face. "Mary?"

And then she saw them. Two tiny holes on the left side of Mary's throat. Barely visible, they would have gone unnoticed by most people.

But Savannah had similar marks on her own neck. She knew what those marks meant, what they were—

A wave of nausea rolled through her. "Dear God," she whispered, her face full of horror. It hadn't been an accident. There was no way it could have been. Not with those marks. Geoffrey had done this; he had attacked Mary.

Mary's lashes lifted. She moaned, the sound harsh and full of fear.

"It's all right, Mary. I'm here." Savannah tried to soothe her.

Mary began to thrash in the bed, her arms lifted, trying to

jerk free of the restraints that held her.

Her IV flew across the room. Blood poured down her arm.

"No! Stop! You're going to hurt yourself!" Savannah frantically pressed the call button.

Mary's lips trembled. She tried to speak, but a groan emerged from her lips.

Patty ran into the room. Her eyes widened as she hurried to the bed, pulling Mary's arms down and securing them with Velcro straps. Mary struggled against the confinement, her eyes huge and tear-filled. Another long groan slipped past her lips.

"You've got to leave," Patty said while pushing the call button and demanding that the doctor be summoned.

Mary began moaning. Her head thrashed.

"Calm down," Patty told her. "You're safe. You were in an accident, but we're taking care of you now. Everything is going to be all right, Ms. Todd." She began to insert another intravenous needle into the back of Mary's hand.

Savannah took a step back from the bed.

The doctor, an older man with steel gray hair and horn-rimmed glasses, appeared at the door. He took a quick look, instantly assessing the situation.

"Morphine, *now*," he ordered.

A nurse hurried in from behind him, a long needle in her hand.

"D-d-d-d—" Mary's teeth clenched and frustration flashed across her face.

"You need to leave," the doctor told Savannah.

The machines beeped, faster, louder.

Mary's pain filled gaze locked on Savannah. "D-d-d-dev—"

"Now, Miss!" The doctor's tone was sharp.

A nurse grabbed Savannah's arm.

"I'll be back," she promised Mary. She hated to leave her. She wanted to stay, to make certain that Mary was all right.

"You've got to come with me," the nurse insisted.

"D-d-devil!" Mary screamed, her face twisted in fear. "The d-d-devil s-s-said he was c-c-coming for y-you!"

Everyone froze.

"What?" Savannah's voice was a whisper of sound.

"H-he's c-c-coming. B-be r-ready." Mary's eyes snapped shut and her body fell back, limp, against the bedcovers.

Patty crossed herself.

"Mary?" Savannah stepped forward, breaking free of the nurse's hold. "Mary!"

The machines beeped, slow and steady, in the quiet room. The doctor leaned over the bed, checking Mary carefully.

"Is she going to make it?" Savannah asked, fear nearly choking her.

The doctor straightened slowly. "I don't know."

Savannah pressed her lips together to control their trembling.

"What was she talking about?" Patty whispered, taking a quick step back from the bed. "The devil—"

The doctor frowned at her. "She was delirious. You know how patients get—"

No, Mary hadn't been delirious. The good doctor was very, very wrong. The devil had attacked Mary, and now, he was planning to come after Savannah.

Savannah stared at Mary's still body. Poor Mary. What she must have gone through! "Is she going to make it?" she asked again.

The doctor ran a tired hand over his face. "Maybe." He shook his head. "I just don't know. It's hard to tell for certain in a case like this, and I don't want to give you false hope." He sighed. "She's getting the best care. We'll do everything in our power to see that she pulls through."

Savannah nodded. She stared down at her friend's pale face.

"You have to leave, Miss. She's got to rest."

Savannah leaned forward and kissed Mary's cheek. "Fight, Mary. Fight for me." *Fight the devil who stalks you.*

She stepped back, gazing at her friend's wan face for a moment more. Then she turned, and walked slowly out of the room.

As she walked down the long hospital corridor, she could hear other patients and nurses talking. She could hear the faint murmur of their voices. The people passed by her in a blur. She stared down at the shining white floor, moving through the hospital completely by memory.

Mary's words echoed in her mind. Savannah knew the devil that her friend spoke of was Geoffrey. He was coming after her. And she was afraid that she wouldn't be strong enough to defeat him.

Her steps were slow, wooden. Her head pounded. She ignored the pain, ignored the chorus of voices and machines.

She kept walking. Slowly, steadily.

As she rode the elevator down to the first floor, she stared at her reflection in the glass, wondering at the fragile looking woman before her. Her eyes were sunken, glassy. Her skin chalk white. She lifted a hand, driven by some strange impulse to touch her image, to comfort the sad woman who stood before her.

The elevator chimed and the door opened. She forgot the sad woman who'd stood before her, and she walked toward the small chapel. She'd always gone to the chapel when she needed strength. When she needed hope.

She pushed open the wooden door and stepped inside. The chapel was empty. Elaborate gold crosses were hung on all the walls, and several cloth covered pews were arranged in the middle of the room.

She walked toward the altar, staring with wide eyes at the image of Jesus at his crucifixion. She fell to her knees, closing her eyes. "Please, God," she begged. "Help Mary. Give her strength."

A cold wind blew through the chapel. The crosses trembled.

Savannah's eyes lifted. A soft chuckle sounded from behind her, and she stopped breathing.

"Foolish woman," he said, his voice a wicked drawl. "Even your God can't help you."

She recognized his voice. The voice that haunted her dreams, her nightmares.

She stood on legs that trembled and took a deep breath. She wouldn't let him see her fear. *She wouldn't.* She turned around slowly, gathering her strength, her courage.

The chapel's door was open, and he stood on the threshold of this holy place, hidden in shadows. She couldn't see his face. Just the outline of his body. Tall, strong. Deadly.

"Stay away from me," she ordered, lifting her chin.

He laughed again. "Foolish human. What makes you think that you're the one I want?"

What was he talking about? Of course she was the one he wanted. Who else would he want? Oh, God, Mary!

"I know where she is," he whispered. "Dear Mary. Such a...sweet woman."

No, no—she couldn't let him get to Mary. Her gaze flew around the chapel. She needed a weapon, something—

"She tasted so sweet. So pure. I think I might just have to

have another taste…"

She grabbed one of the heavy wooden crosses from the wall. "Stay away from her!" Her fingers clenched around the cross and she took a step forward.

"She's just above us, isn't she? Perhaps I'll go upstairs and see her again. Just for old time's sake."

"I said stay away from her!" Savannah snarled, straining to see him through the shadows.

"Make me," he invited, his voice a purr.

Savanna lunged, swinging the cross in front of her.

In a flash, he vanished, leaving the echo of his foul laughter to fill the chapel.

Eleven

When I look into his eyes, I see only evil.
-Entry from the diary of Henry de Montfort,
December 13, 1068

She'd warned the hospital personnel. She'd told them that Mary's life was in danger, that she needed constant supervision. They'd called in two extra guards, and they promised Savannah that Mary would be safe.

She hadn't told them that the man who was after Mary wasn't exactly human. They wouldn't have believed her if she'd said a vampire wanted to kill her friend.

So, she'd lied. She'd told them that Mary's ex-boyfriend was at the hospital and that he'd confessed to attacking her. After that, it had been easy to arrange for Mary's protection.

Once she was certain that Mary was safe, Savannah had searched the upper levels of the hospital. She didn't think that Geoffrey had left, that he'd just given up and decided to leave. No, she knew he was still there, waiting on her. Waiting *for* her.

She couldn't find him. She looked, in every room and in every closet. She hated the idea that he was there, waiting for the perfect moment to attack. To possibly kill Mary.

She had to draw him out. Draw him away from the hospital. Mary needed time to recover. She wouldn't be able to survive another attack from him. She had to lead him away. She had to protect Mary.

She pushed open the door to the stairwell. Only two flights stood between her and the parking garage. A red overhead light illuminated the small area. She hurried down the steps, wanting to get away as fast she could. She absently rubbed her temple. Her head had been pounding steadily from the moment she'd slipped into the hospital. She wished she hadn't left her pills at William's.

She walked down three steps, and the world suddenly seemed to swirl before her. She grabbed the iron railing, holding on tightly. She saw a brief flash, and then darkness surrounded her.

She closed her eyes and heard the sound of her pounding heart. Had he found her? Was he doing this to her?

She counted to ten and opened her eyes. The darkness was

gone. She once again saw the red glow of the light and the concrete stairs.

She began walking down the stairs, not taking her arm off the railing. She didn't know what had just happened, but she didn't want to take any chances. Luckily, she only had to go down one more flight to get to the garage.

She'd take her jeep and drive as far and as fast as she could. She knew he would follow her. And Mary would be safe.

The concrete steps ended in front of a red door. She shoved the door open, hurrying into the garage.

She could see her jeep sitting on the far side, right under the security camera. The long, florescent lights flickered faintly overhead, casting shadows on the pavement.

No one else was in the vast garage. No visitors, not even a security guard.

She had to hurry. She had to get away. Before he—

There was a man standing beside her jeep.

She couldn't see his face. Just his body. And his hair. Long hair, pulled back at the nape of his neck. He stepped forward, into the light, and she gasped, stunned. He had William's hair. William's face. William's eyes. His cheeks. His sensuous mouth.

He could have been William but for one small detail. The man before her did not have William's slashing scar covering his cheek.

He's my half-brother. The memory of William's words slipped through her mind. Brother. The two men could have been twins.

He smiled at her. "Hello, Savannah. I knew you'd come." He rubbed his face lightly. "Didn't dear William tell you about the resemblance?" He advanced toward her like the hunter that he was.

In her visions, his face had always been cloaked by darkness. She'd never known, never dreamed that he shared the face of her lover.

"I'm told we're quite alike," he murmured. His nails lengthened into razor sharp claws.

His words snapped Savannah out of her shock. "You're nothing alike. You're a killer, a monster! William is—"

His face tensed. "What is he?" He snapped.

Good. The word whispered through her mind. *Decent. Strong.* "Something you'll never be," she said instead. "Something you can't even understand."

He sprang forward, his arms outstretched. His fingers looked like knives.

Savannah stood her ground. Waiting for him, waiting for the perfect moment. She could see his long, sharp teeth. See the red of his eyes. See his rage. She slid her hand into her pocket. Just a moment longer...

Now!

She yanked her hand out. Her fingers were wrapped around a small can of mace. She aimed for his eyes, those red, glowing eyes—

He howled in rage and pain. His hands fell away from her and moved to cover his burning eyes.

She didn't stand around and wait for him to recover. She ran straight for her jeep. If she could get inside and lock the doors, she might be able to get away.

"You'll pay for that," he snarled behind her.

Her fingers fumbled, dropping the mace as she searched desperately for the keys hidden inside her purse. She heard his footsteps, pounding on the concrete after her. Where were those damn keys?

Her fingers curled around them. She pulled them out, dropping her purse as she fled. Just a few more feet...

He grabbed her from behind, spinning her around and shoving her against the back of her jeep.

She brought her keys up, aiming for his injured eyes. She wasn't going to let him take her without a fight! She struck out with all of her strength.

His arm lifted, slamming into her wrist. She hit back, gouging with the keys. She missed his eye by an inch. But she left a bloody trail down his left cheek.

"You bitch!" His fingers locked around her wrist, squeezing the bone and tendon. She heard a sharp, sickening pop. The keys slipped from her suddenly nerveless fingers and fell to the ground.

The blood dripped down his cheek. He pulled her imprisoned wrist high over her head. She hit him with her free hand, pounding against his chest, his neck. He laughed and bent his head toward hers.

"I love a good fight," he whispered, pressing his lips against hers.

She could taste blood. His, hers, she didn't know. She twisted her head back, feeling the cold metal behind her. She kicked him, over and over, using her shoes to pound his shins. He didn't even seem to feel the blows. He pulled her forward and captured her free hand. Wrenching both of her arms behind her, he held her effortlessly with one steely hand.

He forced her to move back into the dark corner of the garage. She strained, struggling against him, against his overwhelming strength.

He was relentless. In seconds, he'd pressed her against the garage's cold brick wall. His legs pushed between hers, leaving her body open, helpless. She couldn't kick him. She couldn't hit him, so she opened her mouth and screamed as loud as she could.

His hand clamped over mouth, driving her lips back against her teeth. This time, she knew the blood she tasted was her own.

She stared up at him, hate consuming her. This was the murdering animal that had killed her brother. Killed Sharon. Attacked Mary. Her body shook with rage.

He smiled.

"I've waited a long time for you," he whispered, bending forward and licking the skin of her neck.

She tried to jerk back, but her head just rammed into the wall. He laughed at her efforts, obviously enjoying the thrill of the fight. He began to nuzzle her neck, biting her lightly. He inhaled deeply, drinking her scent.

Pulling back, he gazed down at her with eyes that flashed. "I can smell him on you," he snapped. "He's all over you."

His left hand was still clenched tightly around her wrists. His right hand rose and locked around her throat. His hold tightened. She gasped, struggling for air.

"My brother's lover," he murmured, staring at her with disgust. "How I will enjoy killing you…"

She slammed her head forward, catching him in the chin. He swore, but his grip never wavered.

Tears swam in her eyes. Her head throbbed, pounded. Pain radiated from her temples in a blinding rush. She couldn't breathe. Her throat burned. Her lungs ached. He was killing her.

William! The cry echoed in her mind. He had been right. She wasn't strong enough to defeat Geoffrey. She wasn't strong enough to kill the monster. And now, she would die. She wished she'd had the chance to tell William good-bye. William. Her dark knight.

Geoffrey's head suddenly jerked up and his nostrils flared. He released, spinning around to scan the dark garage.

Savannah fell to the floor, landing in a tangled heap. She gasped, desperately trying to take in precious oxygen.

Geoffrey took a step forward, crouching low. She pulled herself to her knees, pushing up with her hands. She knew her wrist was broken, she could see the bone pushing out at an odd angle. She swallowed. It didn't matter. The pain didn't matter. She had to block it. She had to fight.

Geoffrey's back was to her. She could tell that he was searching the garage, using his sharp senses to hunt.

He was obviously waiting for someone. For another kill.

She couldn't let him do it. She couldn't stand by while he murdered another person.

She sprang forward, throwing her body against his back. He snarled, spinning around. With an almost casual wave of his hand, he hurled her back against the wall.

She slid slowly down to the floor. The pounding in her head intensified.

He stalked toward her.

William. His name was a whisper that never slipped past her lips, a scream that echoed in her mind.

Geoffrey leaned down and pulled her to her feet. His fingers tangled in her hair, jerking her head back and exposing her throat. "Are you afraid to die?" he asked softly.

She stared into his eyes and saw her death. "No," she murmured, knowing her time had come. She wasn't afraid of dying. For years she'd lived with the grim specter of death looming over her. She didn't mind dying. And she certainly didn't fear death.

But she was angry, fiercely and completely enraged, that her brother would go unavenged and William would be forced to slay his brother alone.

Her answer seemed to catch Geoffrey off-guard. He paused, staring into her eyes.

She swallowed, tasting death. "Are you?"

His eyes narrowed in rage. He opened his mouth, exposing his long, glinting fangs. They lowered toward her throat.

She felt the scrape of his teeth against his throat. At the same moment, a fiery burst of pain seemed to explode inside of her mind. She burned, her mind a whirlpool of twisting agony.

A ball of light flashed before her eyes. And then she saw

only darkness.

She didn't feel his teeth as they sank into her throat. She didn't feel her throbbing wrist, or the aching of her bruised and battered limbs.

All of the pain had vanished, disappearing into the enveloping darkness.

Her body fell limp, hanging weakly in Geoffrey's arms.

And just as she slipped into the waiting abyss, she heard her brother's voice. She head Mark call her name.

***

"Savannah!" William burst into the parking garage, fear nearly overwhelming him. With every second that passed, he could feel Savannah slipping away from him. He'd felt her the moment he'd reached Seattle. Felt the waves of pain and fear that enveloped her.

Felt the cool touch of death wrapping around her.

Savannah didn't have much time. Her body was rebelling against her, refusing to continue fighting.

When he ran into the garage, he could feel his brother. He felt the sick, twisted rage that clung to Geoffrey like a cloak.

But, like a light being switched off, he could no longer feel Savannah. Not her warmth. Not her spirit. Not even a flicker of the pain that seemed to haunt her so.

He simply could not feel her. And that terrified him.

The scent of blood teased his nostrils. The faint smell of lavender tormented his soul.

He saw Geoffrey, his arms wrapped around Savannah, his mouth feeding at her throat.

William snarled in rage, launching himself at his brother.

Geoffrey whirled, sensing the attack. He dropped Savannah's body to the ground and leapt at William.

They met, eyes red and teeth flashing, in a tangle of limbs and hatred. Geoffrey's claws ripped William's skin, tearing open his chest and leaving a bloody, gaping wound.

William's fingernails lengthened into razor sharp claws, and he slashed out, catching Geoffrey in the shoulder. Blood slid down his brother's arm, dripping from his hand.

"Hello, brother," Geoffrey whispered. "It's been too long." He struck out with his claws, aiming for William's exposed throat. William caught his hands in a steely grip. He clenched his teeth, and forced his brother's claws back.

He saw Savannah from the corner of his eye. She wasn't

moving. Her body lay still and pale over a pool of blood.

"What have you done?" He snarled, sending Geoffrey flying back against the hood of a car. *"What have you done?"*

Geoffrey jumped from the car, landing easily on his feet. He licked his lips, catching the blood that still lingered upon him with his tongue. "I had a taste of your lover," he said, his lips twisted into an unholy smile.

The beast within William screamed, howled in rage. He attacked. He slammed into Geoffrey, pummeling him, over and over. His claws slashed him, leaving deep cuts all over his brother's body. His head. His chest.

Geoffrey lashed out with his foot, kicking William in the stomach. The blow sent William crashing onto the concrete.

He jumped up immediately and flew at his brother. His vision had narrowed. All he saw was Geoffrey. He was going to kill his brother. *Now.*

Savannah moaned, the sound soft, barely a whisper.

William froze.

Geoffrey slammed into him, sending them both tumbling to the ground. Geoffrey lifted his hand, and William realized his brother was holding a wooden stake, and it was hovering two inches over his heart.

Geoffrey's smile widened. "Are you afraid to die, brother?"

William's hand snapped out, faster than a striking snake, and he ripped the stake out of his brother's grasp. He kicked up, sending Geoffrey crashing back. Geoffrey slammed into a truck, denting the side.

William jumped to his feet, the stake clutched tightly in his fist. He advanced on Geoffrey, watching coldly as his brother stumbled to his feet.

Geoffrey's breathing came hard and fast. His face was tense, drawn from the battle and his increasing blood loss.

His gaze shifted frantically around the garage. And then he smiled, his angel's smile. "Do you hear that, brother? Do you hear that sound?"

William froze, becoming aware of a faint, slow beat.

Geoffrey licked his lips. "It's her heart. It's struggling to beat. Hear it?"

He did hear it. It was slow. *Too slow.*

"She's not going to make it. Your lover is dying." Geoffrey pressed his hand against his shoulder, trying to staunch the flow of blood.

William glanced at Geoffrey and then at Savannah. He could hear her heart laboring desperately.

"What's it going to be, brother?" Geoffrey asked. "Her life...or mine?"

William turned toward Savannah, and Geoffrey attacked. He slammed into William's back. The stake fell from his grasp and clattered across the floor.

William swung back, throwing Geoffrey off him with a powerful swipe. He strained, struggling to hear the sound of Savannah's heartbeat. He almost fell to his knees as realization dawned. He didn't hear the beating anymore.

"Savannah!" He ran to her and slipped his hands beneath her, cradling her body against his. Her head fell back, like a broken flower.

"It's too late!" Geoffrey snarled, pushing to his knees. "She's dead!" Geoffrey smiled. "But don't worry, brother, I'll see to it that you join her...soon." His brother stumbled to his feet and then ran for the door, leaving a trail of blood in his wake. As William watched in helpless fury, his brother's body shifted, becoming mist, and he vanished.

William turned to Savannah, desperation sweeping through him. It couldn't be too late. He couldn't, *wouldn't,* lose her.

He cradled her in his arms, pulling her tightly against his chest. Her head slipped back, revealing her bruised and bloodied throat. He touched the marks gently, with hands that shook. The wounds were deep, too deep.

"Savannah," his voice was a whisper of sound. "Savannah, come back to me. Open your eyes and come back to me!"

She didn't move.

He began to rock her back and forth, as if she were a child. "Open your eyes, Savannah. Open your eyes!" He commanded, pleaded.

No response.

Fear burned through him. It was too much like last time. Too much like Henry. He'd held his brother, praying for him to live, only to watch him die.

He sent his mind out, freeing it to search for hers. He would find her spirit and force her to come back to him. He caught the faint flicker of her warmth, and he followed her, stalking her like the hunter he'd once been.

Pain slammed through his mind. Deep. Fiery. All-consuming. It was her pain. Her agony. And he knew that her death was seconds away.

He tried to comfort her, to give her his strength, but he couldn't stop the pain. Couldn't stop the blinding flashes of light.

His gut twisted. Her end was near. Death was reaching out his hungry hands to claim her.

"No!" William screamed. "I won't let you go! You can't leave me!"

Not again. He would not sit by while death claimed someone else that belonged to him.

He stood, holding her slight weight easily, and ran for the parking lot exit. Beyond the concrete walls, he could see the night. He could see the faint light from the stars. The hazy moon.

Just a few more steps.

He erupted into the night, his body shooting up into the sky. Savannah was held tightly to him, locked in his powerful embrace.

Time was running out. He had to find a safe place for her. He had to make certain that she was protected so that the ritual could begin.

He scanned the terrain. "Hold on," he whispered to her still figure. "Just hold on!"

There! He flew down, landing on the deserted rooftop. They would be safe here. Safe from prying eyes and his brother.

He lowered her gently onto the roof. His hand smoothed against her brow, gently pushing back her tangled hair. Her skin was pale, far too pale. She would not live much longer.

"Savannah," her name was a sigh, a prayer. "Sweet Savannah."

He lowered his head to her throat, still listening carefully for the faint beat of her heart. How long had it been since he'd last heard its beat? Seconds? Minutes?

Then he heard a faint stuttering sound. *Her heart!*

He hesitated. Was she strong enough? Would she be able to survive the kiss?

"William."

His gaze flew to her face. Her eyes were still closed. Her cheeks hollowed. Had she spoken? Or had his feverish mind conjured her voice?

He touched her lips gently and saw her bruised throat move as she struggled to swallow, struggled to speak.

"Kiss me, William," she begged. "Kiss me."

His lips lowered to hers. As gentle as the wind, as soft as the night, he caressed her, worshipped her. He breathed into her mouth, trying to give her his strength, his energy, his very soul.

Her heartbeat stopped, and she gasped.

"No!" She would not leave him. He would not allow it! They had made a vow. She'd promised him eternity. He would not lose her to death.

He sank his teeth into her throat. Her sweet blood slid over his tongue, hot, pure. It made him ravenous. He wanted to drink, to drink all of her.

But he could feel her slipping away. Her spirit was leaving. *She was leaving him.*

He pulled back, her blood sliding down his chin. With his teeth, he ripped a long, jagged path across his wrist and put the wound over her mouth, moving her throat so that she was forced to swallow the precious liquid. She had to take his blood. She had to drink from him, or the ritual would never work.

He pressed against her chest, against her heart. Once, twice. He willed her heart to move. To beat. Just once more. Just long enough for her to drink. To transform.

He poured all of his power into her, pushing his psychic gifts to the limit. And her heart began to beat.

Her eyes shot open, blank and frightened. He lifted his hand, forcing her to drink his blood.

Her lips moved, as light as a butterfly, against his skin. Just a little bit more...

She collapsed, her body sinking into his arms.

He stared down at her, fear consuming him. Had it been enough? Had she gotten enough for the ritual?

He couldn't feel her heartbeat. She wasn't breathing.

He spoke quickly, reciting the words he hadn't spoken for over nine hundred years. "I give to you my blood, my life. Take it, become one. One of the chosen. Be of the night. Be of me." He leaned forward, whispering against her still lips. "Be with me, forever, as I give you the kiss." He pressed his lips against hers, tasting blood, tasting fear.

He heard thunder echo in the distance, and the wind howled. He could smell the storm, feel its approach as it whipped around them.

He didn't move. He just sat there, cradling her cold, still body against his.

Had he waited too long? Had her spirit already left? As

Henry's had left? Was he too late, again?

The minutes ticked by in silence. Savannah continued to lay ominously still in his arms.

His hands clenched around her. *Too late. He'd been too late, again.*

Rain exploded from the sky. Torrents fell, drenching him, washing the blood from her body, from his.

Forgive me. The words screamed inside his mind. He'd failed her. As he'd failed Henry.

He kissed her again. Kissed her wet, still lips.

His chest burned. "Damn you," he whispered, staring down into her pale face. "You promised that you'd stay with me." His hand stroked her cheek.

He couldn't believe that she was gone. Not Savannah. She was too strong. Too good.

He would kill Geoffrey. He would see his brother dead before the next sun set. He would—

Her lashes fluttered. Her lips parted, and a soft gasp emerged from her mouth.

"Savannah!" He cradled her against him, using his body to shield her from the pouring rain.

Her lashes lifted. Her eyes, so pure, so green, met his. She smiled tiredly. "Hello, William."

Twelve

Life does not stop with death.
-Entry from the diary of Henry de Montfort,
December 16, 1068.

She could hear the sound of wind chimes, light, soothing music that floated toward her.

She lay unmoving, just listening to the soft sound. The chimes reminded her of home, of her apartment. She had wind chimes on her balcony, and she awoke everyday to their soothing greeting.

But she wasn't at home now. She couldn't be. And she was afraid.

Afraid to open her eyes. Afraid of what she would see. Her last memory had been of William. Rain had pounded down on him, and he'd been soaked to the bone. Blood had mingled with the water and ran down his face in rivulets. His eyes had been red, redder than the fires of hell. He'd looked both furious and frightened. She'd known that he was enraged at his brother. But why had he been frightened?

She'd glimpsed him for only a moment, and then she had fallen back into the dark world that waited for her. What world would she see today?

She took a deep breath and her eyes opened.

She saw her bedroom wall. She saw the mural that she'd painted, the swirling waves of the ocean and the distant lighthouse.

She saw her bookshelves, her computer. Her wicker furniture and her small dressing table.

She sat up quickly, staring at the room in wonder. How had she gotten back—

Her bedroom door opened and William walked inside. He froze when he realized that she was awake.

Suddenly nervous, Savannah quickly ran her hand through her hair.

Her hand. She froze and stared at her wrist in wonder. Geoffrey had broken it. She'd heard the bone snap. She twisted her wrist, waiting for the pain. None came.

"The bone has healed," William said, coming to sit on the edge of the bed.

"How can that be?" She touched her throat, expecting to feel tender skin. She felt only smooth, unmarred flesh.

William just watched her, his gaze steady.

She heard the voices then. The couple below her was arguing. The wife was angry because her husband had forgotten to pick up milk at the grocery store. She could hear a child crying, somewhere on the ground floor. She could hear television sets. Hear phones. Footsteps. Heartbeats.

Her eyes widened as understanding dawned.

Don't worry. William's voice floated through her mind. His lips didn't move. *I'll teach you to block out much of the noise. It's all a matter of focusing. Focus your energy, focus on me.*

She flinched at the mental touch. She took a deep breath and focused her attention, centering on him. The myriad of noises quieted almost at once. "Y-you gave me the kiss, didn't you?" She had to hear him say it.

"Yes, Savannah, I did."

And then she realized that her head didn't hurt. For the first time in over six years, she hadn't awoken with pounding temples. "My tumor?"

He smiled. "You don't have to worry about that anymore."

Not worry about it? What would it be like to live each day without the threat of death hanging over her head?

She rose slowly from the bed and was vaguely surprised to note that she was wearing a pale blue nightgown. She recognized it as a gift she'd gotten last Christmas from Sharon. William must have dressed her. He must have brought her home and dressed her for bed.

She walked slowly toward the closed balcony doors. With one hand, she touched the heavy blinds. "Has night fallen?"

He watched her closely. "Yes."

She lifted the blinds, peering out into the darkness. "He's out there, isn't he?"

He didn't answer.

She opened the door and stepped outside. The night air brushed against her skin, soothing her. She gazed down below. She could see cars driving past, see people walking on the street. She could see a young couple holding hands and kissing gently under the glow of a streetlight. She could see every detail of their faces. And they were two blocks away.

"Is he hunting?" She asked, her gaze locked on the couple.

"No."

She turned to him in surprise.

"He would have gone to ground. His injuries were severe. He would have needed time to recover."

Gone to ground. A shiver slid down her spine. She wasn't sure she wanted to know what William meant by that phrase. "I was injured...very badly," she said, remembering the fiery pain that had shot through her brain. "Why didn't I need more time to...to heal?"

He rose and walked toward her. His stride was slow, purposeful like that of a hunter who has already captured his prey. She stepped back, her legs hitting the wooden frame of the balcony.

His body stopped inches away from hers. "I gave you my blood. Ancient blood. And then you went through the change."

She frowned. "And that healed me?"

"All vampires heal quickly," he said. "It's one of our gifts. In your case, though, it was the transformation itself that repaired your body. In a sense, you can say that you were recreated. Reborn."

She swallowed. "And...how long will it take Geoffrey to heal?"

His gaze was direct. "I don't know. Two days. A week." He shrugged. "He will have to sleep for at least forty-eight hours. After that—"

"He'll start hunting again." Her heart pounded. "He could go after Mary!"

He touched her lightly, stroking her cheek. "Your friend is safe. I've arranged for her to be well guarded until this is over."

Relief swept through her. She'd been so afraid for Mary. If anything had happened to her dear friend, it would have been all her fault.

William's gaze swept slowly over her upturned face. His mouth tightened into a thin line.

"What's wrong?" Savannah asked, instantly sensing the turmoil running through him.

He stepped back, sliding into the shadows. "I almost lost you," he said, his voice quiet and deep.

She remembered the numbing coldness that had swept through her body. She remembered the consuming darkness, the brilliant flashes of light. And remembered her brother's voice.

"I think you did," she murmured. "For a moment." She

walked toward him, into the shadows. "But then you brought me back."

His arms wrapped around her. "I couldn't let you leave me."

He felt so good against her. So strong. So solid. Her arms slid around his waist. "I didn't want to leave you."

His head lowered and he kissed her. His lips were gentle, featherlight against hers as if he feared hurting her.

He drew back, staring down at her. "I can't risk losing you." She could hear pain, anguish, in his voice.

She frowned. "You're not going to lose me. We made a deal, remember? Forever."

His arms tightened around her. "Yes, *forever*."

She stood on tiptoe and pressed her lips against his. Her tongue slid over his full lower lip, teasing him. She wanted to drive him over the edge, to force him to lose his control. She wanted to wipe the lingering fear from his mind and prove to him that she wouldn't break. That she was strong. A perfect match for him.

They were on her balcony. Anyone could see them. She didn't care.

She could feel his body hardening against her.

"Do you know what you're doing?" he gritted, his eyes flashing.

She smiled. "Yes." She rubbed her breasts against him, letting the delicate silk of her nightgown slide over his chest. Her fingers moved lightly, nimbly, and began to unbutton his shirt. She wanted to feel his skin against her.

Desire pounded through her. Her body felt alive. She could feel the blood flowing through her veins. The strength. The power. The passion.

She pushed his shirt down his arms and tossed it carelessly aside. Her nails ran down his chest, scoring his skin lightly. She heard him suck in a sharp breath. She bent down, lowering her head. While swirling her tongue around his nipple, she slid her hand down to the front of his pants.

She wanted him. Here. Now. With the night surrounding them and the stars shining upon them. She wanted to feel William's heat, his passion. She wanted to *feel*. To know that she was alive. To know that death hadn't won.

She lowered his zipper. His hand flashed out, locking around her wrist. She looked up and saw a muscle flex along the hard line of his jaw.

"I don't have much control," he said, his voice guttural. His eyes were flaming red.

She smiled. "Good." She was heady with power. She could do this to him. She could push him to the edge...and beyond.

She lowered the zipper, easing her hand inside to touch his heat. Her hand gripped him, stroking softly.

He groaned.

As her hand continued to caress his rigid length, she kissed him, letting her tongue glide over his lips and into the warmth of his mouth. She loved to taste him. She moaned, the sound low, throaty.

His hands clenched around her shoulders, his fingers digging into her skin. His tongue thrust against hers. Hot. Wet.

She tore her mouth from his and began to lick his neck. She could feel his pulse pounding, throbbing against her lips. She suckled his skin, pulling it lightly into her mouth and biting gently.

William's body shook. "We have to go inside," he muttered. "*Now.*"

Her teeth pressed against him, harder. His pulse pounded.

He swore and lifted her into his arms, shouldering open the door and stepping into her bedroom. He took two long strides and lowered her onto the bed.

He stared down at her, his face granite hard. She lifted her arms, a silent invitation.

His control snapped. He fell upon her, ripping her nightgown away and leaving her in scraps of silk. His hot mouth captured her breast, licking, sucking.

She fisted her hands in his hair, and she lifted her hips, rubbing against him. She could feel him pressing against her, sliding against the fragile barrier of her panties.

His mouth continued to suckle her while his fingers teased her other breast, plucking lightly at her nipple. Pleasure lashed her. It was too much. It wasn't nearly enough.

She pushed against his shoulders, forcing him onto his back. She moved so that she sat astride him and stared down at him, her chest rising and falling rapidly.

Her panties were still in the way. Frustration boiled through her.

Then she once again heard the sound of silk tearing.

William smiled up at her.

She could feel him, feel the tip of his shaft pressing against her, teasing her tender opening.

It still wasn't enough.

She pressed down on him, forcing his rigid length inside of her hungry body. He stretched her, pushing his way deep inside.

They both moaned. And then they began to move. Faster. Harder. Her hips lifted, fell, lifted. The rhythm was wild, frantic. She hit her first climax and felt pleasure rock through her.

William's fingers bit into her hips, forcing her body to continue its pace. The second climax began to build. Faster, harder than the first.

She lowered her head, licking his throat. Her teeth began to burn. Her hips moved frantically against his. Her mouth opened against him, and her teeth scraped against his neck. He thrust deeper into her warmth.

"Do it," he growled. "Do it, Savannah!" There was a dark need in his voice that she didn't fully understand.

He slammed into her body one more time. Her release rolled through her, sending her spiraling.

Her teeth sank into his throat.

His shout of release filled the room and drifted out into the waiting night.

***

He knew the woman had survived. He knew that William had transformed her. He could feel it.

But it didn't matter. He would still kill her. He would drain all of the blood from her body and leave her dead corpse for his brother to find.

Geoffrey's body lay perfectly still, buried deep within the earth. He could feel his strength beginning to return. Soon, he would be able to rise. And destroy.

He would kill the woman first. He'd always enjoying killing women. Their fear was so wonderfully delicious. Maybe he would make dear William watch as he took the life from his lover. Yes, he'd make him watch.

And then he'd kill William. As he should have done so long ago.

He'd tried to kill his brother before. When they were just lads, he'd pushed William into the dark river near their father's hold. He'd watched from the shore as William had struggled to survive, struggled to stay afloat. And when William had screamed for help, Geoffrey had just smiled.

Unfortunately, William's scream had drawn the attention

of a nearby knight. And his brother had been dragged from the water, unconscious, but alive.

Later, when they'd trained with weapons, learning to fight with Guy's men, he'd attacked his brother a second time. William, caught off guard, had no time to avoid the deadly blade that swung toward his face. He'd been scarred ever since that blessed day. When confronted by the knights, Geoffrey had claimed the blade slipped.

He'd been able to tell that William hadn't believed the pitiful lie. The knights had, so they let him continue training. But William had started watching him more carefully after that day. He'd been on guard.

Geoffrey was almost glad he hadn't managed to kill him before. He wanted William to know that death was coming for him. Of the three brothers, William had been the only one who truly belonged. Guy had always told Geoffrey that William was his real son, the only "true de Montfort."

Geoffrey hated William. He didn't deserve the title. He didn't have Guy's lust for power. He didn't have the de Montfort taste for killing.

But Geoffrey did.

Guy had never appreciated him, and, in the end, he'd had to die. Geoffrey proved to the bastard that he was a true de Montfort. He'd killed Guy, and he'd enjoyed moment of it.

Covered in Guy's blood, he'd gone to the seer who had sent William on his quest, and he'd forced the man to tell him the location of the vampire. He'd cut him at least a dozen times before the old fool finally gave him the directions he needed.

He'd sought out the vampire, and he'd been transformed by him. Of course, after the transformation, Geoffrey had killed the vampire. He could still remember the rush of power, of strength that moment had given him.

He'd killed hundreds in his lifetime. Hundreds. But he'd never been able to kill William.

The woman was the key. Once he had her, his brother would do whatever he wanted. William's weakness for the woman would be his downfall.

And in the end, Geoffrey would kill them both.

He could hardly wait. He would make certain that his brother suffered, that he begged for death.

***

Savannah jerked back, staring down at William in horror.

She touched her lips, feeling the wet drops of blood, tasting a coppery sweetness. There were two small puncture wounds on his throat.

She pushed away from him, stumbling from the bed. What had she done? *What had she done?*

"Savannah—"

She ignored William's cry and ran into the bathroom, slamming the door shut behind her. She turned the lock, sagging against the door.

She'd taken his blood. She'd actually drank from him.

William's fist pounded against the door. "Savannah! Dammit, Savannah, open this door!"

She walked slowly toward the sink. Her fingers gripped the marble top, and she forced herself to lift her head and gaze into the mirror.

She expected to see a monster.

But she just saw—

Her eyes. Her green eyes. Her pale skin. The nose that she'd always thought was too small. The lips that she'd always thought were too big.

She looked the same as she'd always looked. But she could still taste William's blood.

She turned on the faucet, catching water in her hand. She had to wash the taste away. She had to!

She sipped the water, swirling it in her mouth, then she spat it into the sink over and over. But still the coppery taste remained.

"I'm coming in!" There was a loud, splintering crash, and then the bathroom door swung open slowly, the lock smashed.

William stood naked on the threshold, his eyes flashing. "What the hell is going on?"

Her gaze fell to his neck, to the marks she had left upon him. "I'm sorry. I'm so sorry—"

His eyes narrowed. He took a step toward her, but he froze when she shrank back against the sink. "You don't have anything to be sorry about. You didn't do anything wrong."

She shook her head. "I bit you. I took your blood!" And she'd enjoyed it. She'd reveled in the rush of power that his blood had given her. And that knowledge shamed her.

"I gave it to you freely," he said.

Her lips trembled. "I couldn't stop," she whispered in despair. "I didn't want to do it, but I couldn't stop myself. I had to drink. I had to!" She blinked away the tears that gathered in her eyes, refusing to let them fall.

William moved slowly toward her. His hands lifted and wrapped around her, pulling her against his body, cradling her. "Sweet Savannah. I should have told you…"

She stiffened. "Told me what?"

He rubbed her back, his hands gentle, soothing. "For a vampire, physical lust, desire, will stir the blood hunger. It will push your control until the need for release and the need for blood are bound together."

She pushed back and stared up at William. "I didn't mean to hurt you."

"You didn't hurt me," he assured her, his voice urgent. "You gave me pleasure, more pleasure than I'd ever thought possible."

And then she remembered the feel of his mouth upon her neck, the ecstasy that had coursed through her when William drank from her.

"You remember now, don't you?" he asked, his gaze watchful. "The blood connects us, lets us share our pleasure."

Her brow wrinkled. "Will it be like that when I have to feed from someone else?"

William tensed against her. "No. You'll only lose control if your physical desire and your blood hunger merge. And since you won't be with anyone but me…"

His sentence trailed off, but Savannah knew what he meant. She'd promised to be with him forever. He expected her to be loyal to him, to desire only him.

"And you won't be with anyone else, will you, Savannah?" His eyes flashed red.

"No. Only you," she told him softly. And it was true. She couldn't imagine wanting anyone else. It was only William. He alone was the one that she desired, the one that she craved.

She felt the tension ease from his body. "What about you?" she queried, suddenly nervous. "You won't be with anyone else, will you?" She repeated, holding her breath and waiting for his answer.

He touched her cheek. "Do you really need to ask that?" He smiled. "You're the only one for me, Savannah. Now and forever."

Warmth spread through her, chasing the chill from her body. He captured her hand and led her back into the bedroom.

"We need to dress. There is much we must do tonight."

She frowned, stepping into her closet. There was a strange urgency to his tone. She pulled on a blue sweater and slipped on an old pair of jeans. By the time she found her shoes and walked back into the bedroom, he was fully dressed.

They exited her apartment and headed down the empty hall. She pushed the button for the elevator, waiting nervously for the car to reach her level.

With a soft ding, the doors opened and they stepped inside. Savannah lifted her hand, intending to push the button for the ground floor.

"No." William's fingers wrapped around her wrist. "We're going to the roof."

Savannah frowned but obediently pressed the button for the top floor. Once there she knew they would have to take a flight of stairs in order to access the roof.

She leaned against the mirrored wall of the elevator. She studied him silently. He was wearing all black, again. A black shirt and black pants. Even black boots. She didn't think he actually owned any colored clothing.

But it didn't matter. He looked good in black. With his dark hair and that scar, he looked dangerous. Sexy.

She felt desire begin to stir once more, and she was shocked. How could she want him again so soon? Her need for him was becoming uncontrollable.

The elevator chimed. She swallowed, "We're here," she mumbled unnecessarily.

William glanced at her, his brows drawn low in obvious concern. She forced a smile and stepped into the hallway. She had to get herself under control.

They walked quickly down the hall. Savannah showed William the door to the stairwell. The door was locked, but, with a strong jerk of his hand, he busted the lock and swung the door open.

They climbed the stairs in silence. Why were they going to the roof? she wondered.

He pushed open a door at the top of the stairs, and they walked outside.

The night air was warm. Stars shone brightly overhead. Savannah walked to the edge of the roof and gazed below, wonder filling her. The city was beautiful. Alive with a thousand different lights. She stared down, awed by the sight.

"Are you ready?" William asked.

Savannah forced her gaze away from the view and turned to look at him. "Ready for what?"

"Your lessons."

Lessons? What did he mean?

"How high would you say we are?" He asked curiously, moving to stand beside her.

"Fifteen stories," she replied as a knot of fear began to form in her stomach. Suddenly, the view wasn't nearly as appealing as it had been a moment before.

He pointed across the street. "And that building? How far away is it?"

Her eyes widened. It was at least fifty feet away.

"Fifty feet?" He nodded. "Yes, I'd say that looks about right."

She flinched, still not used to him reading her thoughts.

He walked to the center of the roof. "This is your first lesson," he said. "A vampire has incredible speed. Incredible strength."

She nodded. She already knew that.

"But there are many dark gifts that come with the kiss. Many, many gifts."

She took a tentative step toward him. "I don't understand. Why did we come up here?" There was a ball of tension, of dread, knotting in her stomach.

"There is much you must learn. Much that you must see."

What could he possibly want her to see on a deserted rooftop?

"They say that seeing is believing," he murmured.

She frowned, as he smiled at her and began running toward the edge of the roof.

Her eyes widened in horror. "No, William! Don't—" Her hand reached for him, but it was too late.

He hurtled over the edge of the roof.

"No!"

Thirteen

Vampires and immortality. 'Tis madness.
Only God can live forever.
-Entry from the diary of Henry de Montfort,
December 19, 1068

Before her eyes, he transformed, becoming a large hawk. He flew high into the air, circling above her. Then he landed, on top of the roof, over fifty feet away.

Impossible. Not even a vampire could…

He became fog. Pale fog that drifted back across the night sky, drifted back to her.

"William…" Her voice was a hoarse whisper. How could he—

"Power comes with age," William said, rematerializing at her side. "Shapeshifting will become easy for you, in time."

She was stunned. "You mean I'll be able to do that, to transform?"

"In time," he agreed. "You'll learn that as you age, your powers change. There will be no limit to the things that you can do."

She glanced back across the street. Fifty feet. A hawk. Fog. Her knees felt weak. "Can Geoffrey do this? The shapeshifting?" Was that hoarse croak really her voice?

"Yes."

That made him even more dangerous.

"But he won't do it often," William continued softly, watching her carefully. "Shifting weakens a vampire's power. It takes a lot of strength to maintain the shape."

She stared at him intently, and then she straightened her shoulders and took a deep breath. "Teach me." She had to learn as much as she could, so that she would be ready for her next encounter with Geoffrey.

He took her hand and they walked to the center of the roof. "Hold onto me. Don't let go, no matter what happens."

She nodded.

"I want you to focus on the roof across the street. Think about reaching that roof, landing on its surface."

Her eyes widened as she realized his intent. "You can't mean that we're going to—"

"Don't look down." A slight smile curved his lips. "Just pretend that you're doing a long jump."

But she'd never done a long jump. She'd never done track or any sort of running activity.

His fingers tightened around hers. "Ready?"

She took a deep breath. She could do this. She *would* do this. "Ready."

"Then let's go."

They began running, as fast as they could. They were almost at the edge of the roof. Savannah concentrated on the building in front of her.

Their feet left the edge of the roof.

She wouldn't look down. She wouldn't!

She kept moving her legs, but she felt nothing but air beneath her. She tightened her fingers around William. She wouldn't look down.

She stared at the building before her. It was close now. So close. She would make it. She *would.*

There! Her feet slammed down on the roof. She stumbled forward, but managed to catch herself before she fell.

"Oh, my God!" She turned back, staring at her apartment building in shock. "I did it! I actually did it!"

William smiled.

She ran to the edge of the roof. "Fifty feet." She exhaled heavily. "We just flew fifty feet."

"And how did it feel?"

"Wonderful." She was dazed, overwhelmed with wonder. "Absolutely wonderful." She laughed softly. "You know, I've always had a horrible fear of heights."

He frowned, his brows lowering. "You never told me that."

"Well, it's not exactly something I like to brag about." She stared below, amazed that she could actually look down and not feel the vertigo that she usually experienced.

"But you came to my home, to my mountain, and you showed no fear."

She shrugged. "I had to see you. There wasn't any choice." But she had been terrified. As she'd driven up the mountain, she'd refused to look over the side of the road, refused to even glance at the breathtaking view. She hadn't wanted to look down, fearing that terror would overwhelm her. So she'd driven, her eyes locked on the road in front of her. She'd forced herself to ignore the height, to ignore the increasing pressure in her ears.

And she'd made it up that damn mountain.

And, now, staring down at the street below, she realized that her fear was gone.

"It's your turn now," William said softly, touching her back.

Her hands trembled. "M-my turn?"

"Go back to your apartment. Do it on your own."

She glanced at him, her eyes wide. "But what if I fall?"

"You won't." He sounded extremely confident. Savannah wished she had his confidence.

She looked back across the wide expanse. Flying with William was one thing. Flying on her own—well, that was a whole different matter. "It's eleven floors, William. If I fall—"

"You'll wind up with some bad bruises," he said with a small shrug.

"Bruises? I could wind up with a lot more than just bruises!" She'd probably break her neck.

"Stop thinking like a human," he said, his voice suddenly harsh.

"But—"

"Thinking that way will get you killed. Don't think of what you were. Think of what you *are*. You can do this, Savannah. You just did it with me, and you can do it by yourself."

He was right. A fall wouldn't kill a vampire. She'd survive, even if she fell eleven stories.

"You won't fall," he said again, easily reading her. "And even if you did, I'd catch you long before you reached the ground."

He'd better not be lying, because if he didn't catch her—well, he'd have hell to pay. "Okay." She straightened her shoulders. "I'll do it." And she would. She took several steps back, wanting a running start. Her gaze stayed locked on her apartment building. She took a quick breath and ran.

Her feet pounded across the roof. Faster. Faster. She could see the edge now. There!

She shot into the sky, her body flying straight toward the waiting rooftop. Wind whipped against her body. Her feet kicked the air.

She didn't look down.

The edge of her roof was so close, so close—

She landed on the rooftop, slipping to her knees.

Savannah laughed, thrilled with pleasure. She moved to stand, but her legs wobbled, sending her sliding back down.

"Savannah?" William was beside her in an instant.

"It's okay." She pushed her hair back with a trembling hand. "My knees are just a little weak."

He supported her with his arm as he helped her to her feet. She wanted to lean into him, into the shelter of his arms. Instead, she took a bracing breath and stepped away from him. They didn't have much time, and she couldn't afford to be weak. She squared her shoulders and asked, "What's next?"

He stepped to the edge of the roof. "Next, we hunt..."

***

They walked silently down the dark street. It was after two a.m., and the road was completely deserted.

"Where are we going?" Savannah asked. She'd lived in Seattle all of her life, but William had taken her down a myriad of twisting, turning streets. She actually had no idea where she was at that moment.

"Do you hear the music?" He asked her.

She frowned. Yes, she did hear music. A faint, pounding beat that drifted on the wind. She'd been vaguely aware of it for the last few blocks.

"We're following it," William told her. "It will lead us to your next lesson."

She swallowed and glanced up at the night sky. A quarter moon hung heavily amidst the shining stars. "I thought you said there'd only be a need to feed when the moon was full." And, besides, she'd already drank from him. The thought caused a remembered shiver to skate down her spine.

"You're not going to drink."

Then why were they following music that would undoubtedly lead them to a club filled with people? A place that was undoubtedly like Jake's?

Because you must learn to lure your prey to you. His voice drifted through her mind. *You must learn to use your psychic gifts to enthrall, to control.*

She shook her head instinctively, then froze. As much as she rebelled against the idea of controlling another person, he was right. If she intended to survive, she would have to learn to use all of her powers.

She marshaled her thoughts and concentrated on William. *I'll learn, but I won't hurt anyone.* She wanted to be clear on that point.

She felt his start of surprise as he received her mental

message. Then his mind seemed to reach for hers, surrounding
her.

Good. Very good, Savannah.

Warmth swept through her. *I've always been a fast learner.*

She felt, rather than heard, his soft ripple of laughter.

Good. You'll need to be.

They walked quietly for a time. The music became louder.
She could hear voices now, laughter. She could smell the people
inside the bar. Smell the alcohol and the cheap perfume. The
cigarettes and the sex.

They walked around a corner, and she froze.

The bar was as she'd expected—small, dark, and full of
people. A flashing neon sign indicated the place was "The Black
Pit." Judging by its rough exterior, Savannah thought the name
was fitting.

There was an assortment of vehicles in the small parking
lot. SUVs, pickup trucks, even motorcycles.

Several of the bar's patrons had stumbled outside. One man
had even passed out on the side of the building. Savannah studied
him with deep consideration.

William looked at her, his gaze hooded. "Far too easy. You'll
have to pick someone who is still conscious."

She wrinkled her nose and then stepped forward, marching
into the bar with a confidence that she really didn't feel. She was
conscious of William following a few paces back.

A bouncer stood at the entrance, his beefy arms crossed over
a barrel-like chest. His left eyebrow lifted at Savannah's approach.

"Hello, little lady." His gaze roamed over her body, lingering
on her breasts.

Anger swept through her. She stared at him, fixing her gaze
upon him.

Concentrate, Savannah. Focus on him. William's soft orders
slipped into her mind.

The bouncer's gaze lifted to meet her dark stare. He blinked,
once, twice, and then his jaw seemed to go slack.

"Open the door for me," Savannah said softly, clenching her
hands to disguise their trembling.

He hurried to obey, nearly tripping in his haste.

She took a deep breath, exhaling slowly. That had certainly
been easy enough.

*It won't always be. The stronger the mind, the harder it is
to control.* William followed her silently.

I don't like this! I don't like controlling someone else's thoughts!

You don't have to like it. You just have to do it. William was implacable.

There was a small dance floor in the middle of the room. A band played a loud, pounding rhythm on a stage encased in a wire fence.

Savannah walked toward the bar. It was crowded but she saw two empty stools.

She eased down onto the first stool, silently surveying the bar. Who could she pick? Who would satisfy William?

"What can I get for you?"

She spun around. The bartender, a woman with streaked blond hair and a tattoo of a snake around her neck, looked inquiringly at her. Savannah really didn't want anything, and she wasn't sure that she would be able to keep it down if she actually had to drink, but she didn't want to attract any unwanted attention. "Uh...I'll take a..." Inspiration struck. "A Bloody Mary. Yes, that please."

William laughed softly.

"And you?" The bartender leaned across the bar, pushing her breasts forward suggestively. "What would you like?" Her voice indicated that not just alcohol was available.

Savannah glared at her. How dare that woman try to come on to William? Couldn't she see that he was with her? She cleared her throat, loudly. The woman looked at her, annoyance flashing across her pinched face.

"What?"

Savannah's eyes narrowed. "He's with me."

The woman blinked, once, twice. She shook her head and stepped back. "Right. Sorry." She hurried to get Savannah's drink.

Savannah watched her with unflinching eyes.

A few moments later, the bartender placed Savannah's drink in front of her with careful hands. "I-is there anything else you need?"

"No." Savannah turned her back on the woman and surveyed the crowd.

Was that really necessary?

Her shoulders tensed. She sipped her drink. *What do you mean?* She hadn't done anything to the woman. She'd just told her to stay away from William.

You used compulsion on her.

She gasped. *I most certainly did not!* And she hadn't, had she? She'd just told the annoying woman to leave William alone.

It was in your voice. The tone, the pitch.

Savannah's face whitened. She truly hadn't meant— Her fingers locked around the cool glass.

Just be careful. William cautioned her softly. *Control your power, don't let it control you.*

She nodded. She would make certain that she used more care.

Her gaze traveled slowly around the room. Her foot began to tap in rhythm with the music.

So what am I supposed to do, exactly? She knew that coming to the bar was some sort of test for her, but she just didn't understand fully what William wanted her to do.

You see that woman, the one in the black leather jacket leaning against the end of the bar?

Savannah turned her head a bit and caught a glimpse of the woman. She nodded her head slightly.

Read her mind.

What?

Focus on her. See if you can hear her thoughts. You have to be able to read the minds of humans. If not, then you may find yourself in serious danger. Don't forget, some humans know of the existence of vampires. Some humans hunt us. You must be able to scan the minds of those around you. You must know if they intend you harm.

She nibbled her lip. She didn't like the idea of invading someone else's mind. It was too personal, too intimate an act.

Do it, Savannah.

No. She couldn't do it. She couldn't pry into someone else's mind, steal thoughts and dreams. She couldn't, *wouldn't,* do it.

She stood abruptly and headed for the dance floor.

Savannah!

She ignored his call and continued walking. A man with short blond hair and a thin moustache hurried to greet her.

"Hey, there, pretty thing! You wanna dance?" She could smell the alcohol on his breath, see it in the glazed expression of his eyes. She thought about refusing, was in fact opening her mouth to do so, when she heard William's imperious command.

Leave him alone. Come back to me!

She lifted her chin and smiled at her would-be partner. "I'd love to dance," she purred softly.

His eyes widened and he immediately pulled her onto the dance floor.

The band began to play a softer, lighter tune, and her partner pulled her close, sliding his hands down her back.

Savannah pushed lightly against his chest, wanting to put more distance between them. "Ah, look, buddy—"

His gaze was locked on her lips. "Bill. Name's Bill." His hands slid down to her hips.

This wasn't what she intended. She'd only wanted to get away from William for a moment, just a moment, so that she could think—

He'd sure love to lay her down, strip the clothes from her hot little body, and—

Savannah gasped and shoved against Bill, sending him stumbling back. She knew the thoughts were his. She could actually feel the waves of his lust pounding against her.

"What the hell?" Bill glared at her and took a step forward, his hands clenched into tight fists.

"Don't come near me," she ordered, her eyes flashing.

Bill froze.

She lowered her voice, trying for the pitch she'd used earlier with the bartender. "Leave this bar, take a cab, and go home. And don't ever come near me again."

He blinked and then stepped widely around her. He walked straight toward the bar's entrance.

Savannah watched him like a hawk, anger still pouring through her veins.

"Problem?" William asked softly, appearing at her side.

"Can we leave?" She asked, her voice a whisper. It was too much for her. The people. The noise. The smells. She just wanted to get outside. To get away.

She had to get away.

She didn't wait for William to answer. She ran for the door.

She shoved the door open and stumbled outside, breathing heavily. The bouncer looked at her, frowning.

Savannah ran. As fast as she could. She didn't care where she was going. She just knew that she had to get away.

Her feet pounded against the pavement. Buildings and trees passed by her in a sickening blur. Faster. Faster.

The sounds chased her. The smells. The voices.

She wanted to scream. To just make it all stop.

She ran into a park, dashing down an old trail. She pushed

bushes and trees out of her way and dodged fallen limbs, stumbling to a halt in front of a small pond. She stood there a moment, gasping for breath.

Then she fell to her knees, staring blankly into the dark water. What had she done? What had she become?

"You haven't changed," his voice seemed to whisper to her from the darkness. "You're the same person that you always were."

He'd found her. She'd known that he would. Her gaze stayed locked on the water. "No, I'm not."

He sat down beside her, and she could feel the force of his gaze upon her. She knew he was waiting for her to tell him why she'd run.

The surface of the water looked so calm, so clear. But what secrets lay beneath its surface? She closed her eyes for a moment. "I don't think I can do this." Her eyes opened, staring fixedly at the water.

She felt him stiffen beside her. "You *can* do this. I wouldn't have transformed you if I'd thought you weren't strong enough."

But she wasn't strong. She'd never been strong. Mark had been the strong one.

"Savannah." His voice was soft, compelling. "Look at me."

She turned her head slowly toward him.

"You are the strongest person that I've ever met. You've lived through disease, through tragedy and death, and you've kept going."

She shook her head. He didn't understand. She'd just done what she'd had to do.

"No." He was emphatic. "You're the one who doesn't understand. You don't see yourself as the woman you really are. You tracked me down. You found me, when I'd been hiding for centuries." A small smile flashed briefly. "And you blackmailed me. Knowing that I was a vampire, with enormous power and strength, you actually blackmailed me."

She flushed. Had she really threatened to go to the press with his story?

His smile faded. "And you faced Geoffrey. Alone, unarmed. You tried to defeat a vampire with a thousand years' worth of power." He shook his head. "And you say that you're not strong?"

He didn't understand. "I had to fight him. He was going to hurt Mary!" She hadn't attacked Geoffrey because she was strong. She'd done it to protect her friend.

"You could have died protecting your friend! You were willing to trade your life for hers. Don't you realize how much courage that took?"

She swallowed. She hadn't felt courageous at the time. She'd felt terrified.

"But you didn't let your fear stop you. You faced Geoffrey anyway. And when you fight, even when you're consumed by fear, that, sweet Savannah, is strength."

She stilled. She wanted to believe him, but—

"It's not about believing me. It's about believing in yourself."

He was right. She turned back to the pond. She had to believe in herself. To believe in her own strength. She'd cheated death. She'd fought a vampire and survived. And she would have vengeance for her brother.

"How long…" She stopped, cleared her throat, and then asked, "How long did it take to you to adjust to being a vampire?"

He laughed. "Ah, Savannah. I'm still adjusting."

She smiled. She picked up a stone and tossed it into the water. A small ripple appeared on the clear surface. "I didn't want to read anyone's thoughts. It seemed too personal. Too much of an invasion." Her lips compressed. "But then I did it anyway, without meaning to."

"To the man you were dancing with?" There was a slight edge to his voice.

"Yes. He was imaging t-taking off my clothes and—"

"Bastard." She could hear the rage in his voice, feel it in the suddenly tense atmosphere.

"When I knew what he wanted, I—" She took a deep breath. "I was furious. And I was so afraid that I would lose control and hurt him."

"An understandable response." William said, flexing his fingers into a tight fist. "I think the fellow deserved a bit of pain."

"I used a compulsion on him," she whispered, staring at the faint ripples still evident in the water. "I told him to leave and to never come near me again."

"Hmmm. Seems he got off lightly."

She clenched her teeth. "I didn't want to know what he was thinking. I wish that I'd never heard his thoughts. I don't want to know what anyone is thinking. It's too much!" She couldn't stand the idea of being bombarded with images of other people's thoughts, their fantasies.

His hands touched her shoulders, caressing her lightly. "I

can teach you to control it. You can learn to block them out."

"I thought I knew how to block out the sounds, but when I was in the bar, I lost control. The sounds were too much. The smells too much. Everything was too damn much!" She'd been afraid that she'd shatter from the pressure on her sensitive mind.

He pulled her against his chest, stroking her hair with a gentle hand. "You've had a hell of an evening, haven't you?"

She nodded, enjoying the feel of his arms around her. "Will it get better?" She asked him softly.

He kissed her temple. "Yes. Every day it will get easier. You'll grow stronger."

"I don't want to read people's minds." She sounded like a petulant child, but she didn't care. She couldn't do it. She couldn't force her way into the minds of strangers.

"Then I'll teach you how to block their thoughts. I'll teach you how to shield your mind."

She pushed herself back, staring into his eyes. "Thank you, William."

He frowned. "For what?"

"For helping me."

He stared into her eyes. His head lowered, and she lifted her face toward him, eager to feel his lips against hers.

Instead, she felt a shiver run the length of her spine. A cold wind seemed to blow straight through her.

Her eyes widened. "William?"

He pulled back, his face hard. "Let's go, Savannah. *Now.*" He stood, pulling her to her feet.

"But I don't understand—"

She heard the sound of a soft laugh. A man's laugh.

William began to run, pulling her behind him.

And then she heard the whisper, floating on the wind.

Savannah.

She could feel him then, feel the darkness of his presence reaching out to her, calling her.

Geoffrey.

But how? William had said that he'd gone to ground, that he was recovering from his injuries. Had he healed already?

He's close. Very close. William's voice, strong and clear in her mind.

How has he already recovered? His strength was amazing. And terrifying.

William led her down a dark street, pulling her at a frantic pace. *He hasn't recovered, not fully.*

Then how—

His resting place is near. He can sense us.

She jerked to a stop. "He's near?" If Geoffrey was close by, and he was weak…then they could defeat him. "Why are we running? We have to find him. Now's our chance! We can—"

William turned to face her, and his hard expression could have been cut from stone. Another shiver slid through her.

"We're not running from him."

Then who were they running from?

"Don't you feel it?" He asked her. "Can't you feel what's coming?"

A shudder ran though her. She felt something, but—

She saw a faint tremor run through his body.

Her eyes widened. What was happening?

"The sun's coming. Dawn is almost upon us. We run from the light, not from Geoffrey." He lifted his hand, and she saw that it shook. "Our bodies warn us of the approaching light. Listen to your body, and always heed its warning." He pulled her hand. "Now, come on, we haven't much time."

They ran, their hearts pounding and their limbs trembling.

How far away was the apartment? How long before the sun—

William grabbed her, hugging her tightly against his chest, and he took to the sky.

They soared, flying over buildings and rooftops, and in mere minutes, they were on the roof of her apartment.

They ran inside the building just as the sun began to rise.

They hurried into her apartment. With a wave of his hand, William sent the blinds sliding down and secured the curtains. Not a trace of sunlight crept inside her home.

They were safe.

William took her into his arms and pulled her onto the bed.

A strange lethargy was already sweeping over her. Her body felt heavy, almost as if it were weighted down. And her heartbeat was slowing, slowing…

"William?" She was afraid. She couldn't seem to take a deep breath. And her heart, her heart—

"Shhh." His arms were tight around her. "Don't fight it. Just relax."

"I-I'm scared," she whispered and then her heart stopped beating.

Fourteen

Today, father asked me if I was afraid to die.
I have heard him ask that question to hundreds of men,
right before he killed them.
-Entry from the diary of Henry de Montfort,
December 21, 1068

His strength was returning.

Geoffrey stretched slowly, feeling power course through him. He needed to feed. Blood would restore him to full strength.

It was a pity that dear Savannah wasn't around. He would certainly enjoy draining her white throat dry. Sensing her the previous night had been an unexpected pleasure. He'd felt her strong mind seeking in the night.

And so he'd had to play with her, just a little.

Trust William to spoil his fun. His elder brother always tried to stop his games. But this time, William wasn't going to stop him. This time, William would be defeated. Destroyed.

He would die, as he should have died centuries ago.

Geoffrey had planned his brother's death, down to the minutest of details. He had the perfect place in mind for his brother's murder. Absolutely perfect. It was a place of life, of hope. Of blood and destruction.

He smiled, preparing to rise and feed. It was time that he and his brother went home.

***

She opened her eyes and found William staring down at her, his gaze intense.

She blinked and took a deep breath. Energy hummed through her body. Energy…and strength.

She remembered the fear that had swept through her last night. Her hand lifted and she touched her chest. She could feel the movement of her heart. Slow, steady.

"Will it always be like that?" She asked softly.

William nodded. "But you'll get used to it."

Would she? Would she really get used to feeling her heart stop beating? Well, it wasn't as if she really had a choice.

He touched her cheek. "It will get easier, Savannah. Believe me. Soon it will seem to be natural. Just like your human sleep."

She certainly prayed that he was right. She glanced toward

the now raised curtain and blinds. Night had fallen. It was time for her to hunt. To hunt Geoffrey.

She shifted, preparing to rise, but William's hands locked around her, holding her captive. She frowned. "William? What is it?"

His gaze searched her face. She noticed that his jaw was clenched, his scar standing out starkly against his skin.

"I want us to go back to North Carolina."

"What? Why?" They were so close to their goal. They knew where Geoffrey was. They'd been so close to his resting place last night. Now was the time to attack, not to run.

"You're not strong enough to do this, to face him." His tone was rough. "You need to wait until—"

"Until he kills someone else? Until he slaughters someone else's brother? Someone else's wife?" She shook her head. "No, I can't do it. I can't wait any longer. He has to be stopped."

"Then let me do it. Let me stop him. Go back to my home and let me take care of Geoffrey." His eyes blazed down at her.

"Oh, I get it. I'm supposed to be the little woman who stands back and lets you take care of the big, bad monster, right?" Anger flushed her cheeks and flattened her speech. "I'm supposed to stand back and let you do all the work, right? Right?"

A muscle flexed in his jaw.

"Wrong!" She snapped, struggling against his hold. She couldn't believe that he would even suggest such a thing. To think that she would just stand back, just sit quietly, while he went after Geoffrey. "You promised me, William! You promised me that I would have my vengeance!"

He pressed her into the bed cushions, controlling her when she struggled for her freedom. "Dammit, Savannah! He's my brother!"

"And he killed mine!" She bucked against him, kicking and scratching with all of her might.

William froze, his fingers locked around her wrists. Blood trickled from a deep cut on his cheek. His eyes flashed red, then black. "I don't want him to hurt you," he said, his voice soft and deep.

"He's not going to hurt me," she promised, locking her gaze with his. "He's not going to hurt anyone else. We're going to stop him!"

His fingers stroked her delicate skin. Her pulse pounded

furiously beneath his touch. "You're still weak from the change. You need more time to recover, to learn about your powers. Come with me to the mountains—"

She could hear the plea in his words, could hear the soft entreaty. But she could not give in. "I'm going after him. With, or without you." She wouldn't let another innocent person's blood be on her hands. She had to stop him.

"The blood isn't on your hands," he told her softly. "It's on mine. It's always been on mine." He released her and stood, gazing down at her with swirling eyes.

She sat up slowly, pushing her hair back with a quick hand.

William gazed at her, but she could tell he saw only the past. "I should have killed him when I had the chance."

She reached for his hand. Her fingers locked with his. "Tell me, William. Tell me what happened."

William exhaled heavily, and the shadows of his past swept into the room. "Henry was dead, but I couldn't just leave him there. I couldn't let those bastards desecrate his body. So I took him down through the tunnels beneath my father's fortress…"

He could still see it so clearly. So clearly.

The tunnels were dank, dark. The odor of death and decay hung in the air. Henry's body was a slight weight against his shoulder, but the grief he felt was overwhelming.

He'd been too late. Too late to save Henry, too late to save the brother he'd always tried so hard to protect.

He didn't know how long he walked through the tunnels. The passageway narrowed, until he had to turn sideways and pull Henry behind him. Then the passage widened again, and he continued this trek, lifting his brother's broken body high into his arms.

His great-grandfather had first found the passages. They were a family secret, to be used in an emergency. The winding passages led to the cliffs on the northern end of his family's land.

He'd visited the cliffs often as a child. Henry had followed him, a quiet, steady shadow. One day they'd discovered a cave nestled in the cliffs. It was small, probably not more than fifteen feet deep.

They had spent countless days in that cave, talking and planning. It had been their secret place. Their refuge from their father's rage.

The cave would now be his brother's final resting place.

Henry would be safe in the cave. No one would find him. He could rest there, for eternity.

The passage shifted, beginning to curve upward. William could smell the sea, almost feel the cool touch of the water against his face.

He walked out into the waiting night.

Something slammed into him, sending him crashing to his knees. He struggled to hold onto Henry.

"Get up! Rise, you bastard!"

William felt the tip of a blade press against his throat.

He moved slowly, easing Henry's body to the ground. The blade pressed deeper, drawing blood.

William's gums began to burn, his teeth began to grow.

He rose slowly, his gaze lifting to meet the burning red stare of the man before him.

His brother Geoffrey smiled at him, revealing gleaming fangs. "Surprised, brother? Did you think you were the only one worthy of the dark gift?"

Horror rolled through William. "Geoffrey! Dear God, what have you done?" He could still see his father's body, see the blood that stained the ground.

Geoffrey's eyes narrowed and the blade bit deeper into William's throat. "What have I done? I have fulfilled my destiny. I have taken the power that I was always meant to have!" His gaze fell to Henry's still body. "The question, brother, is what have you done?"

William blanched. "I tried to save him, I tried, but I was too late. He was already—"

"Henry was the only one I cared about," Geoffrey said softly. "My true brother. My blood."

"He was my brother, too! I tried to save him!" He'd done everything he could to save Henry.

"You killed him," Geoffrey raged. "You killed Henry!"

William wanted to deny the words. He'd tried so hard to save Henry. He'd sought out the vampire. He'd taken the dark gift. He'd done everything, but...Henry was dead.

"You were never the strong one, despite what Father thought." Geoffrey's lip curved into a snarl. "I should have been sent first. If Father had sent me, Henry would be alive now!"

A dark suspicion grew in William as he stared into his brother's hate-filled gaze. "Did you know what Father was doing to Henry?"

Geoffrey didn't answer him.

"Did you know that Father was torturing him?" William roared, impervious to the feel of steel cutting into his throat.

"I knew what the bastard was doing. I always knew."

Geoffrey and his father had been alike in so many ways. They shared the same dark lust for power, for blood. William's gaze fell as he stared at the sword before him. It was Guy's sword. "You killed Father, didn't you?"

"Of course, I killed him. I should have killed the bastard long ago! I was never good enough for him. Never strong enough. Not like his precious William!" Geoffrey spat. "He always thought you were so strong. 'His only real son!'" He quoted with a look of disgust.

"Geoffrey—"

His brother didn't appear to even hear him. "I should have been the firstborn son, the favored one, not you! I was the one meant for greatness. Not you!"

William slowly moved his right hand toward the hilt of his sword.

"You should have died long ago." Geoffrey's face was a mask of rage. "You should have died in that cursed river. Then I would have been the next de Montfort. I would have been the next leader!"

You should have died in that cursed river. A chill swept through William. He remembered that day. The water had felt like ice. He'd struggled, fighting desperately to stay afloat. He'd screamed for help, he'd begged Geoffrey to help him.

He'd always thought that Geoffrey had gone to get his father's soldiers. That Geoffrey had tried to save him. But his brother had just wanted to kill him.

William's fingers locked around his sword hilt.

"You did not die then," Geoffrey said. "But you will die now!"

William drew his sword in a silent, deadly rush. Their swords hit with a jarring impact.

"Do not be too certain of that, brother!"

He'd spent his entire life training for battle. Since he'd been given the dark kiss, William was even stronger, more powerful. But Geoffrey was a perfect match for him.

Blade sang against blade as the weapons clashed.

They had trained together, from the moment they were

old enough to walk onto the field of battle. They had learned, side-by-side, the ways to strike, to attack, to kill.

Now, they fought each other.

Geoffrey's sword slashed down, catching William along his arm. Blood poured, soaking his garments.

Geoffrey laughed, his eyes alight with the thrill of battle. "Do you know what the peasants call me, brother? Do you?"

William had heard the talk. The whispers. He swung his sword, blocking Geoffrey's attack. His brother was a strong fighter, a dirty fighter. He could not afford to let his guard down.

"You may be the Dark One to them," Geoffrey said, grunting as he dodged William's sword, "but I am the one they truly fear. I am called the Butcher!"

Geoffrey's weapon flashed toward William's chest. William swung, blocking the blade a second before it would have plunged into his heart.

Geoffrey twisted, lunging up with a knife that he'd concealed in his left hand. The knife sank into William's shoulder.

William groaned as agony lanced through him.

"I am called the Butcher because I do not just kill my enemies." Geoffrey laughed, the sound maniacal. "I slaughter them. As I will slaughter you!"

"Not...if...I...kill...you...first..." William lunged, swinging his broadsword with all his strength. Metal screamed as his brother's sword broke beneath the force of his blade.

Geoffrey fell to the ground, stunned by William's strength.

William grunted, pulling the knife from his shoulder. He stared at the bloody blade and then looked down at Geoffrey.

Geoffrey moved, crouching, waiting for the perfect moment to strike.

William dropped his sword and gripped the knife. He lunged for his brother.

Geoffrey met him head on.

William slammed his fist into Geoffrey's jaw.

Geoffrey stumbled back, and then he turned, lashing out with his booted foot. William jumped to the side, narrowly avoiding his brother's attack.

His fingers were slick with blood as they gripped the knife.

"You cannot kill me," Geoffrey snapped. "You're not strong enough!"

William threw the knife. It sank, hilt deep, into his brother's chest. Geoffrey stared at him, stunned. Then he fell to the ground.

William stared at Geoffrey's prone body. He knew Geoffrey wasn't dead. He couldn't be. It would take more than a steel blade to kill one such as him.

Geoffrey began to laugh. Rich, deep laughter spilled from his throat even as his blood spilled onto the ground.

William took a step toward his brother. One, then another. He moved cautiously, knowing that Geoffrey could attack at any moment.

He stared down at Geoffrey. Moonlight spilled down upon his brother's visage. Blood trickled from his mouth.

"It will take more...than this...to kill me." Geoffrey's lips twisted into his familiar mocking smile.

William reached down and pulled the knife from his chest. "I know." He swallowed. He didn't have a wooden stake. That left only one other way to kill a vampire.

Geoffrey's smile faded as he read William's intent. "You cannot—" He coughed, choking on his blood.

"I will do what I must." William's hands shook as he thought of the grim task before him.

"I...am...the Butcher...not you."

William closed his eyes. Could he do it? Could he kill his own brother?

Geoffrey seemed to sense his thoughts. "You...killed... Henry. Are...you...going...to kill...me...as...well?"

William's eyes flashed open and he stared down at Geoffrey's prone figure. For an instant, a shattering second, he saw Henry's face. Henry's bright blue eyes staring back at him. He could see Henry's sadness. See the plea on his brother's face.

And he hesitated.

Geoffrey attacked. He shot to his feet in a blur of speed. He ripped the knife from his chest and plunged it into William's heart.

William felt the cold touch of death upon his cheek.

Geoffrey touched him lightly with a bloodstained finger. "Tell me, brother," he whispered, leaning close to stare into William's eyes. "Are you afraid to die?"

William's body fell to the ground.

***

William shook his head slowly, trying to shake off the weight of his past. "The sun started to rise then. He left me, knowing that I'd die when the sunlight touched my body. He laughed, and he left me there. He left me there to die."

"How did you survive?" She asked softly.

William glanced at Savannah. She'd sat quietly while he spoke. Her legs were curled beneath her, and her hands were linked tightly together.

She looked so beautiful. So good. He didn't deserve her.

"William?" Her brows furrowed. "Is something wrong?"

He swallowed and forced himself to look away from the understanding and concern he could see so clearly in her emerald eyes. "No," he stopped, cleared his throat and repeated. "No, nothing's wrong."

"How did you survive?" She asked again. He could feel her gaze upon him, its weight like a physical touch upon his skin.

"I didn't have much strength. I'd lost too much blood. But I knew that I couldn't just stay there. That I couldn't wait for the sun to rise and finish me." No, he hadn't been able to just lie there and wait for death. He'd known that he had to survive. He'd known that he had to stop Geoffrey.

"The cave was close. I knew if I could just get in the cave, I would be safe. I would be able to rest until sunset. I managed to get to my feet, and I grabbed Henry's arms. I pulled him with me and I made it into the cave." He shook his head. "It was close. Too close. My skin had already started to burn." He could still smell the stench of burning flesh.

"And when you woke at sunset?"

His lips twisted. "I said good-bye to Henry, and I started hunting Geoffrey." And he'd been hunting him for nine hundred years.

"When you find Geoffrey, what are you going to do?"

William sat on the edge of the bed. His gaze met hers. "I'm going to kill him." The words were a vow. This time, he wouldn't fail.

A small frown line appeared on her forehead. "Even though he's your brother?"

"Henry was my brother. He died a long time ago. Geoffrey…" He took a deep breath. "Geoffrey is evil. He lives to hurt others. To torture them. If there was ever any goodness inside of him, it died a long time ago." Her fingers stroked his arm. He stared down at her hand. It looked so fragile, so delicate. He lifted his fingers, capturing her hand. " Savannah, I'll go after him. I'll make certain that he never hurts another person, I swear I will."

"No." She shook her head, but made no attempt to withdraw her fingers from his hold. "You're not going after him alone. We're doing this together. Remember the bargain—"

"Screw the bargain!" William exploded. "I am not going to let him get near you. He's too strong. If he killed you—" He broke off. He shuddered at the thought of Savannah's death. No. No, it couldn't happen. He couldn't let his brother get anywhere near her. He would protect her.

"You can't protect me from everything," she said, her gaze watchful. "There are things in this world that I must face on my own."

"You don't have to face him!" William snapped.

Her gaze was steady. "Yes, I do."

His hands clenched. He could read the determination so clearly in her voice. "If he hurts you—"

"He's not going to get the chance," she promised. "You and I are going to stop him."

He knew that she wasn't going to give up. She wouldn't let him go alone. He would have to make certain that she was safe. And he would stop his brother. Or die trying.

He leaned forward and kissed her. Hard. Deep. He needed to taste her, to feel her lips against his.

She responded immediately, her tongue thrusting against his and a low moan rumbling in her throat.

He wanted to lay her down. To strip the clothes from her perfect body and sink into her. To join with her. To lose himself in her warmth.

But his brother was out there. Stalking the night. Hunting.

And he had to be stopped.

With a fierce effort of will, he pulled away from Savannah. Her eyes were deep, mysterious pools. She stared at him, waiting.

He took a deep breath, bringing his rampaging body back under control. Now wasn't the time. Later, they would be together. They would have forever.

He stood and with a wave of his hand he sent the balcony doors crashing open.

"Come, Savannah. It's time we hunt." They would find their

prey. They would find Geoffrey.

And destroy him.

***

He sensed his brother the moment he rose. He could feel William's anger. His rage.

Geoffrey smiled. His brother was losing control. Good. His emotions made him weak, vulnerable.

Easy prey.

And he could feel the women. *Savannah*. Her mind was strong. He could sense her anger. Her fear.

He loved it when his victims feared him. Fear tasted so good, so sweet.

He knew they were coming for him. Fools. They actually thought they could defeat him. Didn't they know the power he held?

They would find out. Yes, they would find out very soon. It was time to set his trap.

And time for them to die.

Fifteen

Death is coming for me.
-Entry from the diary of Henry de Montfort,
December 24, 1068

They returned to the park where they'd sensed Geoffrey. His resting place had to be close by.

Savannah watched William carefully. She wanted to weep for him, for all that he'd been forced to endure. He'd watched Henry die. She knew he blamed himself for his brother's death. She could see the guilt, feel it emanating from him. She wished she could take that burden from him. She knew that he'd tried to save his brother. He'd taken the dark kiss, just to spare Henry's life.

But in the end, he'd lost Henry.

And now, he would be forced to kill Geoffrey. To slay his own brother before his brother killed him.

"This way." William began walking down a faint trail, his sharp gaze scanning the area.

Savannah took a deep breath and followed him. She knew that William could sense his brother, and she was desperately afraid that Geoffrey could sense him, too.

"Do you think he knows we're here?" She asked, shivering as she remembered the sound of Geoffrey's voice calling to her. *Savannah.* He'd known they were here the night before. Would he know now?

"He knows," William said simply. "Try to guard your thoughts as best you can."

She nodded.

The path ended at the edge of the park. William's dark gaze swept the area, drifting lightly over the empty street and the old houses. He began walking, his stare intense, as he focused on Geoffrey.

The street was eerily silent. It was fairly early in the evening, just a little after eight, but no one was around. All of the houses were locked up tight, almost as if those who lived there sensed something evil was on the streets.

William turned at the street corner. "Where are you?" He whispered softly. His brows were drawn together, and she knew that he was concentrating fiercely, using all of his psychic power.

"Dammit!" He exploded. "Where the hell are you?" A muscle

flexed along the hard plane of his jaw.

Savannah's heart pounded. She could feel his frustration beating against her. "William?"

He swung around, his expression stark. "It's just like every damned time before. I feel the echo of his presence, but I can't tell where he is." He took a deep, shuddering breath. "Or where he's gone."

In the distance, Savannah heard the wail of a siren.

"Focus, William," she ordered, her voice calm and clear. "Use your power and picture him. See him." *Find him.*

He shook his head. "I can't. I'm not strong enough." He waved his hand toward the houses. "There are too many people in the way. Too many thoughts. Too many voices. They're drowning him out." Understanding flared in his eyes. "He's using them to hide behind. That's why he picked the city. He could disappear here, and the voices, the thoughts, would shield him." *I'm not strong enough,* he finished mentally.

"Maybe you're right," she said softly. "Maybe one vampire's mind isn't powerful enough to track someone like Geoffrey." She hesitated. "But maybe two vampires can do it." She closed her eyes and focused her mind on William, pouring all of her power and strength into him. Into his mind.

"What are you—" His body trembled as he felt her warmth pour through him. "Savannah?"

"Use me," she whispered. "Find him."

William swallowed. Lust flared in his eyes. His need, his hunger, wrapped around her. She could feel him, his emotions, his needs, swirling within her mind.

And she knew that he could feel her. Her thoughts, her dreams, her fears.

His eyes flared red. "Are you sure?" he gritted.

"Yes."

And he took her power, pulling it, pulling her, inside of him. Deep inside.

Their minds linked. Their thoughts, their feelings. They merged and became one. She could feel him, feel his body, his strength. She couldn't tell where she ended and he began.

His power doubled, and his mind flashed as he sent a psychic pulse into the night. Together, they focused on Geoffrey, channeling all of their strength into finding him.

A faint black cloud appeared before them.

Savannah gasped. "What is that?" She could feel evil, dark twisted hate.

The cloud stretched out, heading down the street and into the night. "That's Geoffrey." William's gaze was locked on the dark cloud. Come on, I don't know how long I can hold his trail."

They ran, following the dark cloud, snaking down streets and alleys.

And for every step they took, their minds stayed joined. Completely linked. Their hearts pounded in unison.

They ran forward, knowing they didn't have a minute to lose. The road curved, and then it snaked sharply to the left.

Savannah's eyes widened at the sight before her.

"A cemetery?" She knew William had to hear the horror in her voice. "He's resting inside a cemetery?"

A huge wrought-iron gate surrounded the cemetery. Savannah could see crumbling tombstones and high stone vaults nestled behind the gate. The grass was overgrown, weeds covering many of the headstones.

"I should have known," William muttered, easily leaping over the fence. "A place like this would appeal to him."

Savannah bit her lip, surveying the high gate. It was at least twelve feet high. The top of the gate was lined with sharp pointed tips, like spearheads. She crouched low, keeping her eyes locked on those sharp points, and then she sprang into the air.

She landed on the other side, her knees barely buckling beneath her.

William's gaze swept over the cemetery. The black cloud had led to the gate. There was no trail inside.

"Stay close," he whispered. "And don't let your guard down for a minute."

Adrenaline and fear pumped through her. She knew Geoffrey could attack them at any moment. He could be anywhere. In the ground beneath them. Crouched above them in the branches of the old oak tree. Or waiting, lurking in the old mausoleum.

The wind howled softly. Dead leaves crunched beneath Savannah's feet. And she smelled death. Her body was tense. Her heart pounded.

William walked before her, his body crouched and ready for battle.

She stepped carefully over a broken headstone. "Can you sense him?"

No. I can't feel him at all.

She scanned the cemetery, her gaze drifting over the graves. She saw a faint flash of light, a brief glimmer in the darkness.

Her eyes narrowed and she took a step forward. What was

that? She moved closer. She could see what looked like a handle of some sort, a gleaming handle encrusted with jewels. It was—

"My father's sword." William crouched down and picked up the weapon, removing it from the old headstone. He held the weapon easily.

The long blade gleamed in the faint moonlight. Looking at William, with the broad sword clutched in his hands, Savannah could easily imagine him as he once had been. A warrior. Strong. Deadly.

"Why would he leave your father's sword here?"

"He was sending me a message."

"What kind of message?"

His fingers clenched around the sword. "The last time I saw this sword, I was on my father's land and my brother was using it to try to kill me." He took a deep breath.

Savannah waited silently, wondering what was next.

"He used this weapon to kill my father. He almost killed me with it. He wouldn't just leave it behind for no reason. He values it too much." His gaze swept over the dark cemetery once again. His shoulders seem to drop.

"What is it?"

"Geoffrey's gone. Gone from the cemetery. Gone from Seattle."

"What?" Impossible. He couldn't have gotten away from them!

William gazed down at the weapon in his hand. "Geoffrey returned home. He went back to my father's land. Back to the place where this nightmare began. And he wants me to follow him."

"How do you know that?" She asked, stunned.

He pointed to the headstone. "The sword was placed on this particular slab for a reason. Read the inscription, Savannah."

She glanced down. Time had erased the dead man's name, but she could still see the faint words etched in the middle of the headstone. *Death takes us back to the beginning.*

"The beginning," she whispered as understanding dawned. The beginning of William's life as a vampire had been in a blood-soaked European castle. She lifted her chin and met his stare. "Let's go."

***

They arrived in France three days later. They'd had to charter a private plane. William could have flown on his own, using his powers, but Savannah wasn't strong enough for such a journey.

They'd gotten the plane and made arrangements for all of the back windows to be blackened out. The owner of the plane had agreed to their request with only a raised brow. He'd told them that after flying numerous celebrities, he was used to people's "oddities."

The plane touched down in the airport an hour after sunset. Savannah and William thanked the pilot, and then after giving him a small compulsion, they disappeared, knowing the pilot had completely forgotten about the man and woman that he'd just taken across the Atlantic.

***

William cradled Savannah carefully against, him, feeling her heart pound as they flew across the countryside. He cloaked their presence, so if anyone happened to glance into the air, they would not be seen.

He wished that he could stop, find her a room in a quiet village, and face Geoffrey on his own. He was terrified that something would happen to her.

"I'm going to be fine," she murmured softly, her voice music to his hungry ears. "Stop worrying about me."

Let me take you to safety. I can face him alone.

"No. We'll face him together."

But would they survive together?

He kissed her temple, inhaling her sweet scent. And, for the first time since Henry's death, he prayed. He prayed for God to protect Savannah.

The miles flew past, the countryside little more than a green blur beneath him. Then he saw the river. The winding, black river. And he knew that he was home.

He could see his father's land, could see the crumbling remains of the old keep. The ancient stone wall. The empty moat. But there was no sign of Geoffrey.

He drifted to the ground, placing Savannah gently on her feet.

He walked toward the stone steps leading to the old entrance to his father's keep. "This was where I found my father."

He could still see the red stain on the top step. His father's blood. His hands clenched, and he walked up the steps. For just a second, he thought he heard his father's voice.

"William?"

He blinked, glancing back at Savannah. Her arms were crossed over her chest. Her face was tight with concern.

Concern for him.

He walked back down the steps. Turning his back on the old stone, on the past.

"Link with me," he whispered.

And she did.

Her warmth flooded through him. Her goodness, her strength. In that brief moment, he forgot his past. He forgot Geoffrey. His only thought was her.

Savannah.

He pulled her into his arms, his lips touching hers. She met him eagerly, her passion a perfect match for his.

Their bodies pressed together. Their hearts pounded.

He lifted his head slowly. "Savannah, I—"

A cold wind swept across the land, chilling him. And he heard the mocking sound of his brother's laughter.

He spun around, pushing Savannah behind him. He scanned, drawing on both his own power and Savannah's new strength. He could feel his brother, feel the taint of his presence.

Geoffrey was close. Too close.

If you want me so badly, brother, then come and find me.

Geoffrey's taunt whispered through his mind. Behind him, he felt Savannah shiver. Connected to him as she was, she'd heard Geoffrey's voice, felt his evil.

Abruptly, William severed the link with Savannah.

"William? What—"

"We can't be linked, not now. If something happens—" He ran his hand over his face. If something happened to him, and they were linked at the time, then Savannah would experience his death, just as she'd been forced to share Mark's last moments. He wouldn't put her through that agony again.

"We can't afford the link now," he told her, carefully shielding his thoughts. "It will drain our powers too quickly."

He could feel her confusion and fear. But he knew she struggled to contain herself, to be strong.

In that moment, he wanted nothing more than to pull her into his arms and hold her. Just hold her. But his brother was waiting. And death would come for either him or Geoffrey this night.

"Where is he?" Savannah whispered.

William's gaze scanned the rough terrain. Where would his brother hide? Where—

A wolf howled.

William froze. There'd never been a wolf on his father's land. *Never.*

The howl sounded again. Louder.

The wolf was close, and William could feel the beast's overwhelming hunger...and its dark rage.

"That's him, isn't it?" Savannah stepped forward, standing by William's side. "It's Geoffrey."

William nodded. His brother was using his power to shapeshift.

She took a deep breath. "Are you sure that you can do this?"

He glanced down at her gleaming eyes and pale face. "Geoffrey has to be stopped." He couldn't let his brother hurt anyone else.

She nodded.

He turned back to face the night, to face his brother. He could sense the wolf's location, could even hear the soft crunch of leaves beneath the pads of the wolf's paws. The wolf was running, deep into the brush, and he wanted William to follow him.

So he did.

He ran into the night, with Savannah close on his heels. He ran over the dank earth and into the dark woods. Over the fallen trees, over the land that had seen centuries of murder and pain. He ran past the old village. Past the river where he'd nearly drowned. He ran as fast as he could, following the wolf as it led him deeper and deeper into the night.

The trees began to thin, the brush to disappear. The glowing moon shone down upon him, illuminating the sloping land, and William realized where the wolf was leading him.

Death takes us back to the beginning.

The cliffs stood before him.

And there, in the clearing, with red eyes and barred fangs, the wolf waited.

He stopped, staring at the cliffs, at the wolf, and he remembered.

Henry, covered in blood, his body still upon the hard earth.

His father, his body slashed, his blood staining the stone steps.

And Geoffrey, aiming his father's sword straight at his heart. Laughing.

William reached back, and pulled his father's sword from the sheath he'd strapped to his back. The blade gleamed in the moonlight. William swore he could still see blood on the shining tip.

The wolf blinked, and in a flash, Geoffrey stood before him.

"Welcome home, *brother*." His red stare drifted briefly over

Savannah's tense body. "I see you brought me a nice treat to enjoy. And believe me, I will enjoy her...right after I kill you."

William stepped forward, lifting the sword. "You're not going to touch her."

Geoffrey lifted one dark brow. "Let me guess. You think you're going to stop me, to kill me." He smiled and shook his head. "I do not think so. You couldn't kill me before. And you won't be able to kill me now."

"Don't bet on it," William growled.

Geoffrey laughed. "Come on, I'm your brother. Your blood. You can't kill me. You *won't* kill me."

"You're not my brother." William took another step forward. "My brother died on this cliff over nine hundred years ago. Henry was the only brother I ever had. You're nothing to me. You never were."

Geoffrey's eyes flashed, and he attacked, launching his body not at William, but at Savannah. Geoffrey's hands shifted, becoming deadly claws. He reached for Savannah, his face a twisted mask of hate.

"No!" William swung the sword, catching his brother high in the shoulder.

Geoffrey screamed in pain, staggering back. Blood spilled down his arm.

Geoffrey glanced down at his wound, and he smiled, cradling his shoulder. "First blood is yours, brother." He stepped back and ran toward the cliffs.

William swore and lunged after him. He saw Geoffrey bend down and scoop up an old pack. His brother's hand reached inside. He pulled out a gun.

"Now it's my turn," Geoffrey screamed. He aimed the gun and pulled the trigger.

The bullet slammed into William's chest, knocking him back, forcing him to his knees.

No! Savannah's scream echoed in his mind.

His blood poured onto the ground and weakness swept through him. His father's sword slipped from his fingers.

Geoffrey laughed and looked at Savannah. "Before you die, you can watch me kill your woman."

Sixteen

I will never see another sunrise.
-Entry from the diary of Henry de Montfort,
December 27, 1068.

"No!" Savannah's heart stopped when the bullet hit William. She saw him stumble to his knees, saw the blade drop from his hand. "William! No!" She knew that too much blood loss could kill a vampire. She ran to him, frantic.

His shirt front was soaked with blood, the ground stained with it. She dropped to her knees beside him, cradling him in her arms. "William!"

His eyelids lifted slowly, his pain-filled gaze locked on her. "Savannah...I'm sorry."

She felt the touch of death then. Felt the icy fingers on her skin. "No!" She pulled him against her, rocking him. "You're not going to die! I won't let you! *You can't leave me!*"

Geoffrey laughed softly. "How touching. How very touching."

Savannah turned, shielding William with her body. She pushed her wrist against his mouth, carefully covering the move from Geoffrey's watchful stare. *Drink*, she ordered him. *Drink!* There was no way she was going to let William die.

"You're a sick bastard!" She snarled at Geoffrey, trying to keep his attention away from William.

Geoffrey's smile widened. His fangs gleamed. "I'm really going to enjoy killing you."

She felt William's lips moving lightly against her, felt the sharp sting of pain as his teeth bit into her skin. She clenched her teeth, letting the pain wash through her.

She saw Geoffrey's gaze drift to William.

"Are you going to shoot me, too?" she asked derisively, pulling his attention back to her.

He frowned, glancing down at the gun. Then he tossed it over the cliff's edge. "No. For you, I'm going to use a more...personal touch." Once again his fingers lengthened, became claws.

Savannah looked into his eyes. This was the man—no, the monster—who had killed Mark and Sharon. And shot William. She should have been afraid.

She had been, until that very moment. Now, she just felt…rage. She was going to kill him.

"Get up."

William's mouth slid back, freeing her hand. Had he taken enough blood? Would he be able to survive?

"I said, get up!" Geoffrey screamed.

Savannah glanced down at William. His eyes were shut. His body still.

"Don't worry, he's still alive." Geoffrey's lips twisted. "It takes a while for a vampire's blood to drain out. He'll live, at least long enough to see you die."

William's lashes jerked.

"Come here!" His claws flashed out, stopping inches away from William's chest. "Or I'll rip his heart out right now!"

Savannah rose. She could see Guy's sword. It had fallen to the ground, just a few feet away. So close.

Geoffrey grabbed her, pulling her against his chest. "I've been waiting for this moment."

"So have I," Savannah whispered. She concentrated, focusing her energy as William had taught her.

One sharp claw moved slowly down her cheek, down the column of her throat. Down to the curve of her breast.

Revulsion swept through her.

"Do you see this, brother?" Geoffrey called out. "I've got her. And I can do anything I want to her…"

William had managed to sit up. Blood still poured from his wound, and fire burned in his gaze. He began to stand.

Geoffrey met his stare, his eyes narrowing at his brother's increasing strength. "How—"

Savannah's hands shifted, becoming claws. She knew she couldn't hold the shape long, but a second was all she needed. She plunged her claws into his chest.

Geoffrey screamed. His claws slashed against her, catching her along the throat and chest. Pain lanced through her. She wanted to scream, to howl at the agony coursing through her.

Her claws disappeared, and she stumbled away from him and fell to the ground. From the corner of her eye, she saw Guy's sword. She crawled toward it. If she could just get it—

Geoffrey stared in shock at the blood that poured down his chest. "You bitch!" He snarled. "You're going to beg me to kill you!"

He lunged for her.

Savannah's fingers curled around the handle of the sword. And when Geoffrey grabbed her, she swung, slamming the blade into his side.

The blade sliced deep into his skin, tearing flesh and sending blood pouring down his body.

He twisted away from her and grabbed the blade with his bare hands. The steel bit into his palms, cutting deeply into his flesh.

Savannah strained, fighting to control the blade. If she could just hit him again—

She saw William, moving slowly, his face a mask of pain.

Geoffrey jerked the blade from her hand. In one motion, he yanked her forward, spinning her against his chest and locking his bloody fingers around her throat. He faced William with Savannah held tightly against him.

"I'm going to make you beg for death," he whispered into her ear.

In their struggle, the sword had fallen to the ground. But Savannah knew Geoffrey wouldn't need the sword to kill her.

"Let her go!" William's hands clenched.

"No!" Geoffrey's gaze narrowed as it swept over William, over the already healing wound in his chest. "She helped you, didn't she? The bitch gave you her blood!"

William just stared at him, his gaze redder than the fires of hell.

"Well, then I think it's only fair that she helps me, too." He sank his teeth into her throat, ripping her flesh.

Savannah screamed and kicked against him, catching Geoffrey in his shins.

William lunged forward and jerked her from Geoffrey's grasp. He slammed into Geoffrey, and his brother fell to the ground. William grabbed the sword and crouched over him.

Geoffrey panted, his gaze locked on William. William placed the tip of the sword against his throat.

Geoffrey smiled. "Are you going to cut off my head, now, brother?"

William's jaw clenched. "Yes."

"You're going to kill me, as you killed Henry?"

William lifted the sword, preparing to deliver the final death blow. "I didn't kill Henry!"

Geoffrey's smile widened. "I know. I did."

"W-what?"

Geoffrey twisted, kicking out with his right foot. The blow caught William in his midsection, and he jerked, slashing down with the weapon. But it was too late.

Geoffrey rolled away, and the blade slammed into the earth. His brother jumped to his feet, licking his lips. "Her blood is strong," he murmured. "I can already feel my power returning. I think I'll have to have more of her."

"Never." William pulled the blade free and aimed the weapon at Geoffrey. "What did you do? What did you do to Henry?"

"After I killed Guy, I found Henry. He was in the tower." Geoffrey shook his head. "It was really too easy, you know. The fool thought I was there to help him."

"You're the one," William whispered. "You're the one who left him to die."

"He was weak. He was always weak. He didn't deserve the de Montfort name! And neither did you!"

A wolf howled in the darkness. The howl was long, mournful, and full of rage.

Geoffrey blinked. "What—"

A large gray wolf sprang out of the night and launched its powerful body at Geoffrey. Its fangs slashed him, biting deep into his shoulders, his arms, his chest.

William stared down at the beast, stunned. He tried to touch the creature's mind, but found only a world of pain, rage, and hate.

He moved back, hurrying to Savannah's side. She was still, her body limp on the earth. He pulled her into his arms, cradling her softly. The wound at her throat bled sluggishly. He touched it gently. "Savannah?"

Her lashes lifted, and she stared up at him with dazed green eyes. "William, what—" Her eyes widened as she heard the snarl of a wolf.

He pulled Savannah to her feet. "I don't know, Savannah. I don't know where the hell he came from." His gaze drifted over her. "Are you all right?"

She nodded, her gaze locked on Geoffrey and the wolf. As she watched, Geoffrey's claws flashed, cutting deeply into the wolf's side. The animal howled in pain. "We've got to help it!"

Geoffrey shoved the animal away from him and staggered to his feet. The wolf shuddered and collapsed upon the ground.

"Enough of this!" Geoffrey's arms lifted and he began to chant. Thunder rumbled and lightning flashed across the night sky. "I have the dark powers, brother! Me, not you! And I will use them to kill you!"

A ball of fire formed over Geoffrey's head. "Tell me this, brother...are you afraid to die?" The flames flew toward William.

"No!" Savannah screamed and launched herself at William. Her body slammed into his and they rolled across the earth. Savannah felt the kiss of the flames lance over her skin.

"Savannah!" William rolled, checking her body quickly.

She took a deep breath. "I'm all right."

Another ball of flame began to form above Geoffrey. "I won't miss this time," he promised.

William rose to his feet. Savannah stood beside him. "Neither will I," he vowed. And, before Savannah's stunned gaze, a ball of fire began to form in his hand.

"H-how—" Geoffrey shook his head, disbelief etched onto the lines of his face. "Y-you can't! I-I'm the only one who—"

William threw the flame, and it slammed into Geoffrey's chest, knocking him to the ground. He was close to the cliff's edge. Just a few more feet, and he would have fallen into the night.

"With age, comes power." William's red gaze was locked on his brother. "You're not the only one who studied the dark arts." He picked up the sword and walked slowly forward. "Now, *brother,*" he spat. "Tell me, are you afraid to die?"

Geoffrey's eyes widened. Fear and rage flashed across his face. He lunged to his feet.

William attacked, swinging the sword in a swift arc.

The blade slammed into his brother's chest. Geoffrey staggered, stumbling back. His booted heel slipped on the cliff's edge. His face went slack with shock. And he fell back into the air, into nothing.

Savannah expected him to transform, to shift, to fly back up and attack them.

Instead, she just heard the sound of his scream.

"He's too weak," William whispered. "He can't stop the fall."

The screaming ended, choked off abruptly.

Savannah ran to the edge of the cliff. Her eyes searched the bottom, searched the rocky surface, the churning waters.

And she saw him. There, at the base of the cliff, his body dangling atop the old remains of a wooden boat. His head was twisted, his mouth open. His eyes stared sightlessly up at her.

A long sliver of wood from the ship's bow had pierced his

chest.

"I-is he dead?"

William didn't answer. With his fingers clenched around the blade, he leapt off the cliff. Within seconds, he was beside Geoffrey, staring down at his still figure.

He lifted the sword. "Good-bye, brother."

He slashed the blade across Geoffrey's throat, severing his head in one quick blow.

William closed his eyes against the sight. The sword dropped from his fingers, to land in the blood beneath his feet.

Now, it was finished.

He returned to Savannah. He needed her, needed her touch to wipe the darkness from him. To banish the cold sweeping through him.

She was there, waiting on the cliff's edge. He could see the tear tracks on her cheeks. He pulled her against him, desperate to feel her body against his. He inhaled her delicate scent and wrapped his arms tightly around her.

He'd almost lost her. His body began to shake.

"William?"

He kissed her with all the fire and desperation that was in him. It had been too close. He could still see Geoffrey, see him sinking his teeth into her delicate throat.

He shuddered.

He felt her fingers, lightly stroking his back. Soothing him. Reassuring him.

It's all right, William. It's over now. He felt her warmth pouring into him.

"Let's get out of here," he whispered. He wanted to leave this place and never come back.

She nodded, and they turned away from the cliffs.

William froze. He could feel something. Someone. Watching. Waiting.

His gaze searched the clearing. "Where did the wolf go?"

Savannah blinked. "I-I don't know. I wasn't watching—" She hurried over to the rocks and bent down, touching the ground lightly. When her hand lifted, there was blood on her fingers. "He was here a moment ago…"

And now he'd vanished.

But William could still feel him. Still feel his rage.

He's watching us.

Savannah returned to his side, her body brushing lightly

against his. *Why?*

He didn't know, but all his senses were screaming a warning to him. The wolf was waiting. Hiding in the shadows. And he was going to attack.

William didn't know if Savannah could survive another attack. She was weak. He'd taken her blood, and then Geoffrey had savaged her. She needed to feed in order to regain her strength. They both needed to feed. But he knew she wouldn't want to do it, that she would fight the hunger. He would have to force her. He couldn't risk her waning strength. Not when they had another killer on their trail.

He wanted to go after the wolf, to hunt the beast down and destroy it. But he had to take care of Savannah. She needed him.

He scooped her up into his arms, holding her tightly.

He heard a low growl, and he knew that it wasn't just a wolf that was stalking him. He could feel the creature's dark power. Its hunger.

Stay away from her. He knew the creature heard his warning.

William's arms tightened around Savannah and he leapt into the air.

The wolf howled.

***

He took Savannah to an inn on the outskirts of a small village. He knew they looked like hell, but with a small compulsion, he made the innkeeper overlook their haggard appearance and give them the best room that he had available, a room that, he assured William, had strong shutters that covered its windows.

William took Savannah upstairs, worried by her increasing pallor. She needed blood, and she needed it fast.

He locked the door behind him and placed her gently on the bed.

She stared up at him, her eyes wide. "That wasn't a wolf, was it?"

William shook his head. He noticed that her hands were shaking.

"What was it?"

"A vampire." From the instant that the beast had attacked Geoffrey, he'd known that he was dealing with one of his kind.

Savannah nodded. "I thought so." She swallowed and rubbed her head. "Why did he attack Geoffrey?"

"I don't know. Geoffrey spent his life hurting others. Maybe he did something to the vampire, hurt him or someone that he cared about."

She slid back against the pillows, weariness evident in every line of her body. "Geoffrey hurt so many people."

He pulled the covers over her. "He won't hurt anyone else."

Her hand caught his. "Thank you, William."

He stilled. Hunger flashed through him at her delicate touch. "For what?"

"For ending my nightmare."

He took a deep breath. Her weakness beat against him. "Rest, now. Just close your eyes and rest."

She frowned, shifting restlessly on the bed. "Are you leaving?"

"Only for a moment."

She shook her head. "No! Don't leave me."

"Sleep, Savannah." He pushed the compulsion. Normally, it wouldn't have worked on her, but in her weakened state, there was no way she could fight him.

Her lashes lowered and her body stilled.

He couldn't risk traveling far. Not with the other vampire close by. He would have to find food, fast, and return to Savannah.

He would use one of the inn's staff. A maid or a bellhop. He would be quick. Savannah had to drink. And she wasn't strong enough to get the blood on her own.

He hurried to the door. With every second that passed, her strength drained.

And with the wolf out there, she couldn't afford to be weak. Not for a moment.

**

"Savannah. Wake up, Savannah."

She heard his voice, calling softly to her. She tried to open her eyes, but she just felt so tired. She wanted to sleep, just sleep.

"You can't sleep. You have to open your eyes."

She knew that voice. William. She smiled.

"Yes, it's me. And I need you to look at me. Can you do that?"

She concentrated, gathering her strength. William needed her. She focused her remaining energy, and her eyes opened.

William gazed down at her, his black stare intense. A lock of his hair had slipped free and fallen over his forehead. The dark lock made him look strangely gentle, almost boyish. She lifted her hand, wanting to touch him.

He caught her hand, bringing it up to his lips. He kissed her palm, his breath hot upon her chilled hand.

"You made me sleep." Her tone was accusing.

"I'm sorry." He didn't sound apologetic.

"I feel so weak." She tried to sit up, but she slid back against the bedding. "What's wrong with me?"

He smoothed her hair back with a gentle hand. "You lost too much blood. Your body's weak. If you don't get more blood soon..." He shook his head. "You have to drink, Savannah. There's no choice."

She knew he was right. She could feel the hunger within her. The need. But she was so tired.

William leaned forward and kissed her softly. "Drink from me," he whispered against her lips. "Drink from me."

He moved, barring his neck before her.

She could feel her teeth burning, stretching. She could see the pulse beating, throbbing against his throat.

"I don't want to hurt you," she murmured, fighting against the need that rose within her, the need that demanded she bury her teeth in his throat and drink. "You're weak, too. Geoffrey hurt you. There was so much blood—"

"I've fed. Don't worry about me."

She frowned. That was why he'd forced her to sleep.

"I didn't hurt anyone. The innkeeper doesn't even remember uh...helping me." She could hear the faint smile in his voice. "Now, come on, Savannah. *Drink*."

She swallowed. She wanted to. She wanted desperately to taste him, but a part of her held back, still repelled by the idea of actually biting him, of drinking his blood.

She felt the sigh that moved through him.

"I was afraid of that," he said. "Looks like we'll have to try something else."

He grabbed the front of her shirt and ripped the material apart.

She gasped, her eyes widening.

His hand lifted, sliding to caress her breast. "Passion, remember? Physical desire and the dark hunger merge. I am just going to have to make you...hungry...enough to drink from me."

Yes, she remembered. She arched into his touch, a hot tide of desire pouring through her.

His head lowered and his lips locked around her aching nipple. He licked her, sucking lightly. She felt heat pool low in her belly.

His fingers slipped over the curve of her stomach while his mouth continued to suckle her. She heard the rasp of her zipper and felt his hand slide inside her pants. He touched her lightly through the thin layer of her panties. She lifted her hips, responding eagerly to his touch.

And she felt her hunger rise.

"You feel so good. So damn good." He pushed her pants off and pulled her silken panties down. His gaze flashed to meet hers. "If you won't taste me, then I guess I'll have to taste you."

Then, before she could murmur a protest, his dark head lowered and he was kissing her, his tongue licking the most intimate part of her body.

Her body tensed and pleasure slammed through her. She forgot her exhaustion. Forgot her fear. She just felt. Felt him. Felt heat. Need. Desire. Hunger.

Her hips twisted, moving feverishly. The tension within her mounted, churning higher, tighter.

She moaned, tossing her head back against the pillow. "William!"

His tongue teased her. Swirling. Rubbing. She clenched her teeth as his fingers teased her breasts, rubbing and plucking her nipples.

She could feel her climax, feel the pressure as it mounted. Close. So close—

William pulled back and stared down at her. His face was stark. Need was stamped on every hard line of his body. "What do you want, Savannah?" His voice was guttural.

She stared into his swirling gaze. "You," she whispered. "I want you." *I always will.*

He unzipped his pants and slid his hips between her thighs. She felt him, felt the tip of his manhood pressing against her moist opening. "Then take me."

He thrust deep.

Hunger consumed her, spinning her out of control.

He surged into her, again and again. Lifting her legs, he wrapped them around his hips, forcing her to take more of him. All of him. Deeper. Harder.

Her teeth burned. She wanted him. Wanted to taste him. Needed to taste him.

"Do it," he growled. "Do it!"

Her teeth sank into his neck. He shuddered, thrusting deeply into her body. Her mouth moved lightly against him, drinking his essence, and his hips thrust against her. He pushed her deeper into the mattress. Lifted her legs higher.

She screamed as her climax rocked through her.

William kept thrusting, his body locked with hers. His jaw was clenched. He stiffened against her, and her name slipped past his lips. He shuddered, pumping himself into her heat, and his eyes closed.

For an instant, she actually felt his pleasure, felt the strength of the release that swept through him.

She gasped, stunned by the feelings that surged through her.

She held William tightly, her heart pounding. And a whisper swept through her mind.

I love you.

Her heart stilled. But had that thought been her own...or William's?

***

The wolf paced slowly outside of the inn. He knew they were making love. He could feel it, smell it on the air.

He would let William have his time with the woman. He'd been waiting centuries for the Dark One. He could wait a few more hours.

He howled, the mournful sound cutting through the night.

***

William stiffened. He'd heard the howl. And it had been too close. Too damn close.

He pulled away from Savannah, from her tempting warmth and her gentle arms. "He's out there. Dammit, that bastard is out there!"

Savannah sat up, pulling the sheet against her breasts. Her cheeks weren't pale anymore, but flushed with color and health. Her emerald eyes shone like jewels.

"Why would he follow us?"

William dressed quickly. "I don't know. But I'm going to find out."

Savannah jumped to her feet. "Not without me you aren't!"

William's jaw clenched. "You've faced enough danger for one night. Stay here."

She shook her head. "No way. I'm not just going to sit here while you go out there and face this...this thing! I almost lost you once tonight." She took a deep breath. "When Geoffrey shot you, when I saw all that blood, I thought, I thought—"

William pulled her into his arms. He could feel the tremors

that rocked through her body. "It's all right, Savannah. I'm okay."

"You could have died," she whispered, closing her eyes. "You could have bled out. There, on that damn cliff!"

He tilted her chin back. Her lashes lifted. "I didn't die. You saved me." He lifted her wrist, kissing the faint bite marks. "You gave me your blood. You gave me life."

"And I'd do it again," she said, and he could read the truth of that statement in her shining eyes.

"I don't deserve you," he whispered. "You're too good—"

She pulled back and placed a gentle fingertip against his lips. "Stop. I'm not perfect." She laughed softly. "I'm far from perfect, and you of all people should know that."

But she was perfect. Kind. Strong. Beautiful. "I want to keep you safe," he told her. "I've put you at risk already. Stay here, and as soon as I find the vampire…"

"You'll what? Attack him on your own?" She shook her head. "I already told you, no. There's no way you're getting out of here without me."

"Fine, but you stay close to me," he ordered. "I felt his strength. He's an ancient, at least as old as I. I don't want him to get a chance to hurt you."

"He's not going to hurt me." She frowned. "I just don't understand why he's following us. He was obviously Geoffrey's enemy. He tried to kill Geoffrey! I could feel his hate, his rage."

Yes, the vampire had been full of hate and blinding rage. Both had seemed to be directed at Geoffrey. In fact, the creature had almost seemed impervious to their presence.

"I don't understand," Savannah said again. "Why would he now choose to attack us?"

"I don't know." His eyes flashed red. "But I'm going to find out."

Seventeen

I am not afraid.
-Entry from the diary of Henry de Montfort,
December 30, 1068.

Savannah could feel his gaze upon her. Silent. Watchful.

She could feel the vampire, but she couldn't see him. He was hidden in the shadows, hidden in the night.

I feel him, too. He's close. Very close.

Savannah glanced quickly at William's impassive face. They'd searched the village, gone down every street and alley, but still they hadn't found the mysterious vampire. *Why doesn't he attack? What is he waiting for?*

She heard the rustle of leaves, blowing gently against the cobble stone lane.

He's biding his time, William answered. *Waiting for the perfect moment.*

Two drunken teens staggered out of a house, laughing and talking loudly. They saw William and froze, fear widening their eyes.

"Go," he ordered with a wave of his hand. "Get out of here. *Now.*"

They ran.

"Fools," he muttered.

Savannah ignored the boys as they brushed past her. She paced down the street, her gaze searching the shadows. The moon hung heavily in the sky. In a few more hours, the sun would rise.

Her body felt numb with exhaustion. The blood she'd taken from William had healed most of her injuries, but now, she felt a deep weariness.

She just wanted to close her eyes and sleep, to dream. She didn't want to see visions of death, pain and horror.

She didn't want any more nightmares. She just wanted to dream.

"And of what do you dream, my dear?" His voice whispered from the darkness.

Savannah stiffened. She'd lowered her guard, given into the exhaustion, and now he was standing in front of her, his eyes gleaming red, his fangs sharp and white.

William. He's here!

He smiled, stepping forward into the dim street light. He was tall, with muscled arms and strong shoulders. His hair, a light blond mane, curled loosely around his head.

He looked like an angel. A fallen angel.

"Who are you?" Savannah asked, boldly meeting his stare.

He blinked. The red vanished, replaced by a bright blue. "I asked my question first."

"Savannah!" William was at her side in an instant. His fingers locked around her arm.

The stranger tensed.

"Dear God…" William looked as if he'd just seen a ghost. She could feel his fingers trembling against her.

Understanding hit Savannah in a blinding flash. William recognized the vampire, but did he know the vampire as a friend…or as an enemy?

Savannah wasn't going to take any chances. She glanced quickly around the dark street. What could she—There!

An old wooden sign, just a few feet away. She grabbed it, snapping the wood over her knee in one quick move. Her fingers wrapped around one of the pieces, the longest, sharpest piece that she saw. It wasn't much of a weapon, but it would have to do.

She stepped in front of William and lifted the makeshift stake. "I don't know who you are, but—"

"He's my brother," William said, his voice hollow.

Savannah blinked. Just how many brothers did William have running around the countryside?

The vampire smiled. "It's been a long time." He stepped forward, and Savannah leapt at him, thrusting the stake at his heart.

He froze. The stake hovered an inch away from his flesh.

"Don't move," she ordered, her voice soft.

"Savannah." William still sounded shaken. "It's all right. He's not a threat to us."

Are you sure? She made no move to drop the weapon.

"I would never hurt William. He's my brother!" The vampire seemed offended.

"Yeah, well, Geoffrey was his brother, too, and he spent his life trying to hurt William and anyone else that he could."

"I know," he said quietly. "He left me for dead centuries ago."

Left him for dead? Could this be—?

No, impossible. Henry was dead, wasn't he?

"No, I'm quite alive."

Savannah's eyes narrowed. She didn't like it when William read her thoughts. She sure as hell didn't want some stranger jumping into her mind. "And how is it, exactly, that you survived?" She wasn't ready to trust this guy, not yet. She wasn't going to put William's life at risk.

He stared at William. "I was hoping you could answer that."

"What?"

Henry shrugged. "I don't remember much about those hellish days before my transformation. I remember the pain, the blood. But not a damn lot more. The last thing I remember…I was attacked." His jaw clenched. "Geoffrey, that bastard, came to the tower. I thought he was there to help me, to free me. Then I saw Guy's sword. I saw the blood still dripping on the blade, and I knew he was there to kill me."

"But why? Why would he attack you?" William shook his head. "You were the only one he ever seemed to care about!"

"He cared for power, for strength. But he didn't care for me. He didn't care for anyone." Bleak words that rang with the harsh sound of truth.

"What happened after the attack?" Savannah asked, never moving the stake.

"I held on. I knew that William was coming. He'd given his word. William always keeps his word."

Yes, he did, Savannah thought. He'd promised her vengeance, and he'd kept his promise, even though the vow had almost cost William his life.

"I remember seeing you," he said, his gaze fixed on William's face. "You came to the tower. You told me to fight, to hold on. But then I heard the soldiers…" He took a deep breath. "I saw them surround you. There were at least a dozen of them. I tried to help. Believe me, I tried! But I was weak, too weak. And one of them ran me through with his sword."

His story matched exactly with William's. Savannah slowly lowered the stake.

"The next thing I remember was waking up in the cave. I don't know how much time had passed. It could have been days or even weeks. I didn't know how I'd gotten there. I didn't know if you were alive or dead."

"I wouldn't have left you there if I'd known!" William's eyes blazed. "I stayed in that cave with you for hours, praying for you to wake. But you didn't move. I thought I'd waited too long, that the transformation hadn't worked." Softer, "That I'd killed you."

"No, brother. You didn't kill me. You saved me."

She could feel William's pain. Hear it in his voice as he said, "You were alone. You had to learn to survive on your own."

Henry lifted one brow. "As you did."

"I was supposed to protect you," William whispered. "But I just left you—"

"No!" He took a step forward. "Do you think I don't know what you did? You went to the vampire to save my life. You knew what would happen to you when you went to him. You knew the price you'd pay. But you did it anyway. You traded your life for mine."

"I couldn't just stand by and let Guy torture you." William's hands clenched.

"You always protected me, William. Even when we were small lads, I knew I could always count on you."

"I left you alone," William groaned. "For nine hundred years…"

"I've been searching for you," Henry admitted. "I didn't know for certain that you were alive. My last memory was seeing you surrounded by those guards. I didn't know if they killed you, or if you'd survived. I *hoped* that you'd survived. And I held on to that hope for many dark nights."

"I left Normandy," William admitted. "I wanted to get away from all of the blood and death that seemed to surround me."

He'd wanted to get away from his past, Savannah realized. He'd wanted a fresh start, a new life. "But Geoffrey followed you and he started killing," Savannah said. "And you realized that you couldn't get away from him."

"No. I could never get away from Geoffrey. So I started hunting him. I wanted the nightmare to end. I wanted the murders to stop." He shook his head sadly. "But he always eluded me."

And left a trail of blood for William to follow.

"I hunted him, too." Henry admitted. "He'd attacked me. I wanted him to pay. So when I saw him on the cliffs…" His eyes flashed red. "I wanted to kill him. To make him pay for everything that he'd done to me. For every innocent life that he'd taken. For every life that he'd destroyed."

"It's over now." Savannah dropped the stake to the ground and locked her fingers with William's. "He can't hurt us anymore.

He can't hurt anyone." The nightmare had finally ended.

The two men stared at each other. Both were tall, strong and, Savannah sensed, afraid. They had both suffered so much pain, so much tragedy. It was time to heal the wounds of the past. It was time for a new beginning.

She kept her right hand locked around William's. Her left hand reached out to Henry. "My name is Savannah Daniels. It is a pleasure to meet you, Henry de Montfort."

He blinked, staring down at her hand. His fingers lifted slowly, clasping lightly around hers.

She smiled. "I feel as if I already know you," she murmured.

He frowned.

"I read your diary." She looked back at William. "Actually, it was your diary that led me to William." She could still remember how frightened she'd been on her way to that first meeting. But then she'd seen William. "So I guess you could say that I am in your debt."

"No. You brought my brother back to me. It is I who owe you."

"I can't believe—" William stopped, and then he stepped forward, embracing Henry.

Savannah felt her eyes well with tears at the sight. William had been alone for so very long. Walking the earth endlessly. Always alone.

He would never be alone again.

"It's been too long," Henry said.

William stepped back. "Yes."

"I'm sure you guys have a lot of catching up to do." Nine hundred years worth, Savannah thought. Maybe she should give them some privacy.

No. Stay with me.

She rubbed William's arm lightly. "Is there someplace that we can go? Someplace where we can talk?"

Henry spoke quickly. "I have a cottage nearby. It's safe. We could go there."

William nodded.

"Show us the way," Savannah murmured.

***

"So, is she your mate?"

William pulled his gaze from the crackling fire and stared at his brother.

Henry.

It still didn't seem real. Henry was alive. He looked the same. The same blond hair. The same laughing blue eyes. The same slow smile.

But William could feel the differences in his brother. He could feel the echoes of pain. Of rage. He could also feel Henry's strength. His power.

Henry didn't need anyone to protect him now.

"No," Henry murmured, reading his thoughts. "I can protect myself." His lips curved slightly, revealing the tips of his fangs. "But you didn't answer my question, brother. Is she your mate?"

Savannah had slipped from the room moments before. She'd sensed the rising sun and had gone to prepare for the sleep that would come.

Like William's home in the mountains, the cottage was equipped with a series of underground rooms and tunnels. Henry had asked them to stay and sleep in one of the many rooms.

William knew that Savannah had left to give him a few moments alone with Henry and that she would be waiting for him when he returned to the room. Waiting for him with her gentle smile and her mysterious eyes.

"The first time I saw her," he recalled, "she asked me to kill her."

"What?"

"Geoffrey killed her brother and her sister-in-law. And he was stalking her. She wanted to find Geoffrey, to fight him." He sighed, remembering his first sight of Savannah. "She was dying. And she knew she wasn't strong enough to defeat Geoffrey on her own."

"So she turned to you." Henry whistled softly. "Brave one, isn't she?" He rubbed his chest lightly, as if he could still feel the stake that she'd pushed against his heart.

William's lips curved. "She's the bravest woman I've ever met."

"So she *is* your mate."

His smile disappeared. "No. I forced her to stay with me. I told her that I would only transform her if she promised to be my companion."

Henry stilled. "That isn't like you."

"I know. But I wanted her so badly that I would have said anything, done anything, to have her." He would have traded his soul for a moment in her arms.

"You love her."

William blinked. "Of course." There had never been any question in his mind. He'd loved her from the moment his door had opened and he'd seen her standing in the entranceway. "But I have to let her go."

"What?"

"I have to let her go." William could actually feel the pain that lanced through his body at the thought of living without her. But there was no choice. "I can't force her to stay with me." He loved her too much. "Geoffrey nearly destroyed her. He's gone now. She can start her life again. She can be happy."

"And you don't think she'll want to stay with you?"

His heart pounded. "I wish she would." He clenched his hands. "But why would she?"

"Maybe because she loves you, too."

For a moment, hope swept through him. Then he closed his eyes. No, Savannah didn't love him. She couldn't love him. Geoffrey had made her life hell, and he'd treated her little better. He should never have forced her into that ridiculous bargain.

He'd just wanted her so much...

"She cares for you, brother. When she looks at you, I see it in her eyes."

"She's grateful to me," he muttered. He didn't want her gratitude. He wanted her love.

"Will you tell her how you feel?"

Would he? Did he dare? It was almost laughable really. He was an immortal, with immense physical and psychic strength, but he was afraid to tell one small woman how he felt.

"The sun's coming. We should seek our rest." Henry rose and crossed the room. He paused in the entranceway, his back to William. "Tell her. Don't let her walk out of your life without telling her how you feel. You'll regret it if you do."

William frowned. "Are you speaking from experience?"

Henry glanced back, a sad smile twisting his lips. "I've been alone since that day in the cave. I don't even know if I can love a woman. My heart feels dead. It's felt that way for nine hundred years. But I tell you this, if a woman looked at me the way that your Savannah looks at you..." He took a deep breath. "There is no way I'd ever let her walk out of my life. I would do whatever was necessary to keep her with me, *forever*." He walked out of the room.

***

She dreamt of William. They were walking in the moonlight,

their hands entwined.

They were on a beach, an endless stretch of sand. The waves washed gently onto the shore, lightly caressing her feet.

"It's so beautiful here," she murmured, feeling strangely at peace.

William stopped walking and turned to face her. "Yes, beautiful."

She shivered, sensing that he was talking about her, and not the beauty of the land and sea.

He lifted his hand and caressed her cheek.

His eyes looked so incredibly sad.

"What's wrong?"

His face tensed. "We can't stay here."

"Why not?" Everything was perfect. She wanted to stay here forever. With William.

"*I* can't stay here." He took a deep breath. "I don't belong here. I don't belong with you."

What was he saying? Her heart thumped in fear. "Of course you do! We belong together! We agreed—"

He smiled, and the sight tore at her heart. "The nightmare is over now. You're free."

He began to melt away.

"No!" She grabbed him, and for just an instant, her fingers seemed to slip right through his body. "No! You can't leave me!"

His body shimmered. "Kiss me once more," he pleaded. "Just once so that I can remember…"

The waves were louder now, crashing against the shore. Pounding against her feet. Clouds swept over the moon, over the stars, completely obliterating the night sky.

She grabbed William, holding on with all of her strength. She wasn't going to let him go.

She kissed him.

And he vanished.

***

"William!" She screamed his name with the first breath that she took.

She glanced around the room, terrified that he would be gone. But he was there, standing, shirtless, beside the bed, his black gaze intense.

A sigh of relief swept through her. She jumped from the bed, wrapping her arms around him. He felt so warm, so solid. *So real.*

His arms held her close, cradling her against his broad chest. Her fear vanished. She was with William. They were together, as they were meant to be.

"I dreamed about you," she whispered softly. Had it been a dream? Or a nightmare? "At first, it was so perfect. But then you disappeared. You left me, and I was all alone on this deserted beach."

She felt him stiffen against her. His arms lifted, pushing her body away from his.

She frowned. "William?"

His gaze drifted slowly over her face, almost as if he were memorizing her. "You are so beautiful," he said, his voice almost reverent.

A chill swept over her. Why did it feel like he was about to tell her good-bye?

She pressed her lips against his, needing his kiss, his passion, to banish the fear that lingered within her. "Make love to me."

She could see the struggle on his face. Could see the pain and the hunger.

"William?"

Just once more…

The thought whispered through her mind. A memory from the dream?

William pushed her back on the bed, his body pressing her into the soft mattress, and she could think no more. His mouth fed on hers, his tongue sliding past her lips. His hands were touching her, caressing her stomach, her breasts.

He jerked her shirt over her head, flinging it across the room. His head lowered, and she could feel his breath against her skin.

Then his mouth was there. Teasing, sucking the flesh that ached for him.

Her nipples tightened, straining into peaks. He licked her, swirling his tongue around first one nipple, then showing the same careful attention to the other.

Her fingers slid down his back, her nails lightly scraping his skin. She arched into his touch, pressing her hips against his.

"Why can't I get enough of you?" He whispered. "I need you. I hunger for you…" He kissed her again, his tongue thrusting deep.

His fingers were sliding down her pants and easing beneath the elastic of her underwear. He touched her lightly, his fingers stirring her hunger all the more.

She touched his nipple with her tongue, feeling it tighten instantly. She licked him, flicking her tongue delicately over his sensitive skin. She heard him inhale sharply.

Then he jerked her panties down, tossing them out of the way.

"I can't wait," he growled. "I'm sorry, I can't!" He tore off his jeans. She could see his arousal. Strong. Hot. Hard. No, he couldn't wait.

Neither could she.

She parted her thighs, moving eagerly to accommodate him. She could feel the tip of his erection pressing against her. She pushed her hips, rubbing against his heat.

He snarled and thrust deep.

Savannah gasped, pleasure biting into her. She could feel her climax already mounting, rushing toward her, and she wrapped her legs around him, her hips straining to meet the thrust of his. His mouth settled hungrily over her breast, licking, biting.

His fingers slid down into the curling thatch of hair at the juncture of her thighs. And he rubbed her, lightly. And he thrust. Hard.

She screamed, her release shattering her. Fire burned through her body, waves of ecstasy pouring through her blood.

William's arms clenched around her, holding her tightly. He thrust again. Deeper. Harder.

She could see the edge of his teeth. See the red flames in his eyes.

"Savannah!"

She felt the climax that ripped through him. And she shuddered, feeling a second wave of release push through her body.

They clung to one another, riding the crest of pleasure. She could feel his heart pounding against her, could feel the heat of his body burning her.

And, in that unguarded instant, she was closer to him than she'd ever been before. Bound by their psychic link, she was close enough to actually hear his thoughts.

Her breath caught. Pain lanced through her. She pushed against his shoulders, angrily shoving his body off hers. "You bastard! You're planning to leave me!"

Eighteen

I mourn for what might have been.
-Entry from the diary of Henry de Montfort,
December 31, 1068

"Savannah!" William tried to grab her, but she twisted away and jumped from the bed. Her body still ached from his touch. But her heart had been broken by his thoughts.

She wrapped a sheet around her body, her furious gaze locked on him. "I heard your thoughts! I know what you're going to do!"

Pain flashed across his face and he reached for her.

"No!" She jumped back, shaking her head furiously. "Don't touch me!" She would break apart if he did. Crumble into a thousand pieces. "Just get dressed." She couldn't stand to stare at him, to see the incredible beauty of his body. It was like a slap in her face.

His jaw clenched, but he grabbed his pants and slid them on with a quick, rough movement. "You don't understand—"

"What's to understand?" She felt like a fool. An utter fool. "You wanted one more round of sex before you kicked me out of your life. I think I understand that pretty well." She wanted to cry, to scream with the pain of betrayal tearing through her. They had been through so much together. So much. How could he do this to her?

He closed his eyes. His jaw clenched. "I knew I should have left before you woke. But I needed you too much." A sad smile twisted his lips. "I wanted to see you. To see your eyes, your smile, just once more."

Just once more.

The words flashed through her, sending a wave of unease through her heart.

She was missing something. Something was happening that she didn't understand. She tried to read his thoughts again, to uncover his feelings, but she came up against a brick wall. A wall that shut her out completely.

She walked toward him, her gaze narrow and intent. She knew he was aware of her approach, but he didn't move.

"William?"

He opened his eyes and stared down at her, looking sad.

"We had a bargain," she whispered.

His hands fisted. "I never should have forced you into that agreement. I never should have—"

Forced her? Savannah frowned. "What are you talking about? You didn't force me to do anything." And he hadn't. She'd entered into their bargain because she'd wanted to. Because she'd wanted him.

"Yes, I did." He swallowed, and she could have sworn that for an instant, he actually looked haunted. "I said I wouldn't help you hunt Geoffrey unless you agreed to my demands. That I wouldn't transform you unless you became my mate."

"You told me that I would have to stay with you forever," she whispered.

"You don't." He took a deep breath. "Geoffrey is dead. You don't have to worry about him ever again. You can have your life back. You can go anywhere you want. Do anything you want. You can start fresh. Begin a new life."

"Without you." The thought was horrifying.

He nodded.

She didn't understand. "You want me to leave you?"

He didn't answer. He stared at her, his eyes blacker than the night.

"Why?" She had to know. She had to know why he was suddenly pushing her away.

Moments passed in silence. She didn't think he was going to answer. That he was just going to continue staring at her.

"Because you deserve more," he said, and she could hear the agony in his voice.

Her heart stopped beating.

"What?"

"You deserve happiness. Freedom. You've been through hell because of my brother." He hesitated, and then said, "Because of me."

Because of him? "William, if it hadn't been for you, I would be dead now! I would be in a cemetery somewhere with just Mary mourning my passing." Didn't he understand? He'd given her life back to her!

"Geoffrey took your life away. I forced you to change—"

She grabbed his arms, making him focus his attention on her. "I was dying, William. The doctors were wrong. I didn't have six months. If you hadn't changed me when you did, I would be dead." She shook her head. "I wanted you to change me. I begged you to do it."

"And I told you that I would give you the kiss only if you became my mate." Disgust was written on his face.

Her eyes widened. "Is that what this is about?"

"I don't want you to stay with me because I took away your choice."

"But what if I choose to stay?" She touched his cheek. "What if I want to stay with you?"

Hunger flashed in his eyes. Need. Hope. But then he stepped back. Stepped away from her touch, away from her. "Geoffrey killed your brother and your sister-in-law, and he almost killed you." He ran his hand over his face. "How can you stay with me, knowing what he did?"

"Because you're not like him," she said simply, honestly. "You're nothing like Geoffrey."

"After what I've done to you, how can you say that?"

Her temper snapped. "You haven't done anything to me!" She screamed. "Stop saying that! You didn't force me to do anything that I didn't want to do. Yes, you transformed me. I begged you to do it! You saved my life when you gave me the kiss. You helped me hunt Geoffrey, your own brother. You helped me stop him."

"The bargain—"

"Oh, yes, the great bargain! Let me tell you something, I didn't agree to that bargain just so I would gain my vengeance." She shook her head. "I knew you would help me stop Geoffrey, whether I agreed or not. You knew that the killing had to stop, and you would have helped me, regardless. I know that."

"What?" He was stunned.

She punched her finger against his chest. "Listen to me! I agreed to that bargain for one reason and one reason only." She took a deep breath. "Because I wanted you. And I would have done anything to be with you."

He grabbed her arms, his fingers biting into her skin. "What are you saying?"

She stared into his blazing eyes. "I'm saying I love you." Her words spilled furiously from her lips. "And I'm saying that I won't let you just force me out of your life. I won't! I know things have been hard, but it's over now, and—"

"You love me?" he whispered, sounding dazed.

She nodded once.

"Savannah!" His arms swept around her, almost crushing

her. He buried his face in her hair. His body shuddered against hers.

"William?" Her arms cradled him. It was hard for her to breathe, but she didn't care. Hope flared in her breast.

"I wanted you to be free," he said softly. "Free from the past, free to start a new life."

"When I'm with you, I'm free. Don't you understand that?"

He pulled back, staring down at her. "This is your last chance, because I don't think I'll ever be able to let you go again."

"I don't want you to let me go. I want you to hold me, to love me, forever."

He swallowed and the hand he lifted to caress her cheek trembled.

"Do you love me?" she asked him, gazing solemnly into his dark eyes.

"More than anything." His thumb brushed across her lips. "From the first moment that I saw you, I knew that you were the one. The only one that I would love."

"You knew from the beginning?" She was shocked.

"I knew when I looked into your green eyes. I tried to send you away because I was trying to protect you." His lips curved in a sardonic smile. "I was trying to protect you from me."

She couldn't believe it. William loved her? He actually loved her? "Why didn't you say something sooner? Why were you just going to walk away from me?"

He kissed her lightly. "Fear. Pure, unadulterated fear."

William, the ancient vampire, had been afraid of her?

"Yes," he said. "Because if I admitted my love, and you turned away..." A bleak look entered his eyes. "There would be no hope for me."

"I would never turn away from you."

William stared down at Savannah, overcome with emotion. He could hardly believe what was happening. She loved him. She really loved him.

And she didn't want to leave. She wanted to stay with him, forever.

"You're not going to be alone anymore," she said, seeming to read his thoughts. "We'll be together."

Forever.

Every moon-filled night would be spent with Savannah. He would have her warmth, her laughter, her passion. She would be his. *His mate. His love.* For eternity.

"I can't believe you were going to send me away." She frowned at him.

"I thought I was doing the right thing, even though the thought of living without you nearly tore me apart."

"Being with you is the only right thing for me. You know that, don't you?" She asked, her voice soft.

And, staring into her beautiful green eyes, he finally understood.

Her love was a rich pool, glistening and pure. Endless. He could feel her love, feel the waves of it emanating from her mind, from her heart.

She opened her thoughts to him freely, letting him know, letting him see, how she truly felt.

And he was humbled. Humbled by the strength of her love.

And awed. She loved him. She truly loved him.

She loved the monster. She loved the man.

"I love you," she said. "All of you."

He smiled. He had given Savannah the dark gift, the kiss of the vampire, but she had given him something far more precious.

She had given him love, and it would last forever.

Epilogue

I no longer fear the darkness.
-Entry from the diary of Savannah Daniels de Montfort,
January 1, 2005.

Savannah stared down at her brother's grave, a dozen red roses clutched in her hands.

"It's over now, Mark," she whispered. "He won't hurt anyone else."

The wind moaned softly in the night.

"The nightmare's over."

She placed the roses on his headstone, touching the cold stone with a gentle fingertip. "May you find your peace." *As I have found mine.*

She stood, wiping a tear from her cheek. She turned and saw William standing in the shadows, waiting for her.

She walked toward him, needing his warmth to ward off the night's cold chill.

His arms wrapped around her, pulling her against his chest. As always, he felt so good against her. So right.

Yes, the nightmare was over. It was time for a new beginning. A new life.

A life that she would spend with William.

She glanced back over her shoulder, staring at her brother's grave.

Good-bye, Mark.

And on the whisper of the wind, she'd have sworn she heard her brother say, *Good-bye, Savannah.*

Breinigsville, PA USA
07 October 2009
225440BV00001B/32/A